WITHOUT BENEFITS

A NOVEL

NICOLE TONE

M P

WITHOUT BENEFITS

Cover design by Yonderworldly Covers at covers.yonderwordly.com

Interior formatting by Ashley Ruggirello at www.cardboardmonet.com

Electronic ASIN: B01CF47ON4

Paperback ISBN: 978-0692629857

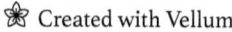 Created with Vellum

To the women who dare to fight for their turn in the spotlight.

"I will seize fate by the throat;
    it shall certainly never wholly overcome me."

— Ludwig van Beethoven

.

1

The photocopied piece of music mocked her as it sat on top of the kitchen table. Emma thought she'd have the original, had been hoping she had the original of the whole song instead of just the first page. The song in its entirety was a not-too-distant memory in her head, a melody she hummed to herself as she walked through Whole Foods or through the sacred halls of Benaroya Hall.

"Emma, you should stop cleaning," Connor, her sweet boyfriend, called softly over the gentleness of Ophelie Gaillard playing Bach's *Prelude to Cello Suite No. 1*. "You've done enough, you're going to wear yourself out."

She looked up at him, the blue glow of his laptop setting ugly shadows on his classically handsome face. Evening was beginning to settle into the city, even though the days were still getting longer. The bright gold of a sun getting ready to set barely touched the white of the carpet, of the couch, of the picture frames on the gray walls. The living room had fallen into the shadows of the buildings outside their windows. It made the electronic glow of the laptop more harsh than normal. Still, she could see the kindness in his eyes that she found a decade ago, the kindness and understanding that made this life — this non-musical life — worth it.

"I know, but I'm really almost done," Emma called back, "and it'll be good to get rid of all of this."

Getting rid of *this* included years and years of forgotten paperwork, of things from her dorm, of essays on musical theory, and of sheet music filled with songs that she had written but was too afraid to play for anyone.

This was her past, sorted and ready to go to the recycling bin.

It was a useless gesture more than an actual act of purging, and Emma knew it. Even if she set their whole overpriced apartment on fire it wouldn't purge the memory of Owen out of her.

The ghosts of the things that she used to love were taking up too much space here. They nestled in the curtains that hung around the large windows that looked out at the Puget Sound. They curled up in bed with her, stealing her dreams, especially on those nights that Connor worked late. The music, piano, New York City, Owen — they haunted her, always. Recalling the memory of one caused a landslide and the rest followed: standing in Times Square while the skyline changed forever, the song that was playing in her head, the song that she wrote with Owen, Owen's hands as they touched her face, her hair, her lips that night.

"Are you okay?"

Emma jerked her head up from the pile of music, eyes wide with the panic that comes from getting too lost in those particular thoughts. Connor had left the blue glow of his laptop screen and was here now, not touching her, but making his presence known. Making sure that she was okay, that she was safe.

"Yeah... yes, I think so."

"You're okay. You're safe." It was a decade-old mantra, one that he repeated over and over again whenever she felt this way. "What can I do?"

Shaking her head, she cleared out the smoldering ashes of the memories. Getting back to work, getting back to doing something other than wondering if she should e-mail Owen back, was best.

"I'll just finish with these and then I'll be done."

Connor smiled, weak and nervous, and returned back to his normal spot on the couch. Their after work routine was always the same. He would pour a small glass of red wine and go over e-mails that had been sent since he left the Amazon compound. She'd consider what to make them for dinner. With the number of lunches and dinners and drink invites she had to accept as part of her job, there was something comforting about coming home and cooking. On nights that she didn't want to, or was too tired, Connor took up the task, his skills limited to comfort food.

"Am I cooking tonight or are you?" Emma asked as she put all of the papers — the songs, the memories — back into a neat pile and placed them back into the box that she'd taken them out of. She'd throw them out another night.

"Actually, I just got a text from Rachel. Is it okay if I go and meet her?"

Rachel. She, like Owen, was a recently manifested ghost of their collective past. She was Connor's ex, one who had broken his heart when she moved away, but had recently come back and was also working in the same department Connor was. Emma wanted to believe that it was all pure coincidence but knew it was a naive conclusion to come to. A hot flare of jealousy shot through her chest. As much as she was okay with Connor getting meals or drinks with his female co-workers, Rachel was in a different territory than the others.

"Ah, so we're not catching up on *House of Cards* tonight?"

"If you'd like, I can reschedule. It's not a big deal."

"No, no." Emma looked over at him, unnerved by how he was watching her with such intensity. He was sincere in what he was saying; she could feel it in her gut. "Netflix will be there when you get home."

"Are you sure? I don't want to leave you all alone for dinner."

Emma shook her head. "I actually got an invitation I've been sitting on for awhile now. I'll have to see if he's available."

"He?"

"Owen."

"Ah."

As the red of the same jealous flair Emma had felt only moments ago flashed across Connor's cheeks, she could only feel satisfied that she could draw out the same emotions in him as he did to her.

"With Tara's engagement party on Friday, he thought that it might be a good idea to rip off the band aid now . . . You know, since its been so long since we've seen each other."

Connor nodded but the red was still there. "No, it makes sense. And I shouldn't feel jealous, but I do."

"Maybe I like that you still get jealous," Emma teased.

"And it's not like I'm not going to dinner with my own ex."

"Yes, but Owen wasn't an ex."

"He might as well been."

Even though Connor was smiling, the chill in his voice betrayed his true emotions. Emma knew the old argument was right beneath the surface. The argument where Connor thought Emma was more in love with Owen than she was with Connor, the argument where Connor thought that Emma was cheating on him with Owen. They were insecurities that Rachel had planted during their time together and ones that, if Emma looked back now, knew that she hadn't done much to help stunt the growth of.

"It's just going to be weird, with him being the best man at the wedding. But I don't want you to feel uncomfortable," Emma admitted. "If it's a problem —"

Connor pulled her in for a hug. Cheek pressed to his shirt, she could hear his heart beating the steady lullaby that she calmed her down in the middle of the night.

"It's not a problem." The words were a rumble in his chest. "It's not. We'll come back here later and we'll watch some shows, just like normal. Just like always."

Emma nodded, breathing a sigh of relief. Pulling away, she sat down at the table where her laptop sat hidden behind boxes and piles of paper.

"I don't even know if I'm going to go to dinner. He sent this e-mail a week ago and I haven't answered. What should I say to him?"

"Just send a 'yes' back, that you're free tonight. If not, then we'll see him on Friday."

"When did you become so reasonable?" Emma grinned, raising an eyebrow. The Connor she first started dating wouldn't have been like this, wouldn't have let go of his jealousy so quickly. He would've been angry, irrational — not the understanding man that stood before her now.

"Since I started actually listening to you." He came over and kissed the top of her head. "But I should head out. We're just going to a bar a few streets over. If you need anything, just call. Okay?"

"Okay."

"I love you."

"I love you too."

She meant it, meant it every time she said it and knew he meant it when he said it. But expressing how they feel didn't help ease the pain of the shift in their routine. It wasn't like either of them never went out with other people. It was just these people, the ones that came with history and pain, that made everything seem off key.

Hearing the door click, Emma re-opened the blank draft of the reply that was meant for Owen. Even though he wasn't there, that she hadn't seen him in years, it was as if he was sitting across from her, staring, waiting to see if she'd rise to this challenge.

"I don't even know what to say to you," she said out loud, fingers tapping the edge of the keyboard. On one hand, yes, she could just send a simple yes as Connor suggested and see if he was free now. On the other, she could just ignore it and go back to cleaning or lining up more calls with potential donors or start to plan the next fundraiser and wait for Connor to get home.

I'm available now if you are. If not, I'll see you at the engagement party. Cheers.

She typed the message out quickly and hit send before she had time to talk herself out of it. It was done; the ball was in his court now.

Maybe it had always been in his court.

She'd seen him in passing so much: at the Market, at the Symphony where she handled the fundraising. They'd catch each other's eye, she'd smile, but he didn't approach her even when she was alone. They just kept moving forward, occupying the same space, breathing the same air, but never getting close.

Emma knew that getting close, close enough to smell his cologne, to see how he'd aged, would've been dangerous. It would've brought back the memories and the feelings that she knew still lingered in the loneliness that came when she went to a fundraising event without Connor. In the loneliness that came with walking through the halls of Benaroya and knowing she'd never grace its stages. She didn't need to relapse into a life where she pined after another man, where she entertained the idea that being a musician was somehow going to bring her the financial stability and lifestyle she had now.

The e-mail alert went off on her laptop and her phone. Expecting it to be work, she glanced over, but instead saw Owen's name.

Purple Cafe. Eight. See you there.

Emma looked at the numbers in the corner of her screen. Six-forty-five. Not enough time to go shopping, to buy a new wardrobe, to buy a new, Owen-approved life.

Walking into her bedroom, phone in hand, she tried to find something mature, sophisticated, and sexy. She needed to find something in the color-ordered designer silk and cotton tucked away in her closet that showed her life was even close to the one he, Seattle Symphony concertmaster and last year's most eligible bachelor, was living. She shot off a quick text to her sister, Leah, not wanting to make this decision on her own.

Thankfully, Leah's response came quickly:

Owen, Really?

Casual dinner. Just catching up between old friends. Emma knew Leah's appetite for details about what was really going on with her younger sister wouldn't be appeased through one text. Maybe just this one time, Leah would let it go.

Conservative, casual. Remember that this isn't a date. Call me tomorrow.

Leah's suggestion was lacking any sort of direction. Jeans felt too casual and the dresses she normally wore for work functions felt too formal. Finally, she took a dress out of the lineup and held it up against her hourglass shape. The dress was simple, A-line, gray with a white hem. It wasn't a dress she normally wore to dinners, but it was comfortable. It felt more like the Emma Owen might expect. More like who she was in college than who she presented herself as now. Flats, a scarf, a trench — the outfit came together in two seconds in her mind.

But did college-era Emma outfits say what she needed them to say?

Did it make her look the part of the trendy Seattleite crowd that'd rather not drive into Bellevue to go to the other Purple Cafe location? Or, did it show her as what she was now: a woman who was part philanthropist, a woman who spent free time with women whose sole responsibility was to take care of husband and houses. These were her friends now. They were mostly well-kept women whose discussions centered around weddings and engagements, on childcare, on the stresses of aging, and of balancing careers and children. It wasn't the long, late-night conversations she shared with her roommates in undergrad, or the debates she got into over the merits of modern music. But, it helped her stay on track; content with the life she was living now. They'd approve of this dress.

But the way her neighbors saw her and the way Owen saw her were two different things. They saw the quiet, put-together future Mrs. Connor Dolan. Owen saw her as the pianist who ensured his salutatorian spot, who got helped him get YouTube views. Who helped him get where he was today.

2

———

"Thanks," Emma said, closing the car door. The Lyft driver smiled, waved, and drove the mustached car away, onto the next pick up.

Having someone else drive her to dinner should've been the easier choice. It was going to give her the time to touch up her makeup, to let her get into a zen mode that would make this dinner easier. But she'd forgotten about the evening traffic, the streets backed up to the point that it took an hour to go a mile. The city of gray clouds and glass buildings turned red from all of the brake lights. It was days like today where she couldn't see why New York had been able to figure out what Seattle couldn't. Now she was running late when she thought she'd get there early.

She walked fast, heels clicking quickly against the pavement. Emma crossed her arms in front of her chest to stave off the anxious chill that had set in on the drive over. With record temperatures, even for early June, she didn't think she would've needed anything heavier than her lightest trench coat.

"Emma?"

The voice caught her off guard. She stopped and turned her head, finding a man — an older man than she thought would be calling her name — leaning up against the building. Of course he'd been waiting outside for her. Of course he wouldn't look the same as he had ten years ago. Whenever she had seen him before now, she'd never been close enough to see the details of how he'd aged. Now she saw the gray peppering in his dark hair, and the crinkled lines at the corners of his bright eyes. Her heart beat too fast, the way it used to when they were together. She wondered if she'd aged too.

"Owen." She smiled, glad she remembered to put on lipstick. Like paint on a warrior, she'd hoped it would dispel the nerves and, instead, project confidence. The nerves were still winning. "It's good to see you. It's been too long." She leaned into him, lips brushing against the stubble on both of his cheeks. "Sorry I'm late."

"It's no trouble. I wasn't waiting long."

"The Lyft driver took the scenic route," she explained as he held open the heavy-looking metal door.

"A Lyft?" he raised his eyebrows.

"If I have a glass or two tonight, I don't want to chance driving home."

He grinned and said nothing. Instead of commenting on whether he thought Emma still played it too safe, of whether he thought she was being ridiculous like Emma expected he would, he turned to the hostess. She was dark skinned and beautiful. Her hair sat just above her shoulder in a wild bunch of tight curls.

"Reservation for Gibson?"

"Of course, Mr. Gibson. We have you at your usual table. Will you need menus?" She went to grab two, but hesitated.

"Please bring at least one. My date hasn't been here — "

"No, that's not necessary," Emma interrupted, "I'm more familiar with the Bellevue location."

The hostess smiled. "Of course. The menu is the same. I'll just bring one with me just in case you need to refresh yourself."

"Thank you."

Emma's stomach twisted as they walked through the restaurant. A soft yellow glow illuminated the restaurant as the city outside of its glass walls meandered by in time with the steady stop and go of the traffic lights. Uniform oak-topped tables were set apart in a symmetrical manner in the circular dining area, with the bar at its center, flanked by dark chairs boasting thick red cushions. If this were a date, it would've been the perfect place.

But a date this was not.

"You have your own table?" Emma raised her eyebrows at him, with only a hint of a smile, as she shrugged off her jacket and sat in her chair. She pulled her phone out of her clutch and placed it on the table out of habit.

"I do. I come here after rehearsal." He smirked in a way that made Emma sit up straighter, old competition lingering beneath the surface. He was still the same Owen — the same Owen she'd spent four years of college with, rehearsing with, breathing, sleeping, and playing in synch with. He had a beard now, more stubble than anything. But it was still him.

"Every night?"

"Most nights."

It hadn't occurred to her that he'd spend most of his time alone. She'd assumed his successful career had carved himself a spot into the most elite corners of the city, full of beautiful people, beautiful women, smiling at him. It wasn't a lonely life, but a fulfilled one with his dream job cemented down so recently out of college.

"Mr. Gibson, your usual bottle?" A man walked up to the table, hands behind his back, voice low. His smile seemed genuine, but tired, with dark circles rimming his eyes.

"Not tonight. Champagne?"

"Champagne holds too much expectation. We aren't celebrating anything." Emma looked over the extensive wine list that the hostess had left with them. The guilt she was feeling earlier in flashed again. It wasn't that she was out with a man, but that she was out with this man that intoxicated her even before she'd had anything to drink.

Owen looked amused. "Then what will we have?"

"We'll take a bottle of the *Alvise Lancieri*."

The waiter took the list as Emma handed it back to him, asking, "And any appetizers?"

"My usual," Owen answered. "Thanks."

Emma settled back into her chair. She was glad she'd chosen to wear a dress, as opposed to anything more casual. The patrons were a mix of casual and formal, of locals and tourists. Sometimes it was hard to tell the two apart, but tonight was an exception. A middle-aged group of four women sat in one of the longer tables, their eyes bouncing excitedly from face to face as they talked in fast, hushed tones. They were dressed low-key for dinner, one woman wearing a white t-shirt with "Grey Sloane Memorial" on it under a loose fitting blazer.

A city full of musical history and the world knew them only for two things: *Grey's Anatomy* and rain.

"It's good to see you." Owen broke the silence first.

"You too. I'm sorry that it took so long to get back to you."

He nodded. "I assume your life is busy. You don't have to apologize."

The waiter returned with the bottle of sparkling wine, euthanizing their painful conversation. Even though he sat right across the table, Owen still felt like a memory. He was a daydream and, instead of having dinner by herself, she was just making it all up in her head.

"Do you still play?" Owen asked, looking over the waiter's hand as he poured the light, golden liquid into their glasses. "*Salud.*"

Emma smiled and sipped the wine. With a hint of sweetness, the carbonation rolled over her tongue, but didn't create an instant warmth the way champagne did for her. The perfect Prosecco. It was exactly what she'd been hoping it would be. As perfect as the drink was, his question left a trace of bitterness in her mouth. She expected the question, but not so soon into the evening.

"Not as much as I should."

She gave up piano the same year she had given up Owen: her final year of college. When it came time to make decisions about whether to stay in Seattle or move on to the next city, her heart had pushed her towards Connor.

"You should?"

She took another sip of wine. Living with Connor had taken her more away from the music world than she had anticipated. "I can't remember the last time. There's no room in our place — "

"Ah, you're living together then."

"We are. I moved in with him a few years ago."

He leaned back in his chair, one hand playing with the stem of his glass. "So you're content with working for the symphony, but not being apart of it?"

"Oh, don't say it like that," she sighed. The disappointment in his voice, in his eyes, settled deep in her stomach. "The only way I could've kept playing after college was if I taught kids after school, and I refused. I'd sooner kill myself."

"You've never been one for the dramatics. Did you trade your music degree in for a theater one?"

"I'm not kidding, Owen." She laughed. "I can't listen to poorly played 'Fur Elise' every day. I would strangle myself with piano wire. That's not a life; that's a death sentence."

"Fair enough. So what are you doing?"

"Making sure your paycheck comes in."

"Seriously?"

"Seriously. I organize a lot of the fundraising for the Symphony."

"And here I thought you were always around because you missed me."

Emma grinned and rolled her eyes. "No, not exactly."

He chuckled. "Last I heard you were in Bellevue with your sister. I'm guessing that's not true anymore."

"Belltown. And Leah's over in Queen Anne with her husband."

"We're neighbors." He smiled, his head nodding towards where they both knew the Space Needle was. "Belltown loft and you don't have a piano? Even I have one."

"Why?" Her heart dropped.

Violin was what Owen played, not piano.

The woman who watched too much primetime television thought that, after all this time, he might've wanted her, too. That the piano in his apartment was meant for her, that he'd held onto some glimmer of hope that they'd still end up together. That there had been something there that she'd missed back then.

"Best for composing. I'm working on a new piece for my concert."

Their alma matter would be including him as part of their fall concert series. The news had come in the form of a headline in their monthly e-newsletter. The school touted him as one of their most accomplished alumna and explained how excited they were to have him back to perform. The e-mail was the catalyst that sparked the death of her favorite mug. Ceramic didn't hold up well when it was thrown against her dining room wall. When Connor asked why there was a drywall patch on their formerly perfectly painted wall, Emma showed him the e-mail. He never asked about it again.

"A little late in the game to be still trying, isn't it?"

"Well, when I say trying, I mean I'm working out the final kinks. You remember how I work."

Nostalgia got the better of her and she grinned. "I do. How many bottles of rum have you gone through?"

"None yet."

She laughed as the waiter came back, placing the long plate filled with an assortment of cheese, crackers, and dried fruit between them.

It had been a long time since she had done something she felt was worthwhile. Her fundraising work was rewarding and she enjoyed it, but it wasn't the life she'd pictured for herself. She'd wandered past the curved face of the Experience Music Project a few weeks ago, blending in with the other tourists. It hit her hard that she could be living in a city with such a rich musical history and not find some way to contribute. It was the day of her thirtieth birthday. It was there, looking at her distorted reflection, that she realized her chance of contributing may be over. Playing now would only be something temporary. Like Owen, the piano would never be a permanent fixture in her life.

"Ready to order?" the waiter asked.

Emma looked across the table. "Whatever the chef recommends?"

"I'll do the same."

"Very good." Michael bowed again and moved into the background.

"You should come play with me, Em." Owen's face softened as he leaned forward, elbow on the table as he picked up his glass. "It wouldn't be a showcase of my work without our song, and I won't play it without you."

"Funny you should mention it. I found my copy of the sheet music today."

"It's fate then."

Emma chuckled but shook her head. "I don't think so."

Her phone vibrated on the table, Connor's name popping up on the screen. His text message was the reminder she needed. She wasn't part of Owen's life anymore and didn't need to become part of it now. His handing her what she always dreamed of wouldn't satisfy her jealousy of his professional accomplishments. She wanted to earn it.

"Ah, he summons," Owen, said taking a long swallow of wine.

"I thought you were a fan of Connor."

"If he makes you happy. But you don't look happy. Are you?"

Emma looked out the window, unable to meet his eye.

"I am."

"I never pictured this life for you, a life without music." He frowned. "You need to come play. At least come practice. Or even watch us. I've been able to secure one of the stages at Benaroya."

Emma turned her gaze back to him. "I'll consider it."

Her phone went off again with another text message, but she tucked the device back into her bag. She wanted the distraction, but didn't want to know how things were going with Connor and Rachel. The night was becoming more uncomfortable than she anticipated, her mind wandering to a place where Connor was fighting the same feelings of attraction, the questions of what if, that she was.

"I think," she added, "I need another glass."

"If you insist." Owen reached for her glass as Michael brought their food, arranged in an ornate manner, and set their plates in front of them. "Ah, finally something to soak up this delicious wine."

"It's probably a good idea. Getting drunk with you was always . . . messy."

Owen laughed, loud and deep. "No, you're right. But if it wasn't for the rum, or the whisky — whichever it was, our song might not have been born." It was his turn to blush.

Emma looked down, still unsure if he remembered everything that happened that night. The music, sure — of course he remembered that. But the next morning he acted normal; hung-over and clinging to both sides of a toilet. He never brought it up. Neither of them did.

"Indeed." She felt her phone vibrate again.

"Does he know you're out with me?"

"He does." Emma took a bite of her food.

Owen set his fork upside down on the edge of his plate. "Answer something honestly for me."

"Anything."

"You know, I've seen you: at the market, the mall, just . . . different places. I've never come up to you, partly because you're usually with him, but also because you never look happy. I never see you smile. Is this the most you've smiled in a while?"

"Yes."

"What do you mean?"

Emma picked up her glass and raised it in his direction now. "This is the first time I've been able to talk to you in ten years."

Owen smirked. "Ah, is that the only reason?"

"It's nice to have a distraction. It's nice not to be worrying about where the next big donation for the Symphony is coming from. Or chatting with the women in my building over things that really don't matter. It's just . . ." she trailed off for a moment, her attention caught by the couple at the next table over. Their hands touched across the table. They were young, mid-twenties if Emma had to guess, with a whole life ahead of them. "This is good. I'm glad that we were able to do this."

"You could have reached out at any point over the years. I never would have turned you down."

"I wasn't sure I wanted to see you. I thought it'd be easier to just stay away." Emma looked down.

"Easier isn't better."

"True," she said, her chest tightening with emotions she tried to will away. "But easier is what I needed. What I still need."

"No," he shook his head, "whoever told you that is wrong. Very wrong. You need to be challenged and pushed." He pulled his phone out of his pocket and swiped through a few screens before placing the phone between them. It was a video of her playing *Comptine d'Un Autre Ete*. The music cut through her, each key a slice against her heart. "This is who you are, Emma. It's time to get back to that."

She looked away from him, an ache building inside of her that she couldn't ignore. The last time she'd played that song had been at a concert her senior year: her last solo.

"I can't."

"I don't understand." He tossed his napkin on the table.

"I know you don't. But I'm not a part of that world anymore. It's not who I am. I have Connor, and — "

"And that's all you have. Why? Explain it to me."

"I'm engaged."

3

The silence that followed was suffocating; the noise of the other patrons enveloping them, closing around the awkward moment. This wasn't what she meant when she said she couldn't play right now, that marriage was taking over her life. She was comfortable with her life. Playing again felt like a step backward, not forward. Owen wouldn't understand.

"Well, I don't know what to say," Owen leaned back against his chair. "I guess congratulations are in order?"

Emma's cheeks burned with embarrassment, his question biting, rather than congratulatory. She was playing defense. "We haven't set a date or anything yet . . ."

"I see."

The waiter brought the check over, but Emma didn't move. Owen reached for it, placing the black credit card in the clear pocket and set the leather book back down on the table. Emma went to grab it, but he waved away her hand.

"No, no. This one is on me."

"Oh," Emma pulled her hand away. "Well, thank you. You'll have to let me buy you dinner sometime."

Owen smiled, soft and kind, residual anger subsiding. It was the exact opposite of what he had been only moments ago. "The gesture is nice, but I don't expect it to happen. I'm sure we'll see each other again, but I'm not sure in what capacity."

"Other than at the cocktail party on Friday, and the wedding."

"Ah, yes. You're right. And you can't avoid me at those events." He winked.

"I don't . . ." Emma stopped, took a breath, and re-started. "I meant what I said. I'd like to do dinner with you again. I want to hear how your concert is coming along. I want to hear about your life."

Owen nodded. "Yes, I'd like that. To see you more. I'm sorry, I was just surprised. I hadn't heard you'd gotten engaged."

"It's very recent. Two days ago, actually."

"The ring. Let's see it," Owen said, extending his hand out towards Emma's.

"It's being sized."

His hand moved to the stem of his wine glass. "I'll see it Friday then?"

"Yes." It was all Emma could say.

"Perhaps this is where we should end tonight." Owen signed the receipt and stood.

"I agree."

She could feel the wine in her knees as she stood. Her cheeks flushed as she looked at him. She wanted to start the dinner over, to keep it on the wedding instead of talking about a path she never followed. It would've been better. It would've kept whatever feelings she had for him buried where they had been since they graduated.

As he helped her into her coat, hands brushing against hands, she blushed deeper.

"Have you arranged for a ride home?" he asked as he led them out of the restaurant. The distance between them, and the ice in his voice, faded the color in her cheeks.

She reached for his arm as they got outside, pulling him towards her. "I didn't want tonight to be like this."

"We haven't spoken in a decade. You're . . . so different now. You've lost your music. Your moxie."

"Of course I'm different. I've grown up. That's what's supposed to happen."

He frowned, his hand taking hers. "Not so drastically."

Around them, cars sped down the road, oblivious to their conversation. People walked down the sidewalk, too fast to appreciate the beauty of the city night. Buildings were lit up, pushing out the darkness, creating long shadows across the concrete. In the darkness, the mountains had disappeared. There was no differentiating between water and sky, the peaks of mountains and the endless expanse of stars that hid behind the light pollution the city provided.

Emma felt her phone vibrate again.

"I'm sorry I didn't live up to your expectations." She walked towards the street and pulled out her phone, opening the Lyft app and hating herself for not doing it sooner. "I'll see you on Friday."

He jogged over to her, hands in his coat pocket. Pulling out a folded yellowed piece of paper, he handed it to her.

"What's this?"

"Open it when you get home. And think about my offer from earlier." He paused, his eyes flicking between hers and her mouth. She parted her lips, expectant, but the kiss never came. He leaned in and kissed her cheek instead. "It was good to see you again. And please, take my car instead of waiting for a ride home."

"Your car?"

A black sedan pulled up in front of them. She looked at him, confused.

"It's already here. I can walk."

"Couldn't we drop you off on the way?"

He smiled but it never reached his eyes. "No, I want to clear my head."

"Are you sure?"

"Yes, please," he said, opening the rear door for her.

She hesitated, lingering in the open space, wanting desperately to recreate the moment from earlier. But she slid into the back seat, the leather cool against the bare skin of her legs. "Thank you."

He closed the door and held up his hand to her as a goodbye.

"Where to?" The driver asked, peering at her through the rearview mirror.

"The Vine Building."

"No problem."

They pulled away, the sounds of the city muted by the glass and the music in the car. She looked at the well-worn piece of paper still folded in her palm, and carefully pulled it open. She recognized it immediately: it was the piece of music they had first worked on together. Taking a deep breath, she folded the paper back up and slipped it into her bag. It would go with the rest of their music, in a box somewhere, tucked away with the rest of the papers she couldn't bring herself to get rid of. She didn't need a constant reminder of what could have been. But she couldn't bring herself to close the door on him, either.

Her phone vibrated again, validating her choice to tuck the sheet of music away. That wasn't her life anymore. Connor, whose name was glowing on the screen again, was her life now. Sliding her finger across the screen, she answered. "Is everything okay? I just checked my phone."

"I just . . . I was worried."

"I'm sorry, my phone was in my bag the whole time. I didn't think to check it."

"No, it's fine. This whole night was just weird. Where are you?"

She couldn't decipher his mood from his questions. He seemed rushed, but his tone was even. He had seemed comfortable with her going to dinner earlier. Maybe it was too much for him after all.

"I'm coming home now, just from Pioneer Square. We went to Purple Café."

"Are you driving?"

"Oh no. I took a Lyft in. After all the wine I drank at dinner, I'm glad I did." Emma laughed. "But he gave me his driver for the ride home. I think I'm almost there."

"Well, that was generous." The bitterness she'd been expecting had finally crept into the conversation.

"Where are you?" Emma asked.

"I'm heading home now too."

"I'll see you soon?"

"Yup. Soon. Love you." He hung up.

Her nerves buzzed, stomach churning with adrenaline, the closer the car got to her building. It was different when she was out doing fundraising activities, or seeing friends. There were clear boundaries where work, friends, and home were concerned. Owen, and the lines around him, had never been clear. She knew that she didn't do anything wrong tonight, but it still felt like she had.

The car shifted into park with a jolt. The wide street looked too dark, quiet even, despite the fact that she lived in the heart of the city. A homeless man made his way up the thin, tree-lined sidewalk, pit bull walking next to him, no doubt in search of the perfect doorway to sleep in for the night. His options were limited here. Too many residential buildings and restaurants had taken over. He'd have to go further into Belltown if he wanted refuge.

"Thank you so much," Emma said as the driver opened the door for her. Pulling a few dollars from her wallet, she tried to pass it to him but he waved it off.

"Have a good evening, ma'am." He dipped his head, got back into the car, and drove back off into the night.

❈

WALKING INTO THE TWELVE-STORY BUILDING, she took the elevator four floors up and wondered what it would take for someone to get a baby grand up to her apartment. She'd settle for an upright; it would probably he easier to move, easier to focus the living room around. This was the effect Owen had on her. He made her want to re-arrange everything just so she'd have a shot at beating him at his own game. If he was doing it all, she most certainly could too.

"Hey babe."

Emma turned around. Her thoughts, still heavy with Owen, made it jarring to see Connor walking towards her instead. His eyes were glassy and heavy-lidded. His smile was more of a grin, as if he had a secret. She hated how attractive he looked when he was drunk.

"Hey you," she leaned into him for a small kiss before turning back towards the door. She tasted the alcohol on him. "Did you drive home?"

"Oh yeah." He laughed, pushing the door open as she unlocked it. "But it was close. It was fine."

"One of these days," Emma teased, "you're going to wish you'd embraced ride sharing like the rest of the city."

"I know, but I only had a few drinks."

Emma looked up at him, smile gone. "Please, promise me that next time you'll get a ride. I don't want anything to happen to you."

He pulled her close, arms wrapping around her, and she could smell rum and strange perfume on him. Emma wrote it off to him having hugged Rachel at the end of the evening. She was sure there were traces of Owen's cologne on her, too. Maybe Connor was just the right amount of intoxicated not to notice.

"Okay, okay. I promise. I can't make you a widow when I just asked you to marry me."

Pulling apart from their embrace, Emma opened the apartment door and tossed her keys onto the table in their entryway. The only light in their apartment came from the small Tiffany lamp on the table and the light above the stove which, combined, threw strange yellow-edged shadows across the kitchen floor and into the living room. As she pulled off her heels, his hands wrapped around her waist.

"Connor, let me take my shoes off."

"I'm sorry I scared you. Can I make it up to you?"

Turning around to face him, she held her shoes by the heels. She couldn't remember the last time he looked at her the way he was now.

Whenever he got home late, he'd fill Emma in on every detail, down to every bit of conversation, during the commercial breaks as they watched *The Daily Show*. They'd fall asleep together, curled up, and in the morning he'd leave a note on the table by the door before he left for work. She kept them all in a shoe box in the closet. It was as if they'd been married for years; almost too comfortable to let themselves get caught up in passion anymore. Tonight was different.

"Come on. You have an early morning."

He reached out for her, his large hand against her thick hips. He had always commented on them in the beginning, how much he loved her hourglass shape. How good she'd look pregnant. In the beginning, all he wanted was to get to know her: both her history and her body.

"I don't need sleep," he whispered.

He kissed her cheek, her jawline, and then her neck. Each flavored kiss was slow and deliberate as his hands gripped her hips tighter.

"Come to bed with me," he said, and he kissed her, his mouth tasting too much like rum. It reminded her of his college apartment, of her dorm room — of a time when things felt much simpler than they were now. She didn't answer him. Instead, she continued to kiss him as they moved through the living room and into the kitchen. Opening her eyes, she could see his face reflected in the stainless-steel appliances. Lust, and perhaps love, had taken over.

He pulled away for a moment, his forehead resting against her cheek. "I love you so much."

"I love you too."

Letting him take the lead, there was a moment where she felt herself outside of the situation, experiencing it through some stranger's eyes. Owen's eyes. Here was Emma Bishop, graduate from one of the top music schools on the West Coast and bonafide New Yorker, paying room and board for her boyfriend while she organized fundraisers that kept her college crush employed. Guilt raged through her. She grabbed at Connor: his shoulders, his hair. She didn't want to think about Owen right now.

"I was thinking," he began as he kissed her collarbone, "we should spend tomorrow night together. Start thinking about dates."

"Oh?"

"I want this to be real. Us. Married. You're my everything. You don't know how much I love you."

She hated when he drank and drove home, but she loved what he said when he was this tipsy. It wasn't that she didn't know these things, that she meant so much to him, but it was rare that he was this vulnerable with her.

"I love you too."

He picked her up, arms wrapped around her sides as she crossed her legs behind his back.

"You're going to be my wife."

"I am."

He carried her into the bedroom and laid her down on the bed. As he undid his belt, she heard his phone start to ring.

"Shit." He pulled the phone out, looking at the screen. "I need to take this."

If it was this late, it was work. If it was work, it was an emergency. There was no other reason he'd walk away from her now.

"Okay."

"Stay here," he said with a grin, "I'll be right back. I promise."

Taking a deep breath, Emma rolled over as he walked out of the room. She could hear him talking fast and low in the other room. It was like listening to a sound machine where, instead of listening to a heartbeat, or a rainstorm, she could hear the sound of him working. Of him doing what he could so he could afford the Tiffany ring, the perfect proposal — so he could give her almost everything she wanted.

*

EMMA WOKE WITH A JOLT. For a moment she had no idea where she was, or the time. Sitting up, dress still on, she turned towards the balcony door to see small rays of sunlight coming through the curtains.

Standing up, back sore from the strange sleeping position, she walked through the apartment looking for Connor. All she found was a small piece of paper on the kitchen counter with a note scratched onto it:

Had to go. I'll call you. I love you. Dinner tonight. Start thinking about dates. Maybe April?

She smiled.

Walking to the front table where her bag still sat, she pulled her phone out. The screen was clear of everything but the time: seven-oh-three. He'd been gone all night.

Sending a quick text, she told him that she got his note and that April sounded perfect.

Have anywhere in mind for tonight?

His response came too quick.

Can't tonight. Something's coming up with work, will have to stay late. I'll call you later. I love you.

Emma tossed her phone onto the kitchen counter. Hope was never something she'd latched onto, not even as a child. There were certainties in the world: weather, holidays, when her mother planned trips. Everything else hinged on whether or not she worked hard enough to deserve things turning out in her favor. The colleges she got into, for example, and even the job she'd settled into after college — these were all testaments to what she was capable of when she set her mind to something.

Connor's work schedule was something she didn't have any influence over, even if her brother-in-law got Connor the job. She wished she had that kind of power, to call up and say that whatever new project they were working on could wait because she wanted to make wedding plans with her fiancé. But that wasn't something that happened in reality and she knew that. Still, it hurt to know that she'd be on her own tonight. That it would be another day, at least, before they could finish what they started the night before.

Her phone lit up again with an e-mail alert. This time it was Owen.

Concert Wednesday at 7:30. I'm sending you tickets.
Please come.

4

APRIL 2007

There were rare days in April when the bad weather gave way to good and highs reached up into the seventies. Today was one of those days. The warmth had continued into the evening despite the sun disappearing behind the mountains.

Emma was too angry to appreciate it.

This was the fifth time they had fought in the past two weeks.

"There's nothing going on. Nothing's *ever* gone on," Emma said as she walked quickly down the street, arms crossed in front of her. She didn't count what happened sophomore year.

Some anniversary this was.

"Em, you spend all of your time with him. What am I supposed to think?"

Emma stopped and turned towards him. "You can trust me. I'm not Rachel. I'm not going to sleep with someone behind your back."

Just saying it pissed her off even more. It wasn't even that Rachel had cheated on him — she hadn't, not really. The way Emma understood it was that he and Rachel hadn't even been exclusive when she started sleeping with someone else. It was an honest mistake, but one that rocked Connor to his core. Trust didn't come easy to him.

"I told you. I can't. It's hard for me."

"Well, this is getting hard for me."

She turned away from him, angry and hurt that this was how they were spending tonight. Emma had a few boyfriends in high school, but they had never made it this far. She bailed on them, or they on her, because the pressure of keeping someone past prom season was just too much when college applications were due. Making the one-year mark was supposed to be romantic.

"I'm sorry." He stepped towards her. Around them, the night traffic was weaning. People moved around them, ignorant or ignoring, as Emma and Connor stood on the corner of 1st Avenue and Pike, where their faces were bathed in the red glow of the Market's sign.

"I don't know how much longer that's going to cut it."

It was the sadness that she felt after she said it that surprised her the most.

"Look, I know. I've been really shitty. I've been jealous and I don't even recognize myself right now. I never used to be like this. I just . . . Emma, I love you. I'm terrified of losing you."

"If you love me, you need to trust me."

"Can you . . . can we just go somewhere, have a drink? Can you explain what you've been doing with him? Not in . . . I don't mean that accusingly. I just mean I want to understand. I'm jealous of the guy. You guys have this connection or something."

Emma looked around. It was too late to get a drink anywhere inside the Market. Everything classed at sunset. "There's The Pike?"

"Where we had our first date." Connor smiled.

"Yeah. I mean, it's close. It's open."

Connor offered his hand to her and she took it.

"This doesn't mean that any of this is okay. I mean it. This . . . it's a huge red flag for me. You can't dictate who I work with at school. I'm a month away from graduating."

"No, I know. I know. I just want to go sit down, and we'll talk."

Emma raised her eyebrows. What would talking fix? They'd had the same discussion hundreds of times. But maybe that was the sign that things between them weren't meant to work out, that she should've gone into this telling him there was an expiration date.

After graduation, she'd have to travel around the country auditioning anyway. Seattle would be her home base, but not her home. Maybe ending things now would be better.

"I'm sorry, Emma. I really am. You don't deserve this."

"No I don't."

Walking past the Northwest Tribal Art, they ducked into The Pike, momentarily bathed in the same red glow as they had been when they stood at the Market. Sound — music and people — created a great mix of chaos that enveloped them. The hostess smiled as they approached her and she held up two fingers. Emma nodded.

"Follow me," the hostess shouted. They obliged.

Moving through the pub, across wooden floors that were littered with shells and dust from discarded peanuts, Emma could feel Connor walking close to her, but not touching — at least not on purpose. His hand brushed against hers but she pulled her arm away.

"Your waiter will be right over," the hostess said, handing them menus as they sat down at the small table.

When they had been here on their first date, they hadn't been able to stop talking. What was supposed to be a simple breakfast and walk through the Market lasted through dinnertime, where they ended up here, learning everything they could about each other. Now, as Emma shrugged off her coat and put it on the back of her chair, she did so just because she wasn't sure what to say.

They stared at each other for a minute and then looked away. Frustration flashed through Emma. If she had known this was how the night was going to go, she would've stayed in. She could've been practicing with Owen.

But maybe that was the problem.

"So, you want to understand the whole Owen thing?" Her guilt got the better of her and she broke the silence.

"I get it, kind of. I mean, I know you guys are working on your senior thesis together and I know that's important. But this is the first time I've seen you in three weeks."

"I know. He's just . . . a perfectionist. He wants to make sure we have everything right for the concert. It's our last chance to be on a stage for a while."

Connor laughed darkly. "You're smarter than that."

Emma just stared at him.

"Come on. You have to . . . you see it, right? The way he is around you?"

It was her turn to laugh. "Listen — "

"Hey guys how're you tonight?" the waiter asked, notebook already out, ready to take their order. "Can I get you guys a drink?"

"I'll have the pale," Emma said.

"Kilt Lifter for me," Connor said, handing the waiter his ID. Emma pulled hers out and did the same.

"New York, huh?" The waiter asked, handing her license back to her.

"Yeah. I'm here for school."

Despite living in Seattle year-round now, she had never bothered to go through the process of becoming an actual resident. With the way tonight was going, the reasons for her even stay in Washington were becoming slim. Maybe she'd finally end up in Boston after all.

Boston still had a certain allure to her. It was far enough away from New York, but still ticked at the same tempo as the rest of the east coast. Seattle, while great, was a few beats off of what she was used to. She embraced the competition with, and the attention from, Owen because he was the thing that pushed her back to a New York-styled pace. But to say that out loud, especially to Connor, wasn't something she was ready to admit.

"Oh yeah? UW?" the waiter asked.

Emma shook her head. "The Conservatory."

"Arsty. Very cool. Great school. I'll be right back with those drinks."

She turned back to Connor, shrugging. "Anyway, about Owen. You think you see him look at me a certain way, but it's not. He doesn't see me."

"I've been in the same room as you two. I've seen the way he looks at you."

"No, he looks at me, sure. But he doesn't *see* me. The whole me. He only knows the me who plays the piano. Nothing beyond that matters to him."

"But that doesn't mean you don't want him to see you." Connor leaned back against his chair and looked away from her.

"I don't. Not anymore." As she said it, she realized how true it was.

"Why?"

"Why what?" Emma asked as the waiter arrived with their drinks.

"Ready to order?" The waiter asked, setting tall glasses of beer with thick foam on top in front of each of them. Emma hadn't been twenty-one for long, but just long enough to appreciate when someone could poor a decent beer.

"Just an order of fries," Emma said.

Connor smiled. "Same for me."

"Right on, well, you guys are easy enough. I'll put that right in for you."

He left again and Emma took a sip of her beer. This conversation was too focused on Owen. She was struggling to figure out what, if anything, she could do to ease Connor's fears, and if it was worth the argument. As open as she had been able to be with Connor before, it had been tempered.

"So you really have no feelings for him?" Connor asked, looking down.

"No. He's . . ." Emma trailed off, fighting to find the right words. She did have feelings, but she did what she could to deny them. He wasn't right for her. He didn't want her. "I don't want to be with someone who only sees me as one thing. I don't want to just be the girl he wrote a song with. I want to be the girl that the guy wants to go home with after the song is over."

"Owen's not that guy?"

There had been a time where she wished he'd been that guy. The guy who was someone she could spend time with doing something more than creating music with. The guy who wanted her for more than the way she played piano. It was intimate, what they did, but it never went beyond writing on sheet music or debating which music genre they'd be using as an influence. What he did when they weren't together, she didn't know. She had heard rumors of him with dancers, theater majors, but never actually saw him with anyone.

"He hasn't even asked where I'm from. If I have siblings. If I do anything other than play the piano. I don't want to be with someone who doesn't want to know those things about me."

"I'm sorry. I just . . . you're amazing. You really are. And I just always feel like I'm right on the edge of losing you."

She was surprised at how in tune with her he actually was. It wasn't that he was losing her, though. It was just that it was inevitable that they were going to go their separate ways. It was the same with Owen. Except where Connor was concerned, he actually cared about her. When graduation day came, she was sure Owen would forget about her. Connor was different. He was everything she wished Owen would be.

"If you were, I'd let you know. I'm not Rachel. I don't know why I need to keep telling you that. I'm not going to sleep with your friend, or with Owen. That's not who I am. I thought you knew that about me."

"You're right. I'm being an ass."

"This just isn't how I thought today was going to go."

"It's not how I wanted it to go." He sighed, picked up his glass, and took a long sip.

"How did you want it to go?"

"We were going to walk down the waterfront, go to Ivar's, and I was going to give you this." He pulled the small box out of his jacket pocket. "It's not . . . It's not an engagement ring or anything, just . . . something."

Emma reached across the table, picked up the little white box, and pulled the top open. Inside was a small silver Claddagh ring. It looked almost identical to the one her father had proposed to her mother with, unofficially. It had been a placeholder before he could afford the real thing. If this was an indication of where he thought that they were headed, Emma wasn't sure if she agreed. It was too early, she was too young, to feel okay with settling down with someone. But there was no denying that he was in this for the long haul.

"It's beautiful."

"You like it?"

"I do." She smiled. "Thank you."

"I can take you to go have it sized, but I had Molly — "

"Molly knew about this?" Emma was surprised that her room-mate had a hand in this. Connor and Molly had met before, in passing, but nothing to where Emma would consider them friends. It wasn't like Molly had the best opinion of him, either.

"Yeah. I messaged her on MySpace." He grinned as the waiter came back with the fries.

"Can I get you two anything else?" the waiter asked.

"No, we're good." Connor picked up the ketchup bottle. "Thanks."

The waiter walked away and Emma took the ring out of the box. It was small in her fingers, delicate even, as she turned it over in her hand. Finally she put it on her finger — the ring finger — and was relieved that it fit.

"So it fits?" he asked between bites of French fry.

"It does. Perfectly."

He grinned again and went back to his fries. "I was trying to figure out something to get you, and you said how your dad gave your mom one when they were dating — "

"I think I said that, like, once."

"I know. But it sounded like you liked the idea of it."

"Of what?" Emma raised her eyebrows.

She needed to remind herself that this had an expiration date. Graduation. Until then she'd enjoy him, their time together, but that was it. Even with Owen out of the picture, she still couldn't see a sustainable future for them.

"Just something to let you know how the person you're dating feels about you?" He blushed.

"And how do you feel?"

She heard him earlier when he said it. He loved her. He was terri-fied of losing her to the person who understood a side of her that he couldn't. It didn't excuse his jealousy, but she understood it. She understood what it felt like to lose someone you love. Maybe that's why she was so ready to bolt now.

He rolled his eyes, smiling. "I love you."

"Good." Emma took a sip of her beer. His face fell.

"That's all you have to say?"

She put her beer back down. For her, there were so many different kinds of love. There was the kind of love she felt for the way Owen played, and the kind of love she felt for New York City. But what she felt for Connor was bigger than those things. It scared her. It scared her to think that she could let herself be so open, and so honest, with a person who wasn't sure if he could trust again. It scared her to think that he'd never be happy with the life that she wanted to live.

But the thing Emma was learning about relationships, and trust, and even love, was that you had to take the chance on someone sometimes. You had to be patient and understanding of the baggage they came with. Whenever a plane went overhead and she started shaking, he'd hold her until she stopped. She needed to help him through his shit too.

"No," Emma reached her hand across the table, touching his. His palm was warm with sweat. "I love you too."

5

"Wow," Connor said as he walked into the large bathroom.

Emma looked up at his reflection in the mirror as she finished applying her mascara. She'd barely seen him the past two days. Event planning meetings for the summer season had kept her out late, while he, too, had been stuck at work. Their time together was a quick kiss hello and goodnight before falling asleep to the television. She missed him and their normal pattern. It made her want to skip the symphony altogether.

"Where are you off to?"

"The symphony. Would you like to go with me?"

"I'm sorry . . . I'm meeting Rachel again. Is it for work?"

"No, Owen sent tickets for us, but I wasn't sure if you'd be free. I have Molly in reserve."

She could see him hesitate, hands in his pockets. As much as she wished she could demand that he go with her instead of meeting Rachel, she knew she couldn't. If he had changed his answer, Molly would've happily stayed home. She had been Emma's roommate in college and unlike many of their other classmates — who had moved to New York or Los Angeles — Molly had stayed in Seattle. It was something that Emma was forever thankful for. Molly knew her better than Danielle, or Leah. Sometimes Emma was sure Molly knew her better than she knew herself.

"That's fine. Like I said, Molly's free tonight to go with me, anyway."

"That'll be nice. You haven't seen her since, what, March?"

Emma nodded. "I have to tell her about the news."

He came up behind her and put his arms around her. She put her mascara down on the counter and smiled at his reflection.

"Oh, that's right. I proposed to you."

"Yes, yes. You must've forgotten with all of your important work business."

"Plus you're not even wearing a ring yet," he said as he mock-rolled his eyes. "No one even knows you're officially off the market."

"I guess I'll be able to scout out a sugar daddy tonight then. Since I'm not officially engaged to you," Emma teased back, smiling the whole time. This felt good, like they were *them* again, even if it was just for a few minutes. Three days of living a different life felt like an eternity. She didn't like it.

He stepped back from her and she turned to face him. He winked and got down on one knee, pulling a black velvet box from his pants pocket.

"Emma Avery Bishop," he began as he opened the ring box. Inside was the ring that he had picked out for her, that he had proposed to her in a similar fashion at a bed and breakfast in the San Juan Islands the weekend before. He said he had wanted to wait until dinner, or sunset, but when they woke up that first morning he couldn't wait.

"Yes?"

"Do I really have to ask you to marry me again?" He laughed, and Emma laughed, and the sound filled the bathroom.

Standing up, he took the ring out of the box and slipped it onto her finger. It was still a little loose, but the jeweler had insisted on the bigger size.

"Does it fit?" he asked.

Emma nodded. It would, when the weather was warmer. "It does. I didn't think it would be ready so soon."

"They called me today. I picked it up on the way home from work. That's why I was late."

"I hate that you got home late. But I love that I finally have my ring."

He kissed her cheek and then her mouth, soft enough and brief enough to leave her wanting more.

"You still owe me from the other night," Emma half-teased. She didn't want this moment to end, for their real life to begin again. Their real life involved too much work, too much Owen and Rachel, and it got in the way of them actually being able to celebrate being engaged.

"Dinner, you mean?" Connor teased back. "This weekend, I'm all yours."

Her phone chimed and she turned around, pulling away from him. "Molly's downstairs."

"She can wait, can't she?"

Emma shook her head. "She, and the symphony, will not wait for me. But remember that you owe me more than a dinner. I miss you."

It wasn't even that she was a particularly sex-driven person. The physical act itself was something she didn't care for. It was just the time with him, those moments where it was just them and nothing else mattered. She wanted the world to melt away and work deadlines, people, her parents being a world away, and airplanes crashing to disappear. Even if she were to sleep with him right now, it wouldn't be what she wanted. It would be quick, and good, but just sex.

"I miss you too. And I owe you the world. Thank you for being understanding about tonight."

"I wouldn't be me if I wasn't." She kissed him on the cheek. "But now I really need to go."

❀

37

TAKING the elevator down to the first floor, she passed the usual neighbors coming home from work.

"Emma, god, I haven't seen you in weeks!" Amy, who lived in the apartment below theirs, came up to her and air-kissed her cheeks. "You need to come for drinks next week. Everything's in chaos."

"Tuesday night, right?"

Emma knew when it was, but it was the only thing she could think to say. A night with Amy and the other women in the building wasn't at the top of her priority list at the moment. The distraction was usually nice. They were different than Emma's college friends, focused on their husbands or finding one, settled in their careers, in their life. Danielle and Molly both were just starting to get settled. They were Emma's peers at a time when she needed mentors.

"Yes! Eight on the balcony like usual. You know, as long as the weather holds. Would you be able to bring an appetizer?"

"Sure thing. I'm off to the symphony right now, though. Can I call you tomorrow?"

"Oh, of course. Connor must be waiting for you. I'm sorry for keeping you!"

She went to correct Amy but stopped herself. "It's not a problem. See you!"

Outside, the ground was wet from the recent rain. The clouds were still thick and low over the city, the tops of the skyscrapers hidden from view. Leaves, ripped down by the storm, tumbled down the sidewalk in the wind, the scraping skipping sound they made as they went barely audible over the noises of the evening traffic. Breaks from buses screeched as they rounded corners and stopped at their destinations. Impatient drivers honked in the moments between red and green. It was its own symphony; a lullaby that Emma was sure she'd never be able to sleep without.

"Finally," Molly said as Emma opened the car door. "Hunky boyfriend keeping you preoccupied?"

"Fiancé."

"What?! When? Now? Why are you with me and not upstairs doing him?"

Molly was short in stature, but what she lacked in height she made up for in personality. While her natural hair color was blonde, today it was near the color of Emma's: somewhere between dark chocolate and mahogany, but with streaks of fire engine red throughout the short bob.

"He proposed Saturday morning." Emma extended her hand to show Molly the solitaire diamond. "I just got the ring back today from getting sized."

"Why didn't you tell me?"

Emma shrugged. "I've barely told anyone. My Mom and Dad know, obviously. He FaceTimed them to ask their permission. But I didn't want to steal Danielle's thunder."

"Oh honey, Danielle would want you to steal her thunder right about now. I swear, if she doesn't get completely shit-faced Friday night I'll be surprised."

"That bad?"

Danielle had recently finished her Ph.D. in some obscure aspect of literature Emma tried to understand but didn't. When Danielle had originally set the date for her wedding, she had thought she'd have more time. A year and a half to plan a party for two-hundred people wouldn't be that difficult, she'd explained. But she pushed everything off: engagement party, wedding dress shopping, her bridal shower. Emma, as maid of honor, had to pack everything into a four-month span, starting with Friday's engagement party.

At least Emma wouldn't be making the same mistake with her own wedding.

"She's stressed. Big time. She went with her mom to look at dresses yesterday and I think she found one. But of course the florist isn't going to be able to do what she wants with the budget she has, or with what she wants to spend. I don't know. This is all your department."

"Thanks for being there for her this week."

"You seem like you've had other things on your mind," Molly said, grinning as she slowed to a stop at a red light.

"Oh, it's not even like that. I've barely seen Connor since this weekend."

"You two really know how to be romantic," Molly deadpanned.

Emma laughed. "We've just both been busy. Work's been hell for him. And I had dinner plans Monday night. So did he."

"So where is he tonight? Not that I mind getting to see you."

"Out with Rachel. It's who he saw on Monday."

Molly was silent, but her silence said everything.

"I'm completely okay with him spending time with Rachel. Just like he's okay with the fact that I went to dinner with Owen on Monday."

"Owen."

"That's who gave me these tickets."

"You're finally over him and you start seeing him again?"

Emma looked out the passenger side window. Belltown flew by, trees and buildings blending together as Molly weaved through the steady stop and go of the evening traffic.

"I have to. He's Tom's brother, and the best man. I can't avoid him with all of this."

"I know, but still. You're finally . . . " Molly trailed off.

"What?"

"Content with your life. Not happy, but you're comfortable. And I know how hard that was for you to get to."

Emma knew Molly had a point. The conversation was lost, however, as they pulled up in front of Benaroya Hall. The front was floor to ceiling windows, lit up against the dark Seattle skyline. People, dressed up and down, were walking towards the doors while people in black stood, ready to take their tickets.

"Wow, I forgot how big this place was," Molly said, leaning over the passenger side to get a better look at the building.

"Mol, just drive. Pull in there," Emma pointed at the parking garage.

"Twenty-five dollars? Fuck no."

"No, no. He gave me a parking pass, too."

"Your man friend treats you better than your boyfriend," Molly joked.

"Hey, Connor did give me a ring."

"Well, we can't really argue with a diamond. But you never were the kind of girl who cared about that shit."

"I could never afford it before. Student loans cover meal plans, not shopping trips to Bellevue Square."

"I know, but still. It would've been more romantic if he proposed to you with a piano or something. You've wanted your own since the day I met you."

Emma shrugged, unable to deny with Molly was saying. Still, Connor was trying: he picked out a beautiful ring, he proposed, he was doing everything he could to show her he loved her, even if he was busy. Wasn't he?

Parking and getting out of the car, the girls linked arms, just as they had in college.

"He does try. I know it all gets mixed up sometimes, but he does try."

Molly shrugged. "Whatever you say, boo. It's your life. I just want to make sure that you're happy. This is just a very different life that I thought you would've had. You're so busy with work and fundraisers and your league ladies who lunch, or whatever."

"Yeah, yeah. My life is fancy."

"It'll be nice to have everyone back together for the wedding."

"Me too. It'll be nice spending more time with everyone."

"Even Owen?" Molly grinned, too much like the cat who ate the canary.

"Yes. And no, not really. It's dangerous. Like I said, I like where my life is now but Moll — he looked like he wanted to kiss me that night. And I don't know if I would've turned him down."

She finished her sentence while they walked into the grand lobby. Grand, of course, was too small of an adjective to describe the room. What looked beautiful from the outside was more beautiful on the inside, filled to the brim with people. Even though her entire life revolved around the symphony, she couldn't remember the last time she went to a function for fun. It was strange, being a part of it, but still being on the outside looking in.

"Can't say I blame you there," Molly glanced back at her as they stood in line to hand in their tickets. "I don't think I would've given him the option. If he still looks at you the way he used to, I don't know how you would have just let that go. I mean . . . have you even bothered to look at where we're sitting? He clearly missed you."

She looked at her ticket. Founder's Tier Box.

"Enjoy the show, miss." The older woman smiled as she scanned Emma's ticket.

"Thank you."

They wove their way into the right entry to their seats. Emma's breath caught as they walked into the auditorium. From where their seats were they could see more stage than auditorium. The conductor wasn't out yet but the rest of the symphony sat in their chairs, instruments at rest while they waited for the show to begin.

Emma felt overwhelmed being here. She had avoided seeing the symphony for this long for good reason. Sitting down, she could see Owen in the first chair, waiting. If he saw her, she couldn't be sure.

"It's not like these were special seats he picked out for us," Emma explained. "He gets the same seats every year."

"Hey, I think he sees us! Should we wave?"

Rolling her eyes, Emma shook her head, but looked back at him. "No, no. Just sit down."

"You're blushing, girly."

"Shut up."

Closing her eyes, Emma sat back in the plush chair and listened to the rustling of material and wrappers as people made their way to their seats. She was waiting for the house lights to dim, for the rustling to stop, for the music to begin.

"Do you even know what they're playing tonight?" Molly's hoarse whisper rose up above the din.

"No."

The lights dimmed and the crowd quieted. The conductor came

out to uniform applause. Emma still kept her eyes closed, her mind caught in a distant memory. She was doing her best to keep her emotions at bay but the bitter ache of a life she had given up consumed her now more than ever.

They opened with Vivaldi's *Spring* and Emma's fingers started moving against her own leg, her muscles still remembering how to play. But as they began to transition into the next season, the ache Emma had been feeling exploded.

"Em, why do I know this song?"

"*Sh.*"

It would be about forty minutes of this. Of Owen leading the piano, of the piano leading the symphony, through the last songs Emma had ever played. *Summer* had been the last song Emma had ever played. It had been the final night of college and she was back in an empty auditorium with Owen before she went to meet Connor. He wanted to play one last song with her and they'd settled on *Summer*.

Emma focused on Owen now, watching his face as he moved through the song. He'd been amazing in college, sure, but that didn't compare to the way he played tonight. He had been so reserved then, the emotion he'd show on stage nothing compared to the man she looked at now. Frankly, she was surprised that she didn't see tears running down his face.

It only reaffirmed her need to stay away from seeing him, and seeing him play.

As they finished the first half of the program, the audience applauded neatly, not moving from the position they had been in as they listened. Emma, too, clapped along with them, nodding to Owen as he found her in the crowd. He smiled back, big and wide. He'd known how these songs in particular would get to her.

She shook her head twice.

He would have to do more than make her feel this way to get her to play again.

6

S moothing the material of her dress, Emma looked around the room. They had been at the party for a couple hours now and guests were still arriving. What had once been quiet conversation was now a louder sound rising above the music that played through the speakers by the DJ's table. Familiar faces kept flowing in, smiling and waving at Emma, before they made their way to Danielle and Tom. It was like a never-ending receiving line; practice for the real thing, no doubt. Connor, though, was nowhere to be found. He'd left her standing there, promising to be right back with drinks. That'd been what felt like ages ago.

She knew she shouldn't feel this out of place, this naked without being attached to Connor's arm. Being that in need of his company was not how things usually were. But Emma was still shaken after Owen and Molly's response. She'd expected something more from Molly than mild excitement. Emma took it as disapproval but couldn't understand where it came from.

Emma's family was excited, of course. Leah had already given Emma the wedding planning books that she had used when she got married. Even her parents wanted to get a jump-start on planning. They already booked flights out to visit this summer with the hopes of helping Emma look at venues. There were also hints of house hunting on the last phone call. After all, she couldn't have children and raise a family in her downtown condo. In a matter of a week's time, her life had gone from her own to everyone else's. Maybe she and Connor didn't want kids. They'd never discussed it. Careers were their focus. Working, fundraisers, charity events — their life felt full enough already without the addition of children.

What Emma did want to plan for was spending more time with her fiancé. They had finally been able to spend a night together, just the two of them, with little distractions. Wedding plans weren't mentioned, but that was fine. He'd brought home a wedding magazine for her, but once they made dinner and put the television on, coming up with concrete ideas had fallen by the wayside. It could all wait until after Danielle's wedding at least. Emma was in no rush.

"There you are!" Molly said, coming up next to Emma.

"Hey."

"Have you seen Owen yet?"

Emma nodded. Of course she had seen him. He was a magnet, pulling her in whatever direction he was heading. She was too aware of him, of where he was in the room, of his eyes on her. It only made her want Connor at her side more. Owen might be a magnet, but Connor was her anchor. He helped her to stay focused on what she needed to get done and reminder her that she was happy in this life. Owen confused her. Being around him chipped away at the foundation she'd built this life, her and Connor's life, on.

"I just haven't talked to him yet."

"Have you even talked to him since the concert?"

Emma shook her head. "I sent a thank you."

"A thank you?"

"Of course. It was thoughtful of him to invite us."

"You don't think he sent tickets for reasons other than being thoughtful?"

"He sent two tickets, not one. I think you're reading too much into this."

Emma played with the ring on her finger, the metal still feeling foreign against her skin. She looked out over the gray, linen-covered tables, their metallic color a pleasing contrast to the red wine colored walls of the room. Along the bar was where most of the guests had gathered, glasses of wine or mixed drinks in their hand. Music played, but not too loud to interrupt conversations. She wondered what her own engagement party would be like, if she had one. Would Owen be there too?

"If you say so," Molly said. "Come on. Let's get a drink. I need to find my girlfriend." Molly linked arms with her and they navigated the groups of people as they made their way up to the bar.

"Captain and Coke for me," Molly said before leaning away, allowing Emma room to give her order, too.

"Spritzer for me, please. Pinot Grigio."

"Oh come on, live a little," Molly teased. "Get yourself a grown up drink."

"Wine *is* a grown up drink," Emma teased back.

A woman came up to her and kissed Molly just then and kissed her cheek. Laurel was everything that Molly was not: quiet, low energy, blonde, and tall. At least tall compared to Molly. They had met at an art event a year ago. Molly had been showing her work and Laurel had been looking to buy. Since then their two separate lives had blended into one and grown from there. Laurel still worked for one of the tech companies in Bellevue and Molly switched jobs and was now working at a glass blowing studio. Molly even moved in with Laurel not too long ago. Their differences — business and art, structure and lack thereof—worked for them. It was an imperfectly perfect match. One that Emma still struggled to understand.

"Not everyone drinks like you, babe," Laurel said. "It's so nice to see you, Emma. It's been too long."

"It really has. I'm glad you could make it. And besides, I've barely touched hard liquor since college."

"That's a shame. You were always so much fun when you had rum," Owen teased. He had approached them without Emma noticing.

"I'm surprised you even remember. Most of the time you were passed out by the time I even started drinking."

He laughed, full and deep. His head tilted back and the sound moved through his whole body. That was one thing that hadn't changed from college.

"All right, that's fair. Molly, it's good to see you."

"Same! And this is Laurel — "

Laurel held her hand out to Owen, who shook it.

"Owen Gibson."

"I've heard a lot about you. It's nice putting a face to the name." Laurel smiled. "Molly said you were great the other night."

"I'm glad she and Emma could make it."

"Owen, buddy, good to see you." Connor approached them now, his hand held out toward Owen. Molly looked to Emma, who shrugged. Owen had never been Connor's *buddy*. He'd always been Connor's competition.

"You too," Owen said, grabbing Connor's hand.

"It was really great of you to send Emma those tickets the other night. I'm just sorry I couldn't use them with her."

The tension between the two men electrified the air, prickling against Emma's skin. The bartender put the wine glass next to her and she had never felt more grateful.

"Consider it an engagement present. Perhaps if I send tickets again, I'll see you both there." Owen smiled. "Did Emma mention I'm trying to get her to come play with us?"

Emma stared at Owen over the rim of her wine glass as she took a long sip. She hadn't said she'd come play. It was the reason why she never even thought to bring it up to Connor.

"No, she hadn't," Connor said, taking Emma's free hand and squeezing it. "It was nice of you to make that offer. She doesn't play anymore, though. Hasn't in years." He looked around the room, his palm sweaty against her own. Emma squeezed his hand back, trying to reassure him.

"That's what I told him, but he seems insistent on the idea," Emma said.

"Well, you can't blame me for trying." Owen shrugged. "You're a gifted musician and it's a shame that you don't play anymore. But you're always welcome to come to the rehearsals, even if you'd just like to watch."

"That's nice of you, really," Emma answered. "I'll have to see if my schedule allows it."

Connor let go of her hand and kissed her cheek. Maybe that was all he needed to hear. "This has been fun catching up, but I'm going to go see if I can go find Tom."

"Of course," Owen answered. "It was great to see you."

"I don't remember him being that jumpy," Molly said after Connor walked away. "I mean, nervous sometimes, sure. But he just seems tense tonight."

"Yeah, I know." Emma finished the rest of her wine and put her glass back on the bar. When the bartender came over, she waved him off. She wanted to be able to think clearly tonight. "I'm not sure inviting me to come play, again, helped things, Owen."

"I didn't mean for it to be threatening. I thought that your fiancé would want you to do things that made you happy."

"What makes you think I'm not happy?"

Emma turned away from him and searched the room for Connor. Finally, she found him at the far end of the bar talking to the same blonde he'd seen him with earlier. The moment cut into her, a deep slice across her heart. Here she was, standing with Owen, and Connor was across the room talking to another woman. It was the glimpse into a life that she could've had that she wasn't ready for. She had to look away.

"Em," Molly cut in. "Maybe you should go play. I mean it's been years. Maybe it'll be good for you."

Turning back towards the group, Emma shrugged. She had been fine the past decade without playing the piano. Changing that now would only make it hurt more when she had to stop again.

"Maybe we should let Emma decide what's best," Laurel added. "It's her life."

Emma reaching out and squeezed Laurel's shoulder. "Thank you."

She was going to say more, but spotted Danielle coming towards them. Emma had seen her at the beginning of the night, her shoulders hunched up, her hands shaking from nerves. But the Danielle that walked towards them now, was quite relaxed — and quite drunk.

"EMMA!"

Danielle never got drunk. Not since college, anyway. Her schedule was always too full to allow even one night off to have fun. They had been able to squeeze in occasional girls nights during Danielle's school breaks, but they were few and far between. Tonight, it was clear from how red her cheeks were that she was drunk. Wine drunk.

Love drunk.

As close as Emma and Molly were, Emma considered Danielle another sister. Molly was great for checking her conscience. She also didn't shy away from calling Emma out when she was overreacting, or underreacting, about something. With Danielle, it was different. They lost track of each other from time to time, but could always pick right back up where they left off. Danielle was the only one who knew about what happened with Owen. Emma was the only one who knew Danielle had been pregnant when Tom proposed, but they lost the baby soon after. Emma and Danielle kept each other's secrets and promised to take them to the grave.

"I'm so glad you're here! And Owen's here, and Molly and Laurel! My favorite people are finally here and I'm so happy." She threw her arms around each of them, embracing them in sloppy hugs. "Emma I've missed you! I haven't seen you in days and I really need my maid of honor. There is literally so much that needs to get done."

"I know, I'm sorry. But I'm here now and we have this. It's going to all be taken care of, don't worry."

"Good! I need my band back together. I need you guys to help me through all this. Just like old times!"

Emma rarely felt nostalgic, but tonight she was overwhelmed by it. She hadn't been surrounded by this many people, this many friends, in many years. It made her miss the cloistered dorm life, the times when nothing outside the school's boundaries mattered. When music, creating it and playing it, was what got her out of bed in the morning.

The rings she and Danielle wore were signs that the part of their lives that were controlled by GPA's and meal plans was over for good. They were real adults now. The decisions they were making now had a deeper impact than whether they'd be hungover for class the next day.

"I'm not even sure what to do next. You guys need dresses. Now that my dissertation is done, now that I'm done with school forever, I can actually see you! And see my fiancé."

Emma knew the feeling, of wanting to be with someone, near someone, but a drive towards something else pushing you apart. A decade ago it had been Owen and the piano. Now it was just life getting in the way. Maybe she was supposed to cherish the moments with Connor more and accept that this was their new status quo. Something about it all felt off. She wasn't ready to settle for her future playing out the way the week before had.

"Yeah, you're actually going to have to spend time with him. Do you even remember what he looks like?" Molly teased.

"Yes! I do." Danielle grinned. "And I get to see him all day, every day, for however long it takes me to find a job. I get to bug *him* while he works now. Does Connor do that, Em? Does he bug you when you work from home?"

Emma shook her head. Boundaries, professional and personal, were always respected in their home. Whenever they were both home, and Emma was working, Connor never disturbed her. Only now did she think that maybe there was something wrong with how much space she and Connor gave each other.

"TOM! He's here." Danielle yelled, walking towards the Owen-clone. Tom and Owen weren't totally identical anymore, but you could still tell they were brothers. Where Owen kept his hair longer, Tom's was shorter. Owen was free of tattoos, where Tom had two full sleeves that were covered up tonight by his button down shirt. He'd added suspenders and a bowtie for good measure.

"I've been here, babe."

"I know. I just meant I finally found you. I lost you!"

The room quieted, eyes turning towards the couple. The stress in Danielle's life was visible in her cheekbones and too-thin arms. Planning a wedding and writing a dissertation at the same time? It was a level of stress Emma hoped she'd never have to feel.

"Why don't I take you back to your place," Emma offered, placing a hand on Danielle's shoulder. "You seem like you're ready to go home."

"Emma-bear that would be so sweet of you! I'm *exhausted*."

"I'll walk her to your car," Tom said, putting an arm around Danielle. "Thanks, Em."

"It's no problem. Really. The keys are in my coat pocket." Emma nodded towards the unmanned coat-check by the door. "The tan trench on the first hanger is mine."

"Great. I'll see you out there."

As Tom walked away with Danielle, Emma tried to find Connor. Owen, Molly, and Laurel had fallen into conversation so she wouldn't bother them. But, since she came with Connor, she had to let him know where she was going. Maybe he'd even want to leave early.

Finally spotting him, she walked to the end of the bar, where he was still talking to the blonde.

"Connor," she began, walking up to them, "I just . . ."

"Oh, Emma. Hey. You remember Rachel?"

Emma smiled at the woman. The last time she had seen a picture of Rachel, she'd looked different. Not so refined. She was still too skinny, her makeup done just right. She was pretty, conventionally so. It was hard for Emma not to compare herself to Rachel, and envy her. It felt strange, seeing her standing there. All week she'd been nothing more than some abstract thing keeping Connor busy. To see Rachel now made Emma nervous. Jealous, even.

"Rachel, it's so good to see you. I forgot you were friends with Danielle."

"Yeah. Thanks for letting me borrow Connor this week. He's been a big help. I wouldn't been able to move without him."

Emma tried to smile but faltered. "Of course. I know he would do anything to help you, whenever you needed it."

Connor shifted as he placed the empty glass back on the bar. "You ready to go then, Em?"

"I actually just offered to take Danielle home. She's had a bit too much to drink. I was going to drop her off and come back here to get you."

"No, no. I can get a Lyft or an Uber."

"Are you sure?"

"I'll be fine. I'll see you at home soon. That was my last drink — scout's honor."

Emma caught Rachel's expression: the small smile as she lifted her wine glass. If this was a game, Emma was just finding out now that she was a player in it. It was as if just being around college friends bred the drama that ran rampant during their undergraduate years. Emma wanted no part of it.

"That's fine. Owen was going to come keep me company, anyway. I just figured I'd extend the offer."

The lie came out before Emma could stop it. This was exactly what she wanted to avoid. She had no reason to be petty, to make up lies, to force Connor to choose between staying here with Rachel or coming with her. But she wanted him to.

"Oh. Were you going to come home right after dropping them off?"

"I'm not sure. Owen had mentioned wanting grabbing a drink, but it'll depend."

"I'll come with, then. I'd be great to catch up with him."

"Con, you said you were going to take me home." Rachel pouted, each word too sweet. It was the kind of sweet that promised a bad hangover in the morning.

Emma clenched her jaw as she looked back up at Connor. Her patience for this was wearing thin. She wanted to get Danielle out of here before the she was able to make a bigger scene. This back and forth, this power struggle, was wasting time.

"No, Rachel. I said I'd get you a cab." Connor was stern, his eyes narrowing at Rachel. Emma felt too embarrassed for her. She had to save the moment somehow.

"We're more than able to give you a ride home, too, if you needed one," Emma added. "It wouldn't be a problem at all."

"I'd rather not. Thanks though. I appreciate it." Rachel smiled.

"No problem."

"Let us know if you change your mind." Emma added. "It was great seeing you."

"You too."

"I'll meet you at the car?" Emma asked Connor. He nodded his head.

Emma turned and left, spotting Molly on the other side of the bar still with Owen and Laurel. She'd let Connor say his goodbye to Rachel in private.

"Leaving already?" Molly asked.

"Yeah, I'm taking Danielle home. Connor's coming with me, he's just saying goodbye to Rachel."

"I thought she looked familiar," Molly said, her eyebrows raised. "You're okay with this?"

"With them talking?" Emma asked.

Molly nodded.

"Of course I am. I have no reason not to trust Connor."

"If you say so."

Emma blushed. She didn't want to have this conversation with Molly now, especially in front of Owen. Especially after a glass of wine. It was bad enough that he didn't believe that she was happy, that he pushing trying to lead her down a path she knew would devastate her. She didn't need Molly to be doing the same thing.

"You'll let me know about Wednesday?" Owen asked.

She shrugged. Thankful as she was that he didn't acknowledge what Molly had said, she hadn't wanted him to bring up the rehearsal, either.

"I can't make any promises. But I'll see the you guys later."

She hugged Laurel, Molly, and finally Owen. His arms wrapped around her, and he held her close enough so that she could hear what she thought was his heartbeat even over the music and conversation. He held on just a second too long before letting her go.

Walking away from him, and leaving the party, felt strange. It was the same pull she had been feeling earlier. Walking away from Owen felt like playing off-key. She felt off-balanced.

And it scared her.

7

AUGUST 2003

Emma loitered outside the rehearsal hall doors for as long as she could justify. Beginning her first college music class was more terrifying than it should've been. She'd never taken classes like this. The private lessons she took after school had been good enough to get her into the best programs in the country. Today was the first day at her top choice school.

Well, sort of. The Seattle Conservatory was her second choice.

Many of her friends ended up at NYU or Columbia, with a few heading out to Boston or New Jersey. A SUNY school was a choice, but a safe one. Even with some of the music programs that the school system offered, Emma knew she could do better. She wanted the recognition that came from going to a conservatory. But as the dust of 9/11 finally settled, she just couldn't live in, or even near New York, any longer. The constant reminder of what happened was too much. Putting distance between herself and New York, and Boston was the only way she knew how to cope. Emma hadn't even known she had a problem with Boston until she went to visit the conservatory there. The mere suggestion of flying through Boston Logan caused the first of many terrible panic attacks. With her older sister, Leah, living in

Seattle, the west coast seemed like the safest place to run. Still not wanting a state school's style of teaching, Emma settled on The Seattle Conservatory. The rumor was that it fed the top orchestras on the west coast. It wasn't Boston, but she'd still be getting a world-class education. At the end of the day, that was what mattered.

A lone violin started playing and the sound ripped through her, slicing her heart, shredding it like paper. It was Bach — the music, that is — and it drew her into the large room like a moth to flame. She flitted towards it, eyes not on the player but on the fingers. His fingers, she realized as her eyes traveled up the arm and onto the face of the player. His facial expressions matched that of the "Partita": troubled and hurting.

"Good, Mr. Gibson." The teacher, a stout, balding man which glasses as thick as his accent, stood up and clapped a few times. "The rest of you strings, yes," he pointed to a small group who held the tell-tale black cases, "you join him. Follow him."

Emma stood, leaning up against a wall, with the other non-string musicians. This room was unlike any room she'd been in before. Brightly lit, the walls were a mix between soundproofing and sound boosting, with geometric shapes bulging from strategic points in the room. Everything was designed to make the music sound full. Like it took up all the empty space in the room. The students holding their black cases filtered into the seats around the piano and started to tune up. The second chair, the one next to Mr. Gibson, remained empty.

The professor moved his arms and sound filled the room again. First it was Mr. Gibson's violin, and then more violins falling into line. The cellos were last, but their deep notes were what stood out the most. Emma's fingers moved against her leg, playing an invisible keyboard, as she followed along.

"Good!" the professor shouted at her. She jumped, not noticing that he'd been watching her. "I thought you might be my piano. Watch them. Keep playing along. Good skills."

Emma smiled, unsure of how else to respond.

"All right," he said, holding his hand up. Mr. Gibson stopped and held his violin at his side. Emma was finally able to get a good look at him. He was tall, with shaggy dark hair and dark eyes, but a smile that was patient and kind. The expression he wore now was different, less painful, than the one he wore while playing. The others were not so graceful. A few last lingering notes filtered through the air while the professor waited with his hands up.

"For this class you will be paired up, and you will work on a piece together for the end of the semester. What you have all demonstrated is the disaster of knowing a piece too well."

A few students chuckled while others blushed.

"No, I do not mean that as in insult, but as a fact. Many of you come from being able to regurgitate pieces, and not make them your own. I want you to pick pieces and learn them — learn them, and make them your own."

He began calling names and paired students off. Most were different instruments — flutes and cello, cello and violins — but others were the same. Emma waited for her name to be called.

"Bishop, Emma," he said finally. Emma stood up, her seat creaking under her as it folded back into itself. "You are with Mr. Gibson."

He hopped down from the stage and extended his hand after brushing hair out of his face. "Owen."

"Emma."

"What do you play?"

"Piano."

She blushed as his eyes settled on her hands, her wrists, her hips, and finally on her face.

"I should have guessed."

"Why's that?"

He shrugged. "Just the way you are, the way you hold yourself."

"I . . . will take that as a compliment?" Emma laughed. She'd heard it before, that she looked like a piano player. She fit the stereotype and she wore it like a badge. But for some reason hearing it come from him made her self-conscious about her thin wrists, her too-straight posture, and her wide hips. Unlike the flutists, who were all built like ballerinas, she was long and took up space on the piano bench. She'd never be invisible when she was on stage.

"It is one, I assure you." He shifted his weight, his left knee bending now instead of is right. "Do you have any idea what you'd like to work on?"

Emma shook her head. She was overwhelmed by all of this, by the freedom provided by this class, and the way he'd been playing. She had so many questions but didn't want to make it so obvious that she didn't belong here. The empty second chair was still lingering in her thoughts. The first chair she knew was important. Any time she'd gone to see the symphony, they were the ones who led tuning and warm ups before the conductor came to the stage. If there was an equal importance of the second chair, Emma didn't know about it. She was glad that playing the piano didn't involve some strange hierarchy.

"I hear you do a mean take on Schubert."

Emma raised an eyebrow. He must've found the audition tape her sister uploaded onto MySpace. Leah had wanted Emma to see the mistake she was making by not just going to Boston. "Everyone thinks you're amazing," Leah said late one night. Emma had to stay up until midnight to talk long distance. "You really need to keep up with the music stuff. If not Boston, then come out here. There's a conservatory downtown." The same audition tape that had got her into Boston, had also impressed the Seattle admissions board, and now had impressed Owen Gibson.

"I guess."

"I haven't heard it played that way before. It was really good. No wondering you got in here."

"Thanks."

She didn't want to say how it was a safe choice, picking Ave Maria. It was safe and personal. Parts of it she embellished, pushing the boundaries of what the notes dictated.

"I thought you'd like to work on Ave with me. See if we can't give it another facelift. Not that the one you gave it wasn't already good."

Looking at him, at his hair that was perfectly messed up, at his bright, cocky grin. This was going to be an easy assignment for him and he wanted to ride it her MySpace popularity all the way to the Dean's List. No, he'd need to pick a different song.

"As a duet? I'm not sure. What if we picked a — "

"No, no. Just trust me."

Emma took a deep breath in. She didn't trust him. She didn't even know him, beyond the fact that his name was Owen and he played the violin. Playing music and writing it were too different skill sets. Just because he had one didn't mean he had the other.

"All right class, now that you're all paired up and talking, I need to emphasize how important it is that you get to know the person you've been assigned to work with this semester. We need to learn to trust our fellow musicians, to trust ourselves, and our conductor. This bond is an important one. You must be able to discern the needs of the person you're playing with. You must know them better than your significant others, should any of you be lucky enough to have time for one."

This got another nervous laugh out of the otherwise confused group.

"This may sound confusing, may not make sense, but you must trust me. If you do not get it by the end of the semester, you will understand it by the end of your time here. I'll see you on Wednesday."

"Ready to get to know me intimately?" Owen muttered, grinning at her.

"Can't I know your favorite song first?" She felt lame for saying it. It was a question she associated with awkward first dates. It was a question you asked when you didn't know what to say. It reminded her of her first boyfriend, of sitting on a park bench in the middle of summer. Of a time when music was just one part of her life, instead of what consumed it.

"Oh, Emma, I don't think I can share that with you just yet. Way too personal." He turned to place his violin back in the case and closed the lid. "But there's always a chance you'll get that answer tomorrow."

"But we don't have class tomorrow," Emma protested.

"True. But just because we don't have class doesn't mean we can't see each other."

Emma rolled her eyes. This guy wasn't going to hijack her off days so he could pump up his ego by ordering her around. If he wanted to compose a duet for them, fine; she'd spot read the thing when he was done. Besides, she knew Ave by heart. It still haunted her best nightmares.

"How else are we going to practice our piece?" He grinned now, wide and bright. The kind of smile that came from a guy who wasn't used to being turned down. "You're down the hall from me. How about I swing by in the afternoon to get you?"

"All this chivalry, it almost feels like stalking," Emma said sarcastically.

"It's funny how blurred the line is there, isn't it?"

"Funny isn't quite the word I would use for it," Emma shot back playfully, looking up at him. She hadn't noticed just how tall he was. She came to his shoulder and had to tilt her head to meet his eye. "But that sounds fine. It's a good thing with all your stalking you've already learned my schedule."

"I had a hunch we have similar schedules. Tuesdays and Thursdays off?"

"How lucky your hunches are, Mr. Gibson."

"See you tomorrow?" he asked.

"Yep. Where you'll be prepared for me to talk you out of the Schubert and into something more modern while still having a classical twist."

"Like what?" He crossed his arms.

"I don't know." Emma sighed. "Alicia Keyes meets Bach. Somewhere in that area. Anything but the Schubert."

Owen whistled. "Seems ambitious for our first project out, but we'll see. You bring your ideas and I'll bring mine. Best idea wins."

"Fine."

With their class time up, Emma slung her bag over her shoulder and walked out of the room. She had a long night of writing music ahead of her.

8

Pouring herself another glass of champagne, Emma tried to
ignore the conversation at hand. Her Tuesday night "meetings" were always the best source of city gossip. She'd never
gotten involved with drama in college. Her focus had been on Owen,
Molly, Danielle, and then Connor. On playing and writing music. It
was fun to hear the stories of other women misbehaving. She loved
living vicariously through them.

Tonight felt more like a chore than it should've. She wanted to be
back in her apartment, curled up with Connor. Getting back to her
normal life — her normal routine — was more of a need than a want
after the previous week.

" — at the symphony, can you believe it?" Amy finished, coming
up to Emma. "I just can't."

"Sorry, I missed the first part of that."

"She was getting high in the bathroom at the symphony."

"Who was?"

Amy nodded in the direction of the other women. It was a small
group of eight tonight. They all sat around the glass-topped table on
the rooftop balcony of their apartment building. The light sea breeze

blew their straight blonde hair around their thin, tan shoulders. To Emma, it looked like a page out of the Age Issue of Vogue. The women might have been older, but they didn't look it. Their skin looked bright and natural, without the added need for layers of make-up. Most of them didn't look their age, either. So much so that Emma worried that she was wasting her time being so focused on her career.

Their get-togethers had started as a way to plan different events for the building. It was why Emma had gotten involved in the first place: it was another philanthropic activity to add to her resume. As younger couples moved into the building, the amount of people wanting to take part in community building events dwindled. Now the time set aside for their weekly meeting was just an excuse to get together and drink. To gossip. To pretend to be more intoxicated than they were so when they spilled their own secrets, it could be forgotten. Tonight's topic centered on the scandal of the younger group members.

Emma was just glad the celebration of her engagement ended before she started getting questions about wedding plans. It was still a topic that she and Connor hadn't talked about yet.

"Christa!" Amy whispered.

Emma raised her eyebrows. She knew that some of the women indulged in some drugs every now and then, but Christa didn't seem the type. She was another tech company executive's wife, well bred and raised here in the city. Quiet, but funny, Christa was always the one Emma felt herself gravitating towards. Maybe her gut feeling about the woman had been way off.

"Seriously? I just don't see her . . ." Emma trailed off.

"Yeah, she's got this new friend. A co-worker of her husband's, I think, who's a little more liberal than Christa's used to. I mean, if you're going to indulge, at least do it in your own home. Not in the bathroom during a concert."

"So when do we get to meet this mysterious new friend of hers? I'm surprised she's not here tonight."

"Oh, Christa invited her," Amy began, rolling her eyes, "but I'm hoping she doesn't show up. I wanted a quiet night with you girls tonight. Frank's out of town again."

Emma frowned. Amy, like Emma, was alone a lot. But unlike Emma, Amy didn't seem to handle it well. Whenever her husband was out of town, Amy would organize events to pack every night.

"If it makes you feel better, Connor's been so busy with a big work project. It's rare that he's home now."

Amy smiled, sad and small. "At least someone else knows a little what I'm going through. Sometimes," she leaned in closer, "I see these other girls in the group and . . . they have these perfect lives. It's so hard to keep up with them."

"I don't think that it's exactly like that."

"What do you mean?"

Emma looked out over the balcony, over the gold-bathed skyline and the hint of Rainier in the distance. It was a far cry from views of Central Park, or the Hudson. Here, nature still dominated. At any given moment, an earthquake could shake down their buildings, or a tsunami could wipe out their streets. In New York, humans allowed nature to exist within so many square miles.

"I think that it's easy to forget that everyone has things they hide."

Amy chuckled. "Oh yes, because Emma Bishop has a thousand secrets hidden in her perfect hair."

"Wouldn't you like to know?" she teased. Her hand went to her hair, too thick and too dark for her to ever be as beautiful as these women. Maybe that's why it was so easy to fall back into seeing Molly and Danielle: Emma wasn't jealous of them. The three of them had always been on equal footing. "Come on, let's rejoin the group before they think we're having some secret love affair."

"It wouldn't be the first time they thought that."

Emma rolled her eyes, picked up her champagne flute, and sat back down at the large table. She had known these women for three years. Amy had been the one to welcome her into the building and invite her to the first gathering the day that Emma and Connor moved in. This was the first time she even considered the fact that she did hold all their secrets. Where they had been so open, she kept her walls up. They only guessed at who she really was and what skeletons hid in her closet. Not that she minded. To them, she was the cool girl from New York with her modern life and good-looking fiancé. They knew she was a Seattle Conservatory graduate, and that she had lived in New York when it was attacked. They never asked about either. Instead, they threw fundraisers for 9/11 memorial funds and the Conservatory. It made Emma homesick for her friends who went to private school and their WASP-y families. Talking about difficult topics wasn't what they did.

"Em, did I see you at the Symphony last week? I swore I did, but then you were gone as soon as it ended!" Christa looked over the rim of her glass. "The violinist was so good looking you guys. Right, Em?"

Emma took a careful sip of her champagne. "He is. He's single, too."

Christa leaned forward. "How do you know?"

"I went to college with him. He's in a wedding with me in October."

"If I was single, I'd make you introduce me."

Emma blushed. It wasn't just introducing someone from this world to her other one that made her uneasy. She occupied the same city with him easily because she didn't know about his love life. He could be sleeping with Molly for all she knew, and it was fine because she didn't know about it.

"She could still introduce you. You're still allowed to look," Stephanie grinned. She was one of the blondes, one of the women Emma would love to look like. Classic and petite, the woman looked like she stepped out of a J Crew catalog and somehow landed on their rooftop garden party. "Isn't she?"

"I'm sure my husband does." Christa rolled her eyes. "So, sure, fuck it. I can, too."

Amy and Emma exchanged glances. This wasn't like Christa. She never had a bad thing to say about her husband. He was perfect, the way Connor was perfect. And she never swore.

"I mean," Christa continued, her face red, "if he can go to work all day and stay late with fucking gorgeous girls, I'm allowed to, too, right? Rachel, she's — "

"Rachel?" The color drained from Emma's face. It couldn't be the same one. There had to be a thousand Rachel's who lived in this city.

"Yeah, Rachel . . . something. I hung out with her last week. We went to the symphony. She's like, your height, red curly hair, knockout body — that she didn't have to pay for. She told me."

Definitely not the same Rachel. Emma relaxed.

"But you're friends with her, right? So, you shouldn't have anything to worry about," Stephanie reminded her.

"I know, I know. It's just so hard. I don't know how you do it, Emma."

"What do you mean?"

"Connor's always busy with work, isn't he?" Christa asked.

Emma nodded.

"I mean he probably works with loads of gorgeous women. You don't get nervous?"

Emma finished her champagne and placed the empty glass on the table. "No. We both have our own lives outside of our relationship. He's free to look at whoever he wants. You know, as long as he's not touching."

"Like, an open relationship?" Christa asked.

Emma laughed. "No, no. We're just independent people. If he wants to look, that's fine. I'm sure women look at him, too. But I'm the only one who gets him, so it's okay."

It felt like half the truth, half convincing herself. Emma never had a reason not to trust Connor. He'd always been faithful, almost to a fault. Her thoughts about Owen were making her feel guilty, were making her feel like she wasn't the only one with something to hide. Her mother always said that if someone is paranoid about something, it's usually because they're guilty of the same thing. That's all her jealous of Rachel was. She was just projecting.

"I wish I felt like that with my husband," Amy confessed. Stephanie and Christa nodded, though Emma wasn't sure if it was in sympathy or agreement. "I mean he is great. Our sex life is . . . okay, when he's not traveling. But it's so difficult not to wonder sometimes."

"With David, I don't wonder. I know." Stephanie leaned back in her chair. "We decided a long time ago that it's what worked best for us. If he has something on the side, that's fine. I can do the same."

"Seriously?" Amy asked. Stephanie nodded.

"We still spend the night at home, though. And it's never anything serious. It keeps things interesting."

"You don't get jealous?" Emma's brow furrowed. Being in an open marriage wasn't something she thought happened outside of television shows or novels. As much as she'd get jealous of Connor being with someone else, she knew she wouldn't want someone else touching her. Even just the idea of it felt dirty.

Stephanie shook her head. "Sometimes it's hard. But I can't tell you the last time either of us had anything on the side."

"You tell each other?" Amy asked.

"Of course. Only way this thing works."

"I don't think . . . I'd just die if Frank ever wanted to do something like that."

"It really isn't for everyone," Stephanie admitted. "We just got to that point in our relationship. We're not having children, we're both busy our lives, and if we find something to do for fun, we do it. It doesn't mean anything. I'm not falling in love with anyone."

Emma leaned back against her chair. Sex and love, at least in some way, went hand in hand for her. She didn't need sex to feel loved, but she did need to be in love to have sex. The thought of sleeping around just to sleep with someone new sounded tiring.

The only man outside of Connor she even felt attracted to had been Owen.

Of course she had seen attractive men at events or even at Whole Foods. But there wasn't some urge to get them to sleep with her. She appreciated them, but never had the desire to fantasize about them.

"I think Emma should have one of these relationships with Connor, and sleep with that violinist," Christa winked.

Emma blushed again and shook her head. "Oh no. Been there, done that. That hatchet has buried for a long time."

"Wait." Amy leaned forward. "You've slept with him?"

"Oh, this is before Connor. I'm not even sure Connor knows about it."

"You need to revisit this, for my sake," Christa pleaded. "You can't let fresh fruit dangle like that and not pick it."

"I don't even think he's still interested like that. We're friends."

"But you're seeing him, and you're in a wedding together. Everyone always falls in love at weddings!"

"But, she is in love," Stephanie reminded them. "She's in love with Connor."

"I am. I mean, I am seeing Owen again soon, but just in a work capacity. There's nothing there."

"Ah!" Christa squealed. "When? When are you seeing him!?"

"Tomorrow, maybe. I haven't decided yet." Emma hesitated. She had shared much more with the girls tonight than she thought she ever would. "He invited me to sit in on a symphony rehearsal."

It felt good to see it through their eyes: to see the excitement, to hear how juicy this piece of gossip was. And so what if it got around that she'd slept with the concertmaster a hundred years ago? Who would believe it? Who would even care now? This wasn't some Page Six nonsense she'd have to worry about if they were living in New York. She wasn't part of the orchestra circuit, either.

"You two went to college together, right?" Stephanie asked.

"We did. We actually ended up playing a lot of duets together. He's a brilliant composer."

Emma left out the part where she was the reason he was a brilliant composer. That he graduated with the honors, with the offers he did, because she had helped him get there. It was less exciting that way, puffing up herself just because she wanted them to know the truth. No one liked the hero of a story being less than the heroine. He was supposed to be the one who saved her. That's how it worked for these women.

"I swear I just read a romance novel that started out just this way,"

Christa said, her hands clasped together. "You're going to have a brilliant affair. I can feel it."

Emma rolled her eyes. "No. I don't think I'll be having one of those anytime soon. It's just nice to catch up with such an old, and dear friend. I'm quite happy where I am."

"She's getting married. If she wanted to sleep with someone else, she wouldn't be getting married. No offense, Steph." Amy came to Emma's rescue.

Stephanie smiled, a hard line forced across her face. "None taken."

"I just mean that Emma, she would never have an affair. She's too much of a good person," Amy said.

"I appreciate the vote of confidence. I could never do that to Connor. And I know he'd never do that to me. We're both happy with the life we have together."

Christa raised her eyebrows. "The lady doth protest too much."

"What's that supposed to mean?" Emma asked, not liking where this line of questioning was going. Her attraction to Owen now was based on nothing more than missing the way things used to be. That's all it was.

That's all it could be.

"The more you tell us how happy you are, the less I'm inclined to believe it."

Emma laughed. "Or you just really want me to have an affair."

Christa cracked a grin. "Yeah, well, one of us has to try and sleep with him and I think you're more his type than I am."

9

Going to the rehearsal wasn't what she had planned on doing today. She finished making her phone calls and answered e-mails, and was ready to take the rest of her work home. Music had already taken over enough of her life. Just the night before she caught herself tapping her fingers to a jazz song playing while she cooked dinner. Her kitchen counter turned from a granite slab to a piano keyboard. Instead of working in silence like usual, she put on a playlist full of piano and emotion.

She needed music the way an addicted needed their drugs. After almost a decade of being sober, she was flirting with relapsing. If she walked into the auditorium, Emma knew that she'd be a goner. But she pulled open the door to the auditorium and walked in anyway.

Instead of the bright natural light of the Hall's windowed hallways, Emma was enveloped in darkness. It was warm and inviting, the way a chapel was. Closing her eyes, she inhaled deep, taking in the smell of resin, of plush chairs, of everything that made up her version of a sanctuary. Instead of an altar, she needed a piano at center stage. She needed to feel keys under her fingertips and see her reflection in the black face of a grand piano. That's where she found God.

This room mirrored that of what she played in back in college, except bigger. The empty chairs were reflected in the piano's shining side and the lid of the piano was propped up to project the best sound. The man who sat on the bench had his back bent, arms too tense, as he looked up at Owen.

She took a seat towards the back, somewhere that Owen wouldn't be able to see her from the stage. But instead of playing, Owen had stopped the group and began to berate the pianist.

"You're starting wrong. Even before you start playing you need to be feeling what this piece means," Owen said. He closed his eyes and picked up his bow. "Start again."

The man at the piano went to place his hands on the keys and Emma knew it was wrong.

"No," Owen said again.

The rest of the group sat back against their chairs in one collective creak of weight, plastic against metal. Those who held cellos and bases leaned them to the side while the few who held violins set their instruments down. They knew they would be here awhile.

When Owen had put these pieces together he meant for it to just be strings and the piano. Creating pieces of music for a large group wasn't in Owen's skillset, at least it hadn't been when they were in college. The rest of the orchestra was grand, he explained, but with only the piano and strings, the songs were more intimate. Emma never called him out for not being able to see the big picture. Like now, when his whole orchestra was here when he should've been working with the pianist one on one.

"If you can't get this right," Owen began, "then maybe we'll have to find someone else to play this part."

"I just don't know what you're asking of me. I'm playing this the way you told me to. I watched the video. This is the way it's played."

Standing up from her seat, she walked towards the stage. She couldn't stand for watching Owen bully a man for the simple fact that he wasn't her.

"Let me show you," Emma said, walking up the wooden steps and onto the stage. She could feel her heart beating in her ears, in her throat.

The man nodded and moved aside. Emma took her seat on the bench without looking at Owen. It was how this song started. As her fingers rested on the keys, she heard the familiar rustling of paper as the rest of the group readied themselves. The presence she commanded on stage was one that had intimidated her classmates.

This power was something she had missed.

As she began to play, the piece came back to her in a tidal wave too big for her to control. She could feel her body relaxing, moving with the rise and fall of the progressions. It was only in the middle of the piece that she was able to look up at him, but only for a moment.

Blushing, she looked back down at the sheet music. She hadn't noticed before that it was a photocopy of the original with her notes scribbled in the margins. The original was sitting at home in the box she couldn't throw out.

The night they had finished composing the song, it had been too late and she had felt too drunk on life. Her senior year had been spent working towards this moment: this concert, these songs, finally being able to call herself a musician. Owen had been wearing this dark gray t-shirt and was barefoot on the stage. Emma had been trying to figure out the best way to bring each movement of the song together.

"We just need something . . . I don't know. The feeling, it's missing," Owen had said, chin resting on his violin as he brought the bow to the strings once more. She listened to him as he began to go through the piece again.

"Owen, wait," she said, putting hands to keys while keeping her eyes on him. "Follow me."

It was a game they had been playing for awhile just to get warmed up. As she began their normal runs up and down scales, she began to switch over to the piece, notes more fluid, more Debussy than Mozart.

"We're trying to inspire a picture, not paint one."

Putting his violin down he walked over next to the piano. "But what kind of picture?"

Emma shrugged. "You're the composer for this one, not me."

"No, but this is our brainchild. This is as much yours as it is mine."

Grabbing the piece of sheet music she scribbled something into the side and handed it to him.

"That's what you want this to be?"

Looking at the notes now, she could still remember the first time they played the song the entire way through. It had turned into something neither of them had been expecting it to be. Even their advisor had been stunned. Owen wanted strings in the background and Emma manipulated the notes so that the rest of the violins turned into a wall of sound. It had been one of the best songs she written, and Owen had gotten all the credit.

As they finished playing now, she looked back up at him. His eyes were still on her, too intense for her to look at for very long. Hands on her lap, she looked over at the man who had tried to play the song. He shrugged, admitting defeat.

She knew he wouldn't be able to play the song the way Owen wanted him to. The song wasn't his and Owen's. None of these songs were.

"Wow," the man said finally. "Yeah, she needs to be the one to play this with you."

There was a muttering of agreement from the others.

"Scott can't play that like you can."

"He could if you gave him the chance," Emma argued.

"No, miss. I really can't. Maybe if Owen and I were together — "

"Owen and I aren't together."

Scott held his hands up. "I didn't say that. I'm just saying . . ." he trailed off, collecting his thoughts. "It's like dancers, watching you two. My boyfriend is a dancer and he's always just a little off with whatever partner he ends up with because there's no deep connection there. A lot of people think it's a myth. For some people, maybe it is. But you guys, the way I play? I'll never be able to compare to the way you two played together."

Emma blushed but said nothing. She knew what he was talking about. It was the connection that almost ruined her relationship with Connor. It was the reason why she didn't want to come to this rehearsal in the first place.

"Just play the next song with me. Then decide if you want to play or not. The rest of you can go," Owen instructed. "You too, Scott. Thank you."

Rustling of music cases and quiet conversation filled the stage. Turning the pages of sheet music, Emma saw what was next. As the room emptied, she put her hands to the keys and started to play again. She didn't even need the sheet music there; her hands remember the song better than she did. Owen joined her in playing. The lone violin was quiet at first and then picked up speed and strength, taking up all the spaces the piano didn't.

It was the song she hummed to herself every now and then. She tried not to think about it too much, but didn't want to forget it. The fact that she couldn't play the song without crying was why they had never played it during their showcase. It seemed too juvenile, too unprofessional to get so deep into the emotion of a song. They weren't real artists if they were so invested in what the music was supposed to be saying. Looking back, it was a silly philosophy to have.

Looking back, too much of what she had thought then had been ridiculous.

Breaking into the middle of the piece, her fingers moved faster, her notes more full. She could feel her heart aching, her eyes watering. She needed to avoid looking at Owen if she wanted to make it to the end of the piece. Or at least into the final movement. That was when "they," whoever the song was about, knew they would never be able to be together. The princess goes off with a different prince, the soldier comes back in a wooden box, the fire eats the man. Every time they talked about who the song was about, it was a different romantic trope. Never once had they talked about the song being about themselves.

Tears began to fall as they finished the song and Emma sat back, hands folded in her lap once more.

"If you don't come play this with me, I swear, Emma . . ." Owen trailed off, his voice thick with an emotion she couldn't place. Or didn't want to place. Needing, wanting, lust — it was all there.

"I don't know if I should." She stood up, the back of her hands wiping away the tears.

Emma looked over at Owen and then looked back at the empty chairs of the auditorium. It hadn't been full, the night of their senior showcase. Family and friends had been there, but it wasn't anything that she had felt proud of. The MySpace videos had received more views than the people who had seen it live.

But the auditorium would be full the night of his concert. It would get press coverage. He would get more publicity than he already did — as much as a classical musician could hope for, anyway. What was he doing this for? The marginal fame? The recognition by the conservatory and the local music community?

The important question wasn't about him and his motivations, but hers. She needed to understand why she was here. What she was doing.

She knew for too long now she had shunned this part of her life. She had hid away a gift she had put so much time and effort cultivating. If she was going to do this, to play on stage with him, it had to be about her and not about him. Or Connor. Or who parents who made comments in passing about her college career and how it would've been better for her to go for business. She wasted thousands of dollars polishing a talent that she never used again.

"I need to get to know you again first." Emma smiled at Owen and sat back down on the piano bench.

He nodded and began flipping through the sheet music. Rolling her neck, she felt her vertebrae crack. Next, she rolled her wrists, her ankles, and then stretched her arms into the air. She had done this a thousand times before she began practicing. It was true what they said, she thought. Old habits really did die hard.

She started slow, working through their usual runs and scales. It was a better way to warm up than running through the pieces a thousand times. This way she could reacquaint herself not only with the music but also with the feeling of the keys under her fingers and the way the notes sounded when she struck the right chords. After they went through the first piece again, just the two of them, she put her hands in her lap.

This was the high she missed. Not the feeling of being on stage, but of pushing herself to keep playing when her body was too tired to keep going. The feeling of keeping up with, and outpacing, Owen. It was a challenge, physically and mentally. He was right. It was what she needed.

"So, when are practices?"

He smiled. "Are you sure?"

"Are you going to give me time to talk myself out of this?"

Owen laughed and pulled his phone from his pocket. "I'll e-mail you the schedule now."

Emma stood up and pushed the piano bench in. She pulled the cover down over the keys and went to close the top but Owen stopped her.

"I'm glad you came," he said, brushing her hair out of her face. "I missed seeing you like this."

"I know. It felt . . . great. Playing again. I'm glad I came. But I should get home."

Owen nodded. "I'm having dinner at Purple Cafe again tonight. You're welcome to join me."

Emma shook her head. "I've had enough nostalgia for one night. But perhaps a different night."

"I'd like that."

It was hard for Emma to turn and walk away from him. She knew she needed to, for both of their sakes. If she stayed, she wasn't sure if she'd ever go home.

"See you later."

"Yeah," he said. "See you later."

She turned, finally, her ballet flats making no sound against the wooden floor of the stage or the steps. When she reached the auditorium door, she forced herself to keep moving instead of looking back. Their song played on in her head, ripping at her heart.

She hummed it the whole way home, going over the rehearsal in her head.

"Where were you?"

Emma looked up as she put the keys down on the table by the door. Connor was already home.

"I ended up going to the rehearsal Owen invited me to."

"Are you actually going to go play in that concert?"

Emma looked at Connor, at the redness of his eyes and the general disorder of his clothing. He reeked of whiskey. She could smell him even though they stood apart. There was a half-empty bottle sitting on the coffee table.

"What happened? Why didn't you call me?"

He shook his head. "I don't want to talk about it. I thought you'd be home. You said you were coming home early."

"Connor, please. You can talk to me."

"Fucking James got the promotion over me. I needed you to be home when I was home."

The comment was an icicle to her chest. This wasn't like him, but it didn't make his words hurt any less.

"I'm sorry you didn't get the promotion," she shot back. "I really am. But you can't expect me to read your mind. I had no idea what was going on because you didn't call me. I had my phone on me."

She pulled her phone from her pocket. She touched the home button to make sure she hadn't missed any of Connor's calls. All she saw was the e-mail notification from Owen.

"Sorry," Connor whispered. "I'm sorry. I just. I wanted the promotion and I thought I was getting it. I want to be able to give you the best wedding. Your dream wedding."

Emma closed the space between them. "It's okay. You don't need to get a promotion at work to make me happy."

"Are you sure?"

The alcohol had sucked any confidence left right out of him. She wasn't even home that late, maybe an hour later than normal. He had either drunk fast or he'd been home a lot longer than he said he was. Outside, it was still light out. People were on the street, their conversations drifting through the open windows of their apartment. A cloudless sky meant people could enjoy happy hour cocktails on patios. Here, inside their perfect apartment, Emma could feel storm clouds moving in.

"Of course I'm sure. I'm not marrying you because of your job. I'm marrying you because I love you. Why don't you go lay down for a bit?"

"Will you come with me?"

There were moments over the years where she had thought about moments like this. She had leaned on Connor so much in the beginning, when she couldn't breathe whenever a plane went overhead. When they moved into the apartment it had gotten worse. Emma had to get used to the over-the-city flight plan again. But today, right now, was when she could give back to him. She'd bring up the concert later, when he was sober. When he didn't need to be taken care of.

What she'd learned a long time ago was that life wasn't a fairytale. That it was easy to romanticize a life that she could have had. Today, with Owen, she could have imagined a thousand lifetimes for them, each one more perfect than the last. What she had with Connor was real. It was messy and, sometimes, unpleasant.

But this was what a relationship really was.

"Sure. Come on," she said, taking his hand and leading him towards their bedroom. He picked her up and kissed her. He didn't put her down until they reached the bed.

10

DECEMBER 2006

E mma couldn't remember the last time she'd had a normal Christmas. Her dad's work schedule rarely let them have a "normal" holiday. Being a firefighter meant overnights, twenty-four hours, or even being gone three days at a time. They — Emma, Leah, and their mother — got used to him not being there just in time for his rotation to end and used to him being home just in time for him to go back to work. It wasn't the kind of childhood her friends had. They were the daughters and sons of investment bankers or lawyers.

But they'd all looked at her differently after the attacks. Suddenly, the fact that her dad was an FDNY firefighter was better than anything their parents did. He was a real hero, not just another blue-collar worker.

Connor had a normal Christmas every year. This would be his first one waking up in his apartment by himself unless he decided to stay with his parents on Christmas Eve after all. It was a subject he brought up with Emma frequently.

"What about this one?" Connor asked, pointing to the small, Charlie Brown-esque evergreen that stood in a bare patch of the tree lot. They were enveloped in the smell of pine and the bright glow of the Christmas lights that hung from one tall, wooden pole to the next. She'd never been to a tree lot before, let alone had a real tree. Even now that they were older, Leah and Emma made a day out of unpacking the fake tree. The fact that "fake trees aren't as likely to start fires" was a childhood fact that followed them into adulthood.

The tree was always more about the tradition that anything, though. As soon as the Christmas packages started arriving from their parents, Emma and Leah never waited to open them. They just told their parents they did.

"It's small enough to fit in that corner your bedroom."

"That's what I was thinking."

He'd recently moved into an apartment was some guy friends from school. They were business majors like he was and, like Connor, didn't want to pledge a fraternity to score off-campus housing. But unlike Connor, they were from eastern Washington, northern Oregon, and even out on the peninsula. So they went home for at least part of Christmas break, leaving the house entirely empty. It was strange, the house being so quiet. Emma liked that they still stayed contained to Connor's room.

"You know, I sort of imagine you having a tree like this one back in New York. Since you all live in closet-sized apartments, right?" Connor joked.

"Something like that. I think the last Christmas I had a tree in New York was, God, '99?"

"Why that long ago?"

Emma shrugged. "Dad lost a good friend in a fire a few days before Christmas in 2000. Then the attacks happened and he was working a ton of overtime. We didn't get around to putting a tree up that year. After that, Leah moved, and then after that Mom and I bought a candle that smelled like a tree. It seemed silly to put up a tree."

"Oh." Connor looked away. "I thought you lost someone in the attacks and just weren't ready to tell me."

He'd asked the same question the first day they met. Maybe it was the same question that lingered between her anyone who asked where she was from originally. How could she explain that the thing that drove her away from New York hadn't been any one person's death? It would've made more sense. It would've sounded more logical to anyone she explained it to. It was the three thousand people who did die that day who drove her away from the city. It was the panic attacks at the sound of airplanes, the nightmares of melting faces and burning rooms. She hadn't been directly affected by the attacks. Didn't lose anyone that day.

But she sure lost herself.

"No. Things were just . . . different. It's stupid, I know."

"No, I get it," Connor put his arms around her, hugging her tight. "I get what you're saying."

"I've done some after Christmas trips with Mom and Dad."

"Where'd you go?"

"Usually to Cape Cod. No one's there, and the ocean during the winter is just perfect."

"Really? I mean, I've seen our ocean here, but it looks the same as it always does. We always do Christmas morning like when we were kids. Up early for presents, breakfast, and then pass out watching *A Christmas Story.*"

"We'll have to go to Cape Cod some time. The Atlantic Ocean is a little bit more intimidating than the Pacific. At least from what I've seen."

"I'd like that." Connor smiled brighter than the Christmas lights. "I've never actually been to the east coast. I'd love to see it for the first time with you."

"Really?"

"To which part?"

"Either, I guess." They hadn't been dating that long. At least long enough for Emma to seriously entertain the idea of them going away somewhere together. Sleeping over at his apartment was one thing. Getting on a plane and spending a long weekend in a hotel was something you did with someone you were really serious about.

He shrugged. "I've done California, Vegas, the Grand Canyon . . . Never been farther than that. I've always wanted to, though."

81

"I've never been to Vegas," Emma moved closer to the small tree. Her hands were beginning to go numb from the cold. "But warm sounds nice right about now."

Connor laughed. "Doesn't it? I went when I was sixteen, so it wasn't like I could have that much fun while we were there. But it was pretty cool."

"Was it just you and your parents?"

He shook his head. "My parents, my sister, and my grandparents."

"You have a sister?"

"Yeah, older by like two years. Natalie. She's in California now."

Emma took his hand, wanting to feel close to him. He always asked about her, and her life, but she rarely asked about his.

"Are you guys close?"

"Not as close as we used to be. She's crazy busy with school. We hang out when she's home but I haven't gone down to visit her or anything. That's why I'm kind of jealous of you and Leah."

Emma nodded. "Losing connection with a family member sucks. I used to be really close with my cousins but we don't talk that much anymore. We're all spread out all over the country."

"Yeah. Nat's coming home for Christmas, though. So you might get to meet her."

"I'd like that."

So many of her classmates were doing the same thing. They'd cleared out the dorms and were back home, spending a month with their family. Being invited to be part of Connor's life, his real life, meant more to her than she was able to voice. She'd have to tell him that she couldn't come, though. The plane tickets had come into her inbox this morning. She'd be spending Christmas until New Years in St. George, Utah, with Leah and her parents. Hiking and going to a spa was on the agenda. It'd be the first time she spent Christmas with her whole family in years.

"I'd like to get out of this cold." He laughed, putting his arm around Emma. "Is this the tree we want?"

"I think it's the only one we're going to find that's going to fit."

"Perfect."

They paid for the tree and put it in the back of the pickup truck Connor had borrowed from his dad.

While Connor drove, Emma played with the dial on the radio, trying to find a song she could stand. In her head, she could hear the song she and Owen had been working on before break, unfinished and raw. She wanted it finished. Settling on NPR, jazz filtered through the speakers. Tapping her fingers on the dashboard, city streetlights passing over them, she tried to lose herself in the chaos of the song.

"How do you follow that?" Connor asked.

"What do you mean?"

"It just sounds like . . . noise."

"Try breaking it down. I only listen for the piano and follow along with that. If you just focus on that one thing, it's easier."

He was quiet for a few minutes. Emma watched him, waiting for that moment where he'd catch on, where he'd find the beauty in it. But it never came. He shook his head.

"Sorry."

"It's okay. What do you like to listen to?"

"Whatever's on the radio, I guess."

"Oh."

After being enveloped into a world that breathed passion for music, his answer was one she wasn't expecting. It wasn't like they had talked about music before, beyond what she was working on in school. Still, the answer shocked her.

"I mean, I'll like what you play," he added quickly. "I just don't really care about music. I've never even been to a concert."

"Bullshit."

"Scout's honor."

"I know what I'm getting you for Christmas."

"Are you dragging me to the Symphony?" Connor chuckled.

"No. We're going to go to a real concert. There's like six venues in walking distance of the Conservatory. There's bound to be a band playing soon that you at least recognize."

"I'll come and watch you play, you know."

"That's different. I love going to the Symphony and recitals at school, but they're too stiff. You need to go to a real concert. There's just a different energy to them."

"I'll trust you on that one. Just don't take me to a jazz concert, okay? I hate jazz." He laughed like it wasn't a big deal and turned the radio to a different channel.

Emma looked out the window. She was a closet Jazz fan. The perfect date night she had in mind was going to a jazz club. It was also her dream concert venue. Somewhere dark and smoky, where there were tables close together to make room for good conversation. Her heart sunk. As long as she was with Connor, that wouldn't happen. At least he wouldn't go to support her.

"I promise I won't do that."

They drove on in silence, the music filling the space between them. For the first time, there was a distance between them that Emma wasn't sure she liked. He was so different from the world she was a part of — but she couldn't deny the allure.

11

─────────

Sun blared through the sheer curtains. Opening one eye, Emma looked at the alarm clock on the bedside table.

7:30.

If she got up now, she could still make it into the office on time.

"Good morning," Connor said, putting a hand on her bare shoulder.

"We slept in."

"You slept in," he murmured, sounding half-asleep. "I already called in sick."

Emma rolled out of bed and grabbed her bathrobe from the plush armchair next to the bedroom window. A day off was probably a good thing for him, but Emma knew it wouldn't look great to his boss. At least, it wouldn't look good to her if she was his boss.

"Why don't you call in too? We could spend the day together."

"I wish I could. We're ramping up our fundraisers now that summer is here. I have a ton of calls to make and e-mails to send."

"You could do that from here."

Picking up her phone, she scrolled through the day's reminders. Realistically, she could do it all from home. It wasn't like she was expected to work every day at the office. The idea was tempting.

Emma wanted to spend time with him. Since their engagement, they were just ships passing in the night. Most nights, Connor disappeared into the fog. Making time for him was a good thing. Or, it would be, if she didn't feel so guilty about shirking her work duties.

"Give me the morning to catch up on some work. Then we can do something."

Connor grinned. "Want to go to the Market? We could pick up something to make for dinner. You could start looking at flowers. Figure out what you might want to carry."

Leaning back over the bed, Emma kissed his cheek. "That sounds perfect. Go back to sleep. I'll wake you up when I'm done working."

She walked out of the bedroom and closed the door behind her. Hand still on the doorknob, she closed her eyes and took a deep breath. This wasn't like her, compromising her work so she could spend time with her fiancé. It was Thursday. He couldn't have waited two more days to ask her to spend time with him?

It wasn't like she didn't want to spend time with him. She did. But she didn't want to have to re-arrange her work schedule to do it. She would have never asked him to re-arrange his schedule to accommodate hers.

Emma knew she could've said no. She knew it was her decision.

Letting the breath out slowly, Emma walked into the kitchen and started to make coffee. Waiting for the water to boil, she sent off an e-mail to her boss. He'd been ecstatic for her that she was getting married and said that if she ever needed time off to just let him know. As if planning a wedding needed to be the center of her world. So she told him that she had a few personal matters to attend to but she'd be working from home, for at least the morning. As the kettle whistled, he responded that he didn't even expect her to work the morning if she needed it. She rolled her eyes.

Coffee now steeping in the French press, she pulled her laptop out of her work bag and set it on the kitchen table. She opened her work e-mail and pulled up her to-do list like normal, but something was missing.

Music.

Her fingers tapped against the surface of the table. It was an anxious withdrawal symptom. On one hand, she could just cut herself off, cold turkey, tell Owen never mind. Her music-free life was fine. It was comfortable and conflict-free. Both she and Connor made good money and they had everything they could ever want.

Double-clicking on her inbox, Emma got to work. It wasn't as calming as playing the piano was, but it was a temporary fix. At least she could concentrate on something else for the morning other than the million what-if's that kept her tossing and turning most of the night. One minute she was fine with her life, fine with the decisions she was making, and wanted everything to stay the way it was. The next, she wanted everything to change. She wanted to play in Owen's concert and then play more concerts. She wanted more out of life than financial stability. She wanted to play music.

She needed to play music.

❄

"Ready?"

"Mmhm," Emma said as she finished putting the earrings he had bought her in. She hadn't worn them, not since he had given them to her the same weekend he proposed. Now seemed like a good occasion.

"They look good on you." He reached out to touch her ears but she shied away. "What's wrong?"

"You start touching me and we won't ever get out of here."

He laughed and took her hand. "Is that a problem?"

Emma squeezed his hand and walked towards the door. "Do you want to walk or drive down?"

"It's nice. We can walk."

Blue skies and sunshine hadn't been as rare as Seattle's reputation made them out to be and this year was especially dry. Leaving the lobby of their apartment building, Emma took her sunglasses off of her head and pushed them up her nose. There wasn't a cloud in the sky. Walking down the thin sidewalk, city noises bouncing between buildings, she tried to remember the last time they went out together, just the two of them.

They had gone to work functions and cocktail parties, or even the occasional family event. Even their anniversaries came and went without much pomp or circumstance. A night in, take out, television: they tried to keep things simple and easy. Convenient.

Walking under the viaduct, they kept walking up Western, comfortable in their silence. Finally, as buildings cleared, they were greeted by a large green space, full of people on blankets enjoying the sun and an un-marred view of the Sound. Crossing onto the cobbled road, they passed booths of t-shirts and art, set up outside the main market building. In the distance, the giant Ferris wheel turned slowly as a ferryboat made its way to Bainbridge Island.

"Where do you want to go first?" he asked.

"There's that lavender shop just around the corner, but I was thinking we could see what kind of vegetables are in. I could make a stir-fry for dinner."

"Sounds good to me, babe." He took her hand and kissed it as they entered the enclosed part of the Market.

The conversation sounded mundane to be sure, but for Emma it was something that rarely happened. For them to be discussing making dinner at home, in the kitchen he wasn't around to enjoy very much, it felt like she was finally getting the life that she wanted.

The future she would've picked for herself wasn't so domestic or basic, but it was the one that fit around a life with Connor.

As they pushed their way through the main thoroughfare, Emma felt overwhelmed by all the people, the sounds, and the smells. Tables filled with leather goods, with white-matted photography and hand-made jewelry, waited for her attention. The tables with goods quickly changed to more perishable items the deeper into the market they walked. Buckets filled with flowers, their colors loud and vibrant, sat on the edge of the wooden tables, just waiting to be picked. Emma stopped at a bucket of tulips, wrapped in bunches of eight.

"Come on, let's get you some. It's been awhile since there's been flowers in the house."

Emma squeezed his hand. "I forgot. It's Bloomsday."

"Then you definitely need to get flowers."

She went to correct him, but didn't. Him buying her perfume would've been more appropriate. Or going on a pub crawl. James Joyce had been her favorite author in high school. Connor was more of a Tolkien and George R. R. Martin fan. She brought up Joyce once, and Woolfe, but he shrugged it off. He didn't understand Modernist writers. He couldn't follow them. The idea boggled Emma's mind since Tolkien was especially difficult for her to read.

"What about tulips?" he asked, pointing to the multiple buckets brightly colored flowers. "They're good for a spring wedding."

"They are." Emma grinned. A spring wedding was exactly what she'd been thinking of for them. "I love the white ones. Just a simple bunch, tied together. Maybe with some of the purple caspia." She pointed to the other bucket that contained branches of tiny purple flowers.

"Excuse me, we'll take a bunch of these with some of the caspia," Connor said to the woman behind the table. She nodded her head and grabbed the bunch. Wrapping it in brown paper, she exchanged the flowers for his ten-dollar bill.

"Do you want to carry them?" he asked, extending the flowers towards her.

"Sure." She accepted the flowers and brought them to her nose. Closing her eyes, she inhaled deeply.

"Em, look at these."

She opened her eyes to find Connor across the crowded walkway at a vegetable stand. He pointed to the large peppers, fire engine red, and the bright green beans. It seemed too early in the season for such luxuries but Emma would take it.

"Sure, let's get some. But what else goes in a stir-fry?"

"No idea," Connor said. "Let's come back, though. We'll look around some more."

Emma followed him down the walkway, past the woman selling hand-stitched leather goods. At another booth, a man had a variety of bottles set up, all different olive oils in different types and flavors. A large family passed between her and the booth. Watching them go by, she had to ignore a familiar longing building in her chest. She was happy with the way things were, with just the two of them. They didn't need a big family. They just needed each other.

"Here, let's grab some of this," Emma said, walking up to the man's booth.

"All right, girl?" the man asked. Emma nodded. "Is there anything yer looking for in particular?"

"I was looking to sauté some vegetables for dinner tonight but I was wondering if you had anything you suggest that's different from, you know, just plain olive oil?"

He tilted his head to the side and looked at her straight on. She felt strange, vulnerable even, as he watched her. There were lines in his face, dug out from years of living and working hard. As he reached out and picked up a bottle, she saw the gold band on his ring finger looking like it might get swallowed up by his tan skin.

"Here. You want this one. It's simple, light citrus flavor. Good balance."

Turning the bottle over in her hand, she noticed that the label was handwritten with the date that it was bottled. The handwriting looked too nice to be the man's. Emma imagined a woman at home, waiting for him to finish up his day at the shop.

"Is there anything else ya need?"

Emma looked around at the different bottles, wanting to find something else that she could buy from him.

"A bottle of your balsamic?" To Connor, she said: "I'll make a salad, too."

"Whatever you want to do. I'll eat anything you cook me."

The man laughed. "Ya got a smart one on your hands. Happy life, happy wife."

When Connor didn't correct the man, but instead squeezed Emma's free hand, her smile grew. Finally, the engagement felt real. They were talking wedding flowers, this stranger referred to her as Connor's wife. This was better than nights she stayed up late on Pinterest. Better, even, than coming home to finding different wedding magazines Connor picked up for her on his way home from work.

"Yes sir," Connor said. "Especially when you find yourself a great one."

"Especially then," the man agreed. "Do you two need anything else?"

Emma shook her head. "No, this is good. Thank you so much. I'm sure we'll be back to visit again."

"Good, good. Can never turn down an opportunity to see a pretty face."

Paper bag in hand, Connor moved on down to booths towards the end of the hallway while Emma took her time gazing over various goods. One older couple was selling pasta while another booth was selling artisan cheeses.

Looking through the choices, Emma picked up two different bricks. "I'll take some cheddar and some goat cheese," she said, handing them to the woman behind the counter.

"Emma? Emma Bishop?" the woman asked, eyes narrowing as she studied Emma's face.

It took a minute before Emma recognized her. It looked like Brianna Hayes, but the Brianna she remembered was much younger. There weren't laugh lines next to her eyes the way this woman had, or the hint of gray hair in her long, black braid.

"Brianna? Wow. I didn't expect to see you here."

"I know, right? It's been forever. What are you doing now? I haven't seen you since, what, one of the graduation parties?"

Emma laughed, nodding. Brianna was a girl she had been close with in high school who had come out to Seattle to go to UW. It was exciting to have someone from her old life follow her into the new one. But much like the rest of the people in her life, Brianna had fallen by the wayside as Emma threw herself into her work at the Conservatory.

"Yeah, I think so."

Connor had wandered back now, one hand in his pocket.

"Connor, this is Brianna. Brianna, this is Connor. My fiancé."

"Oh awesome. Great to meet you." Brianna said as she bagged up the cheese.

"So are you just visiting the city?"

Emma shook her head, but felt shy about saying where she lived. "No, no. We live here. What about you?"

"Same, for the most part. I went down to California for a bit, did some time in Portland, but ended up back here."

"That's awesome. Do you make all these yourself?"

"Oh yeah," Brianna said, smiling wide. "It's so gratifying. What about you, what are you doing?"

"Oh," Emma said, blushing. "I work with the fundraising department for the Seattle Symphony."

"Oh awesome. Good for you! Well, it was really good seeing you. Add me on Facebook. We can catch up sometime!" Brianna smiled, shaking her head. "Wow. Emma Bishop, as I live and breathe. A Seattle girl."

Connor laughed as they walked away from the booth. "A Seattle girl?"

Emma shrugged. "The East Coast versus West Coast debate is alive and well. I'm just surprised to see her out here still. I would've thought she'd went back to New York."

"Like you?"

Emma shook her head. "No, Seattle is home now. I'm happy here."

The realization made her stomach twist. She wasn't sure when it happened, when she started thinking that Seattle was home, not New York. It was probably around the same time she lost track of everything else she'd wanted to do. Brianna's question hung heavy over her head. Happiness for her had always been about career accomplishments, until she found a comfortable job that lacked upward mobility. Owen's concert would be the biggest thing she's done since she left college. Even that wasn't hers.

"Connor?"

"Yeah, babe?" he asked while preoccupied looking at another booth.

"Do you think . . ." she trailed off as she moved out of the way of a couple pushing a stroller. "Do you think that I'm doing something with my life?"

"What do you mean?"

"Well, I went to school, I got my degree . . . and now?" She shrugged.

"Of course you are."

"But what am I doing?"

He took a second, which only made it worse. That hesitation told her everything: that he had to think of what she did all day was her answer.

"You're doing an amazing job fundraising for the Symphony. You know that your boss wouldn't know what to do without you."

"Yeah, but that's not what . . . " she trailed off again. There had been a time when she was comfortable talking with him, when he had been more closer to her than even Owen. Had it been eight years ago she could have been more honest with him. Now, being too honest would add cracks into their life. She didn't want him to know that she hated taking a half day from work. That her work felt unimportant in the face of his, even though her job paid the rent.

"You've got that concert now too."

"You're okay with that?" she asked, hoping to keep the conversation about music going. Instead, he pulled out his phone.

"One sec. I need to tell Rachel I'm busy tonight."

He turned away from her, answering his phone. There was little she could hear of the conversation until he started raising his voice.

"No. I didn't say I would . . . no, that's . . . Listen to me. I'm spending time with Emma tonight." A pause. "Because she's my fiancée." Another pause. "You already tried that one. I have to go. Bye."

He turned back towards Emma, smiling. "Sorry about that."

"No, it's quite all right." Emma said, eyebrows raised. "I'm just . . . surprised."

"About what?"

"Nothing. I just feel special now, that's all. You usually don't . . . " she trailed off. "I don't know. I'm glad I have you tonight."

"I'm glad I'm with you." He leaned down and kissed her as they blocked the flow of people moving down the walkway. "Come on. Let's get the rest of what we need for dinner. I want to take you home."

"Okay."

Any uneasiness she felt about her lack of accomplishments vanished as he took her hand. Together, they navigated through the heavy throng of people and started the walk home.

12

Emma reached up at the cupboard to grab plates on tiptoes, but Connor grabbed them first.

"I got it. You just worry about dinner."

He kissed her cheek and put them on the kitchen counter. He'd already set the table, complete with placemats and candles. The flowers he bought her were already in a vase in the center. In the background, music played—instrumental and indie, something she knew he liked.

The vegetables sizzled in olive oil on the stove while water boiled, cooking angel hair pasta. The menu had changed from her original idea, but the smell of chicken cooking in the oven made her glad she decided to this instead of the stir-fry.

"If you insist." Emma said, smiling. For a moment, she could see this—their future, them cooking together, going on like this forever. It wasn't what she'd wished for when she was younger and more idealistic. But this was what her life was shaping up to be and she was happy with it.

"So, I was thinking," Connor started, coming up behind her and wrapping his arms around her. "I know we've been waiting to pick a date to get married."

"Yes?"

"And I thought about this fall. September."

Emma didn't look back at him. "I don't want to take the attention away from Danielle and Zach."

"I know, I know. Which is why, I was thinking spring, like I mentioned at the Market."

"You mentioned it last week, too."

"So April 22nd? It's a Saturday."

"Are you sure you want to get married that quick?" Emma turned towards him, one hand on her hip. She brushed her hair behind her ear with the other hand.

He nodded. "It's either that, or we're waiting a few more years before the date falls on a Friday or Saturday again."

"And you already spent money on the ring. Might as well not have a long engagement," Emma joked. Getting married on their anniversary was a cute idea but she wasn't sure how realistic it would be.

"Exactly," Connor said, picking up the pan of pasta and dumping it in the colander Emma had put in the sink. "We could pawn it, go on a really nice vacation instead."

"And continue living in sin?" Emma teased back.

"Might as well. We've gone this long."

"Well, if we're going to hell anyway, what's another few years?" Emma pulled the vegetables off the burner and poured them into a bowl.

"I don't think I want to wait much longer before being able to call you Mrs. Dolan."

Emma almost dropped the bowl. She'd been entertaining the idea of them getting married for so long, she forgot what the end game was. She'd be changing her name and become part of his life, of his family. It wasn't just a change in how they filed taxes, but a change in who she was. Not that she had any idea who that was anymore. When she was in college, her work was always co-signed by Owen. Before that, she was Chief Bishop's daughter. She had traded those in for, what? To be Connor Dolan's wife? She'd spent a lifetime being defined by the men she was associated with.

Getting married meant she'd keep doing everything she was now. That was true. It didn't mean she'd have to quit her job. It just meant that any formal piece of mail she received would be addressed to Mrs. Connor Dolan.

"What?" He put his arms around her. "Did I say something wrong?"

"No, no," Emma shook her head, "I just forgot that . . . you know, that's what this ring really means. That I wouldn't be Emma Bishop anymore."

"You can hyphenate your name."

"Bishop-Dolan feels like a mouthful."

"You still want to be my wife, right?" He stepped back.

"Of course I do. It's just the weight of the decision. This is real, Connor. What we're doing."

He chuckled. "I remember the first time I said I wanted to marry you, you just about had a heart attack."

Connor had been watching her organize their kitchen when they first moved into this apartment. It was a task Emma hadn't thought twice about. Her mother had taught her how a kitchen should be organized, and her mother before her. It was a legacy that gender roles demanded that, as progressive as Emma was, she couldn't ignore.

"You know," Connor had started saying, giving his hand to her to help pull her up off the floor. "This right here. Watching you here, making this home for us. This is why I love you. This is why I know I'm going to marry you one day."

Emma laughed at the memory as she pulled the chicken out of the oven and set it on the heating pad on the counter. It wasn't a memory she looked back on with total fondness. "Oh yeah, bright shining moment of our relationship that was."

"No, it was cute. I think it made my love you even more."

"Oh yeah, because having me throw up after you told me you wanted to marry me was super endearing."

It was one reason why Emma was thankful she aimed for the sink with the garbage disposal.

"Okay, well, at that exact moment it was a little disgusting. But afterwards, it was cute. You were nervous."

"Yeah, nervous is a good word for it."

"What word would you use?"

Emma turned towards him. "Terrified."

"What, of getting married?"

She nodded.

"I'm not that scary, am I?"

"No, just marriage . . . it's permanent. You don't walk away from it. You can't. You have to break up a family if you do."

Connor nodded. "I guess I never looked at it that way."

"I mean, look at my mom—if something were to happen to my dad, she'd never re-marry."

"Because she loves him so much? I think that's a good thing."

Emma shook her head. "The sun rises and sets with my dad for her. She just orbits around him, making sure he's taken care of, not doing anything without him. If anything happens to dad, she's going to be so lost. She's not going to know who she is."

"So you're afraid of loving me too much?"

"It's silly." Emma turned away from him and began to dish up their meals. She wasn't even sure what she was admitting to. Maybe she was afraid of loving him too much, or of depending on him too much. Or maybe she was just terrified of getting to used to him being around—of losing him when they've come so far. "I'm sorry, I shouldn't have brought it up."

"No, definitely not silly. I'd want you to be able to live without me. I think that's why we work so well together. You have your life, I have mine, but at the end of the day we have this. We always come back to this."

"I know. And I do, I do like that a lot."

"What's wrong then? What are you really scared of?" He leaned against the counter, looking at her.

Emma sighed. "I had drinks with the girls from the building, and Christa thinks her husband is cheating on her. Stephanie and her husband have an open marriage. Just neither of those things sound like something I'd want."

"An open marriage?" Connor raised his eyebrows.

"Yeah, they see other people but always tell the other person about it or something."

"Sounds exhausting."

"That's what I thought." Emma chuckled. "But I barely even look at anyone else. I don't think that's something I could pull off. And I definitely don't want to be cheated on."

"I barely have the time to see you, let alone cheat on you." Connor grabbed the plates and put them on the table.

"I didn't say you were."

"We should eat before it gets cold."

"Connor, what's wrong?"

He shook his head, handing her the plate. "Nothing's wrong. Really. Let's eat."

Emma sat down at the table, the music not loud enough to buffer the silence between them. "Do you want me to put something on? We haven't caught up completely with The Daily Show from this week."

"Sure." He smiled. "Sounds great."

"Are you sure everything's okay? I didn't mean . . . I don't think you're cheating on me."

"I know. I'm fine, really. Just remembered I have to go back to work tomorrow."

"Well, cheer up. I'm taking you somewhere this weekend," Emma said. It was impulsive, but it would give the both of them something to work forward to. She'd look into bed and breakfasts with openings this weekend on Orca Island. They'd go whale watching, like they always said they wanted to.

Connor looked up at her from his plate and smiled. "Oh yeah?"

"Yeah," she said, standing up to turn off the music and turn on the television. "But I can't tell you. One of us has to be good at keeping secrets."

13

When Emma agreed to be the maid of honor, she was under the impression that picking out her own dress wasn't in the job description. She'd helped organize the engagement party and the bridal shower. She called and set up cake tastings. When Danielle went dress shopping with her mother, Emma had been there too. This was one decision Emma had hoped that she wouldn't have to help with.

Standing barefoot in the dressing room, she pulled on the third dress. Unlike the other two, this one was what Danielle considered "season appropriate" in color and length. Smoothing the material she stepped out into the small lounge where Danielle and Molly sat, champagne flutes in hand.

"Oh yes. That one." Molly said, raising her glass.

"I don't know," Emma said as she stood in front of the mirrors. The dress was a burnt orange, which went with the theme of the rest of the wedding. But it felt too ostentatious for her. She preferred muted colors to this spectacle—even if she did like the cut.

"I like it," Danielle said. "But try on a few more. Think of it as practice."

"For what?" Emma raised her eyebrows.

"Your own wedding. Duh." Danielle teased.

"Oh yes, yes. If the boy ever agrees with you on a date," Molly teased, waving her hand dramatically.

"April 22nd." Emma blushed. "We talked about it a few weeks ago."

"He picked this? Or did you?" Molly leaned forward, elbow resting on her knee, chin in her hand.

"Oh no, he did." Emma smiled. It had been the second night, in a long string of nights, where he'd talked about their wedding, their future. Kids, too, had been talked about: how many he wanted, what he thought good names would be. Even if Emma wasn't sure she wanted children, she was glad that these were things he was focusing on again. It wasn't just work, and Rachel, and how he could get promoted anymore. It was back to them.

"That's great, sweetie." Danielle said. "You're going to be pro after helping me"

"I'm sure Owen would help you out if you needed him to," Molly teased.

"I don't think that's a good idea," Emma said, rolling her eyes. "Besides, if anyone's going to help me through this thing it's going to be the two of you and Leah."

"How're things going with him, by the way?" Danielle asked, standing up to grab another dress from the pile she had picked out for Emma.

"Owen? Oh, it's fine. I see him at rehearsal, we talk then, but otherwise I haven't heard from him."

"No more amazing symphony seats?" Molly asked.

Emma shrugged. "Too busy. He's been very focused on this project, and I've been busy with Connor."

"Busy?" Molly grinned.

"Not like that." Emma blushed as another woman walked out of a dressing room, a red dress draped over her arm. Emma recognized her immediately. "Rachel, what a surprise."

There was little that could surprise Emma these days. Out of all the dress shops in the entire city and outlying suburbs, she would never have expected Rachel to be here. In fact, Rachel had really been far from her mind these past few weeks. Even with Emma doing drinks with her neighbors on Tuesdays, and rehearsals and Wednesday, their life had gone back to normal.

"Oh, Emma. Hi."

"What're you doing here?" Emma asked.

"Connor. He said . . . he said you come here a lot. That you'd be here tonight. And always says how great you look dressed up. So I thought I'd check it out. He's taking me to dinner on Tuesday to celebrate my promotion."

Emma knew about the dinner plans, but had assumed they wouldn't require cocktail attire. It was flattering, that she'd shop here just because she knew Emma did. Still, the night was full of more surprises than she had anticipated.

"Thank you, that's really kind."

"He usually does. You know, like the things we do together."

Emma stayed quiet and attempted to keep her face clean from emotion. On the inside, her pulse raced and her stomach twisted

"I'm glad. I know he's been stressed with work. It's great that you two have stayed such good friends"

"Yeah. Good friends. That's it." Rachel laughed. "God, he pisses me off. Seriously? Good friends? You have a shitty fiancé, Emma."

"I won't punish Connor because he likes to play a white knight."

"Oh, he tells you that he, what? He has to come save me?" Rachel shook her head, her cheeks turning red.

"He just tells me you've been having a hard time. I trust him. I don't need to know more than that."

Rachel rolled her eyes. "You're really that naive?"

"What do you mean?"

"I wanted to run into you tonight because I needed to tell you the truth, to your face. We've been sleeping together, for like a month now."

Emma shook her head. Her world, what was left to it, crumbled inside of her, crushing her chest. It was hard to breathe.

"I doubt that." Emma whispered.

"Honestly, I wouldn't believe me either. I wouldn't. I know how this looks. If my boyfriend's ex came to me saying that he's cheating on me with her, I'd think she was just being a crazy jealous bitch. But I have pictures. If you ever want them, you know how to get in touch with me."

She went to walk away, and then stopped and turned. "I mean it. Like, I'm pissed off that he's been blowing me off lately. I'd do anything just to make him feel the way I'm feeling right now. But you should know the man you're sticking around for. And know that I'm not going to stop fighting for him."

"You should probably go now," Molly said, standing up.

"I'm just trying to be honest with her. She deserves the truth." Rachel shrugged. "I'm sure I'll see you around. I mean it, Emma. About the pictures. Just ask."

"Thanks girl, we got it from here." Molly took a step towards Rachel. Rachel shrugged and left the dressing room.

Emma's heart pounded in her ears while her stomach churned and squeezed. If she didn't throw up in the dressing room right now it would be a miracle. It wasn't enough to be jealous of Rachel, or to have these jealousies based in something that didn't exist. Now she had a foundation, a testimony to base her argument off of.

"Shit." Molly spoke first. "Holy. Shit."

"Emma, are you okay?" So unlike the drunken bride-to-be the other night, Danielle was composed today. Out of the three of them, Danielle was the one that Emma knew she could count on to stay levelheaded. Molly would kill Rachel right now if given the chance. Danielle would formulate a plan; formulate something to get back at Rachel and to get Emma out of Connor's house—if that's what she wanted.

"I can't . . . I can't breathe."

She didn't know what she wanted.

"Come on, let's get you out of that dress."

Molly and Danielle helped her out of the dress and back into her normal clothes. They walked out of the boutique without buying a dress, leaving Rachel crying at the counter. Emma wanted to say something, comfort her. But Molly and Danielle ushered her outside before she had the chance.

"Now what, sweetie? Drink?" Molly asked once they were in the car. Danielle shook her head.

"No, let's get her out of Bellevue. She needs air."

Emma nodded. Air. She needed to remember to breathe in and breathe out. It was something her brain had trouble processing. The edge of her vision was black with tiny stars and pinpricks across her body.

"Where can we take her?"

"Not home." It was the first thing Emma had been able to say.

"Well, no shit sweetie. We can't take you back there. You're welcome to come crash with me and Laurel."

"Tom's at my place," Danielle said, shrugging. "But we can go there if you'd rather?"

Emma shook her head. Tom or Laurel weren't people she wanted to see right now. She wanted to see the ceiling of a bathroom from the comfort of a bathtub. Checking into a hotel was the most practical option, but all Emma really wanted was to be somewhere that felt like home.

"Leah." Emma said.

Danielle and Molly looked at each other and then back to Emma.

"She'll know what to do." Emma pulled her phone out of her bag and called him. Leah picked up on the third ring.

"Hey stranger!" She could hear the smile in her sister's voice. His world sounded busy, like traffic and other city sounds.

"I ... " she trailed off.

"Emma? Are you okay?"

Emma shook her head. It was lost on her that Leah couldn't see her.

"Emma?"

Danielle reached for the phone and took it ever so gently from Emma's hand. She nodded.

"Hey Leah, it's Danielle." A pause. "Yeah, can we bring her over?" There was another long pause. "We ran into Rachel while we were shopping . . . " Danielle trailed off. Emma looked up at them. Was there no more explanation they needed than this?

"Did . . . did you guys know?"

"No, sweetie. No. I promise." Molly said, turning towards Emma again. Danielle turned around now, too.

"No, Leah just didn't need to hear anymore. She said we should bring you to her."

Emma wondered if Connor would think to even look for her at Leah's. Molly's maybe, or Danielle's. He'd probably even look at Owen's. Emma knew she'd be left alone at Leah's. He was too afraid of Emma's brother in law to even try and go there.

"Okay."

Danielle started to drive and Emma tried to close her eyes. She had bare necessities with her in her handbag: makeup, medicine, and a charger for her cell phone. But she didn't have a change of clothes or even a truth brush.

She wasn't paying attention as they drove through the city. Emma still wasn't paying attention when they got her to Leah's and helped her up into the guest bedroom. Her sight was still blurred, black and filled with stars.

It wasn't until the following morning that she even realized where she was.

The room was dark, but comfortable. The bed was unfamiliar. The sheets were too soft to be the hotels she normally stayed in and they didn't smell like starch or bleach. It smelled like home.

Rolling over, she blinked a few times, the room finally started to come into focus.

Getting out of the bed, she walked over to the window, where heavy curtains blocked out whatever scenery was around her. Peeking through, she saw hills and houses laid out below her with the Seattle skyline off in the distance.

Emma opened up the bedroom door. The house was quiet, except for the gentle sounds of her nephew's giggle floating up the stairs.

"Emma?" Leah called up the stairs. "Are you up?"

Emma walked to the banister and leaned over. "So it would seem."

"Hungry?"

"Not really."

"You should eat something," Leah said as she started to climb the stairs. "You've been asleep for a few days."

"Days?"

They blurred together. Before now, the last thing she remembered was vaguely being helped into the bedroom. Maybe Leah had given her something to calm down.

"What about work? I can't be missing—"

"It's fine. I told your boss there was a family emergency. He said to take all the time you need."

"What day is it? I can still go into the office."

"It's Monday, and no you can't. You haven't eaten. Or showered."

"I don't have anything."

Leah rolled her eyes. "I have one child and a Costco membership. I have extras of everything. And we're the same size. So help yourself to my closet. But only the PJs or yoga pants and t-shirts. Go shower. Or use the tub in my bathroom."

"Why only the PJs or yoga clothes?"

"Because I don't want you thinking that you're going to be leaving this house for work today." Leah said with a stern voice. "You need to decompress a little. Trust me on this. Go to a bath. I'll make some food."

Emma knew better than to argue. She'd do as she was told. Going back into the guest room, Emma grabbed some things--her phone, the towels Leah left on the dresser, along with the toothbrush, toothpaste, razor, shampoo, and conditioner--and went down the hall and into Leah's room.

Opening the door, Emma felt like she was entering her parents bedroom more than going into her sister's bedroom. Putting her things down in the bathroom, Emma went back out to closet and pulled some of Leah's clean clothes off of the shelves. Yoga pants, t-shirt. She grabbed a clean bra and pair of underwear, too. At least

Leah's post-pregnancy body and Emma's normal body were the same size.

She put the clothes by the rest of her things and finally started to fill the tub. Had she, at last, become so much like her literary heroes? Sylvia Plath had once said there was nothing a good bath couldn't fix. Emma wasn't sure it would fix her broken heart. But at least it was a start.

As she settled into the hot water, Emma re-played the whole run-in with Rachel in her head. It was too perfect of a set-up. Rachel said Connor told her that Emma would be there that night. Maybe Rachel was just trying to get back at Connor for not being around as much, and the only way to hurt him was to try and ruin his relationship. Or maybe it happened once, and it was a stupid mistake that Connor regretted. Maybe Rachel was just making the whole thing up. Connor looked her in the face and told her he'd never cheat on her. Hadn't he?

Emma could remember the first time she had met Connor. It was her second year of college and she had gone to the Cherry Street Coffee Shop to work on a paper. The residence hall, as amazing of an experience as it was, had become distracting. Owen, more to the point, had become distracting. She had packed up what little materials she needed—laptop, cell phone, key card, and wallet—and walked the few blocks to the shop.

Connor had been there that day. She didn't end up getting her paper written, but did leave the coffee shop with a date.

Getting out of the tub, Emma went back to her phone to check the messages Connor sent. A few were just question marks, of him wondering where she was. But after a few hour pause, the longer messages started pouring in.

Connor Anderson (9:48pm): *I just talked to Rachel. I can't believe she said that to you. Emma, I swear, it's not true. I could never hurt you like that. I would never do anything to try and jeopardize what we have.*

Connor Anderson (10:05pm): *Just tell me where you are. I just need to know that you're safe and that you're coming home.*

Connor Anderson (1:04am): *I guess you're not coming home. I don't know what*

to do. I guess this is how you must feel when I don't show up. I'm sorry. I'm

sorry for everything. I promise that things will be better when you decide to

come home. I'm really hoping that you do.

Emma put the phone back on the counter. There wasn't much to his text messages, but more than she was expecting. He had given her something to think about; just like he had the day they met.

14

APRIL 2006

Writing essays wasn't exactly what she had in mind when she decided to go to school for music. Emma had anticipated spending hours practicing, learning new music, and pushing herself. She knew she'd be learning how to compose pieces bigger meant for a full orchestra. She expected the long hours of one-on-one time with instructors and piano labs. Planning out the recital at the end of her senior year despite it only being her junior wasn't even a surprise. Spending time researching world music traditions and writing a paper on it was.

She felt awkward sitting with a laptop in front of her, her fingers moving across keys that didn't make music. Her notebook was next to her, flipped open to notes she'd taken during class while her textbook remained untouched in her bag like it had been all semester. This was more difficult than it needed to be. Looking over that rough outline she'd made, she was certain of two things: that this might be the end of her college career, and she needed something else to drink

Standing up, and stretching, she looked around the small coffee shop. It was modern looking, the coffee shop, with wide wooden plank floors and clean-yet-rustic decorations. Yellow globes hung from long black wires lit the darkest corners of the small shop. There was a mix of tables, and of chairs to sit in: small, shining booths and antique wingback chairs. Most of these were occupied today. Emma recognized a few faces from her previous visits: a girl she had seen on campus a few times, an older man sitting in a worn-out chair, nose buried in a book. The guy the next table over even felt familiar. She knew she hadn't seen him on campus, and yet she was sure she had seen him—here, perhaps. The coffee shop was the only place, aside from the practice room, that she spent time in these days. She was sure he had been here, too.

"Excuse me," Emma said, her hands in her back pockets. A nervous habit, one that was developed after years of riding the subway. Underground, she had to trust that she could count on the other people in the car. She always had to have her hands out. Above ground, bracing for the jerk of a subway car was just weird. "Would you mind watching my stuff for me for a second?"

He looked up and her and smiled. "Sure thing."

Emma smiled back. He was boyishly handsome, like the models they used for Hollister ads. But the way he smiled at her made her suspicious of him. He looked like the kind of boy that her mother would warn her to stay away from. The kind of boy that she was sure would be added to the list of kinds of boys she should never sleep with: too innocent looking, which meant he'd probably break her heart at some point.

Blushing, she pushed hair behind her ear, and walked towards the counter. She looked back once, and found him looking at her. Staring at her. Emma looked away, focusing on the menu. Still, she could feel his eyes on her.

"Another coffee?" the barista asked.

"Herbal tea?" Emma asked, feeling too stimulated already. "Peppermint if you have it."

Paying for the tea, and accepting the double-cup, she could feel the heat radiating through the paper. As she sat back down, the boy stood up from his seat.

"So, since I made sure that your stuff wasn't stolen by any number of the various . . . flannel wearing coffee drinkers in here I think you owe me something in return."

Emma looked up at him, eyebrows raised. She had been asked out in a number of different ways by a number of different people. But she'd never heard a line like this one before. If this guy thought she owed him something for being a decent human being, he was going to be disappointed.

"I didn't realize that being nice came with terms and conditions."

He chuckled. "I was nice to you, so you can be nice to me."

"I don't even know your name," Emma said, shaking her head at him.

"And yet you asked me to watch your stuff."

She conceded to his point, smiling and touching her hair. "Well, what's your name?"

"Connor," he said as he extended his hand. It was a gesture that always took Emma by surprise. It was something she had always seen her father do, always a gesture associated with something wholly adult.

Taking his hand in hers, she shook his and then went to pull away but he held on, stretching out her fingers in his palm.

"Your fingers are so long, so skinny."

She blushed. "Piano hands."

"Is that what you do?"

Emma nodded. She had forgotten for a moment that not everyone went to the Conservatory. That not everyone could tell the instrument a person played just by looking at them.

"So, are you a music major or something? UW?"

"Music major is the easiest way to describe it. And no, I'm at The Seattle Conservatory."

He leaned back against the back seat of the booth and she felt her face flush, not used to being the person someone regarded.

"Why here, and not a fancier conservatory on the east coast?"

She flinched, not expecting him to know much—if anything—

about classical music higher education. No one else had ever questioned it. In fact, it may have even considered a rude question, especially if that person hadn't made it into a conservatory.

"Sorry, I didn't mean—"

"No, no. It's fine." Emma shrugged. "It's a long story. It's not that I didn't want to go to one, or that I didn't get into one. I just . . . " she trailed off. How could she explain this story to someone, a stranger, when she hadn't even told her closest friends?

"I was set to go to a conservatory in Boston, but 9/11 . . ." she trailed off.

His brow furrowed.

"I thought I was going to be okay with staying in the city, but I wasn't."

"But Boston isn't New York."

Emma shrugged again. "I know. But to me, it was still too close. I needed to get away from all of it."

"Oh, I'm . . . I'm sorry. Did you lose someone?"

"Not that day, no."

It was hard to explain such a strong connection to something when she had no personal stakes in that day. How she feared the sound of planes, how she hated that the flight plan to SeaTac was right over the city. What was even more difficult was explaining to someone like Owen that she may have compromised a music career because of fear.

Of course, she had, in fact, lost people later on. She got the news, usually second hand gossip on an endless scroll of useless news on MySpace. So-and-so was going home for the weekend because they had a funeral to go to.

"But later?"

Emma shook her head. "I mean, a few people I knew in high school enlisted and didn't make it back. But no one I was close with."

He frowned now. Their once flirtatious conversation had turned too dark too fast. "I'm really sorry, if I had known—"

Emma shook her head. "No, no. It's fine. It's weird, talking about it, but it's good."

"What, no friends?" He smiled, joking.

"No, I think that musicians and artists are kind of . . . self-involved. No one's bothered to ask why I'm out here instead of back there. I think people just assume that the Conservatory is where I want to be, and that I'm from here."

"Have you played tourist yet?" Connor asked, his eyes wide and bright. She could hear his foot tapping against the floor.

"What do you mean?"

"You know, explored the city. You're, what, a junior?"

"Yeah. But no, I haven't. Not really."

"I know what we're going to do."

Emma raised her eyebrows. "For what?"

"Our date."

"Okay." She wasn't sure if he had actually been serious about the two of them going on a date, especially after the turn the conversation had taken.

"Tomorrow morning, are you free?"

Emma glanced at her laptop screen. The amount of work she still had to do was overwhelming. But in the two years she had been in Seattle she had never been to Pike's Place, had seen the Space Needle or gone to the Experience Music Project. She stayed on campus and hid in the coffee shops that were within walking distance. She spent her breaks wherever her parents were: San Diego, Cape Cod, and, most recently, Vancouver.

"Tomorrow morning? I could be free."

"Good. Can I pick you up somewhere, or would you rather meet?" he asked, hands tapping out a hurried rhythm on the tabletop. It was a characteristic she always associated with musicians. With Owen.

At the thought of him she blushed. Of Owen, of his hands, of his eyes and how they never quite focused on her whenever they talked. Here, across the table from her, was someone who was interested, who asked questions, and who looked at her—really looked at her.

It made her blush even more, the heat a cascade from her cheeks down her neck, down her arms, into her toes. It was like getting drunk without even having to take a shot.

"Whichever. I can meet you somewhere," Emma said, trying to stay collected.

"Do you know where Pike's Place is?" Connor asked.

"Um," Emma pointed in the direction she thought it might be. "That way?"

He laughed. "Close enough. Do you think you can find your way there, or should I go just pick you up?"

"I think . . . I mean, the city isn't that big. If I start walking towards the Sound, I should find it."

He laughed again. "Well, here, let me give you my number and if you got lost or do want a ride, I can come get you."

Emma pushed the small, silver flip phone towards him. He took his cell phone out of his pocket, something thick and bulky, and offered it to her.

"Here, so I know who's calling."

"Assuming that I'll call," Emma said, grinning at him as she picked up the phone.

"Just in case. I don't answer numbers I don't know."

Putting her name and number in, she put his phone back on the table and pushed it towards him. He took it and, in turn, handed hers back.

"Thanks."

"Well, I'll see you tomorrow," Connor said as he slid out of the booth seat. "Maybe around ten?"

Emma nodded. "Sure, that sounds good."

"Are you a morning person?"

"I'm a coffee person."

Connor laughed. "That's fair. I'll see you tomorrow."

"See you." Emma said, watching as he went back to his table and started to pack up. She tried to find focus on her work but was distracted by him still being there, and how she could feel him watching her.

When he finally left, he looked back to wave and she waved back. Putting headphones on, she tried to get back to work, hoping the swirling sounds of a mix Owen made her would help her concentrate, but it failed.

She'd have to get the essay written later.

15

The next few days passed without change. She didn't leave Leah's guest room except to eat or use the bathroom. Leah didn't want her going into work, so Emma worked from bed. When she wasn't working, she was replaying the past month in her mind, trying to figure out the exact moment she should have known.

She thought she was overreacting, being jealous of Rachel. At the engagement party, he hadn't been ashamed to be seen with Rachel in public. If something was going on, he would've tried to avoid her, wouldn't he? The night she brought up cheating to him, he'd acted strange, but Emma didn't think anything of it. They told each other everything. She had no reason not to trust him.

Opening up her laptop, she tried not to think about where she would go from here. Work was something she could actually manage. The problem was, if she left Connor, he wouldn't be able to afford the apartment on his own. Kicking him out seemed harsh when she'd just be breaking the lease anyway. Even if he had cheated on her, she was still human. She still loved him and cared about him. She couldn't just ignore their past together even if she was hurting in the present.

Her phone went off with a text message alert. Grabbing her phone, Emma swiped at the screen. It was Connor. Again. This time he wanted to make sure she knew he loved her. Over the past few days he'd sent texts asking where she was, if she was okay, and that understood why she wasn't speaking to him. Her stomach lurched, a ripple of pain spreading like wildfire through her body. That first day, he insisted it wasn't true. Now there was no mention of it, of what Rachel said. He wasn't trying to convince her one way or the other. If he really was sorry, if it really didn't happen, wouldn't he be trying harder? Or was it the other way around? Emma couldn't remember which he should be protesting too much.

Typing quickly, she sent: *I'm fine. Need to clear my head. I'll contact you when I'm ready.* Then, she added, *I love you too.* Clicking the top of the phone, she turned it back over, not wanting to see if he responded. She could at least be adult enough to let him know she was alive.

"Emma?" Leah called through the closed bedroom door. "Molly's here."

Closing her laptop and setting it on the bedside table, Emma got up out of bed. She wasn't in the mood to visit with anyone. But she'd been ignoring Molly and Danielle as much as she was ignoring Connor.

As she opened the door, Leah apologized in a whisper. "I'm sorry, she really wanted to see you and she brought you food. I couldn't turn her away."

"It's fine. Where is she?"

"Downstairs in the kitchen. Henry's down for a nap."

Emma felt a twinge of guilt. She'd been here since Friday and had barely spent any time with her nephew. "Are you coming down?"

Leah shook her head. "No, I'm going to lay down for a little bit. Go spend time with your friend. She's worried about you."

"You're a really good mom, you know that?"

"I'll remember that when Henry's a teenager and hates my guts." Leah patted Emma's shoulder and went down the hall towards her bedroom.

❁

"My visit comes with gifts," Molly said as Emma entered the kitchen., holding up paper bags. "Ivar's."

Molly opened up the paper bag. The room filled with the smell of beer-battered fish and chips, Emma's favorite.

"You know how to coax a girl out of hiding."

"I wouldn't call this you coming out of hiding. Just coming downstairs. I've been texting Leah to make sure you were okay since you haven't been answering me."

"I'm sorry." Emma looked down. "I don't mean to shut you out. I've just been trying to figure this whole thing out."

"You just need to do what makes you happy," Molly said before popping a French fry into her mouth.

"I don't even know what it would take to even make me happy anymore."

"What about playing? You're doing that concert with Owen."

Emma nodded. "But it isn't something that is mine. It's just something else that I'm helping out. I'm just I'm a minor character in these men's lives."

"I'm glad you finally see that," Molly said. "I've seen it for awhile but didn't know how to bring it up to you. How do you tell one of your best and oldest friends they're selling themselves short?"

"Without them telling you to 'get fucked?'"

"Exactly. I want you to be happy and you've really seemed happy. Bored, sure, but I guess that comes with being an adult. But your happiness always—"

"—is dependent on making the men in my life happy."

"Exactly."

Emma knew Molly was right. She'd known it for awhile. It was why she got so angry when she found out Owen was putting on a concert at the Conservatory. Why she didn't want to play with him in the first place. With Connor it was different. She compromised herself in what seemed like small ways—or at least ways that felt like she was working towards some greater good. Connor's happiness, and their happiness as a couple, was what mattered the most. Now she could see how unfair that was. If Rachel was telling the truth, and Connor cheated on her, then Emma had really been compromising for nothing. She had done everything she could to make sure he had everything he could ever want or need. Everything she had to give wasn't enough for him.

"So what now?" Molly asked. "Are you just going to stay in your sister's room forever?"

"I don't know. I don't know who to believe."

Molly looked away. "Connor's a good guy. He's always been a good guy to you, even if he's selfish."

"Are you saying you think Rachel's lying?"

"I think she has a lot of reasons to."

"But so does Connor."

"What is your gut telling you to do?"

Emma shrugged and reached for the Ivar's bag. The smell of the food was finally making her feel hungry. If it was as easy as trusting her gut, she'd already be back at Connor's. She wouldn't even have reacted the way she did. Trusting her gut the way Shondaland heroines did was something Emma always thought she could do. But Emma wasn't Olivia Pope. She didn't have forty-five minutes of a television episode to fix this scandal.

"It's telling me I should eat these fries before they get cold."

Molly laughed. "Well, that's a start."

"Just . . . distract me with something. Tell me what's going on with you."

"Well, there's something I actually wanted to talk to you about other than your boy problems."

"Oh?"

Molly pulled her cell phone from her back pocket, swiped the screen with her finger, and handed it to Emma.

"The Conservatory contacted you?"

"Yeah. They want me to come to do a talk in the fall during their freshman orientation about my experience there, what I'm doing with my life now."

Emma read the e-mail and got to the part where the Admissions Director knew how to get ahold of Emma, too.

"They want me too?"

Molly rolled her eyes. "Of course they do. You're successful and a big supporter of the school still. You actually got something out of your time there."

"So did you. You just don't know it."

"Yeah, I don't think so," Molly said in between bites of another fry. "I have this degree in music production but I'm blowing glass instead."

"But you still have those skills. You still use them. I've seen your work. You can't tell me you don't mix music together to listen to while you work on new projects."

"Guilty." Molly grinned. "Fine, you caught me. But what about you? You keep skirting around the question."

"I'd love to come and talk to the first years. Tell them I'm in. I can give you my work e-mail address to give them."

Molly took her phone back and began typing. "Awesome. This is going to be great."

"Do you think . . . What if we put a project together for this?"

"What do you mean?"

"I came across a ton of boxes of my old sheet music—songs that I've never even played on stage before. What if we put something together to help show why you need to branch out beyond your musical cluster?"

"Please tell me you still have some of those jazz songs you'd keep me up all night working on."

"Actually, I do." Emma grinned.

"I'll see if we can grab some time on campus to work on this. I mean, you donate enough money there every year. They should at least owe you access to the rehearsal room or the recording equipment. Right?"

"It doesn't hurt to ask."

Molly folded over the top of the Ivar's bag and pushed it across the kitchen counter towards Emma.

"Well, my work here is done."

"You're leaving already?"

Emma realized that in the short time Molly had been there, she didn't think about Connor once.

"I've gotta go see Laurel. Date night. We're going to another exhibit opening."

"Well get out of here. Have fun," Emma said, reaching out to hug her friend.

"I will." Molly squeezed back, hard, for moments longer than Emma thought the hug should've lasted. "And you, figure out what you want to do. Just know that I support whatever you decide. I just want you to do what makes you happy. Not anybody else. You got that?"

Emma nodded. "I got it."

And she did. She was excited about something for the first time in she didn't know how long. With Molly's help, maybe she'd finally record music of her own. She'd be able to listen to something that wasn't a combination of her and Owen. She'd be able to work on herself for once.

But she would have to go back to her apartment to get the sheet music.

16

Her hands flew across the keys and she moved through the motions of warm ups. Scales bridged into songs that Owen and the rest of the group tried to keep up with. Her repertoire had cobwebs that were starting to clear. It was the first rehearsal since the incident with Rachel the Friday before. Emma felt like now, more than ever, she had something to prove. That just because her personal life was falling apart, didn't mean her professional one was.

She needed to prove that she was still good.

A few minutes into a new song, a Chopin, she became too aware of the lack of background noise and stopped playing.

"Sorry," she said, looking up at Owen.

"No, no. It's good. We need to get you here more often." He laughed. "Please, continue on. I can give the others a break while you work out."

Emma laughed as she looked back down at the keys. Working out was what they called it in college. It was all muscles and memories of the way the muscles were suppose to move, to pull the music out of the instrument. Instead of going to the gym, she just limited caloric intake. This was all the cardio she had needed then.

"What are you going to play next?" Owen asked, sitting down next to her on the bench. His violin rested in his lap.

"That always seems to be the question, doesn't it?"

He chuckled. "It does indeed. But you are the leader in this round, Emma. I'll follow you."

"You know, in all our time at the Conservatory we never played around with the contemporary past our freshman year. We always tried to mimic the Greats, or forge our own path. Meanwhile, some great music was being made that will never see the inside of a classroom."

"That's true."

"And," Emma continued, tracing a finger over each of the keys in front of her, "there are songs that aren't meant for our instruments that we could alter to fit our needs."

"What do you have in mind?" Owen asked. She could see his fingers tapping the edge of his bow, anticipating the music even before she knew what she wanted to play.

Hands against the keys, Emma pressed down gently and then with more force as she began moving through the opening of the song. Her foot, the one that she didn't use to work the pedals, began to shake, anticipating the change in tempo as she got to her favorite part of the song.

"'Summer?'" he asked. Emma continued playing, fingers moving faster as she got to her favorite part of the song.

"'Winter' seemed inappropriate." She said as she glanced at him, wearing the smallest of smiles.

He picked up his violin and followed her through the song, keeping perfect pace. A chill ran through her body, raising goose bumps down her arms and legs.

Stopping suddenly, he looked at her, eyebrows raised. She winked and moved into Storm. It was one of the songs Owen had always had a difficult time catching up once she started playing. The other was Chopin's 'Fantasie.'

As they finished, Owen put his bow down, out of breath.

"You've upped the tempo on me."

Emma grinned. "I don't know what you're talking about."

"Are you sure you haven't been just playing in secret and you didn't want to tell me? Shouldn't you be rusty?"

"Don't feel bad. You just haven't had me around to make you keep up with."

"That's true."

They fell silent and Emma was too aware of the other members of their small group that had filled some of the empty seats in the auditorium.

"All right, well, I know you said contemporary so, let me try something. Guys?" He motioned for the few in the crowd and then turned back to Emma. "You're going to think it's lame. Beneath us, dear, but it was fun."

Emma shook her head. "I don't think anything you do can be considered lame."

"Just wait."

As the rest of the group came on stage, he picked up his violin and his whole body changed. The formal player, the classically trained musician, had suddenly loosened his body and was stamping his foot to count everyone in. His body moved with each note, facial expressions matching what she was sure were words to the song.

After he moved into the initial round of the chorus the rest of the string orchestra came in with him. Emma recognized the song immediately: Avicii's "Wake Me Up." It was something Emma would've pushed Owen to do in undergrad. Something fun, different, that loosened him up and moved him away from his classical comfort zone.

"So?"

"I loved it. Absolutely. But, did you plan that out, or did you improvise it?"

Owen rolled his eyes. "Does it matter?"

"You did the same four years of Conservatory that I did. You tell me."

A few members of the orchestra chuckled.

"Okay, fair. But we need to focus on the pieces for the concert. I—"

"You need to be moving in synch. You can't do that if you don't trust each other."

Everything she learned over the four years was unlocked from some hidden part of her mind.

"Should I know this song?"

"It doesn't matter," Emma said without looking up from the piano. It was a Sia song that had been stuck in her head for a few days now. "Just start adding in where it feels right."

The cellos caught up first, slow and all minor chords. The basses next and then finally the violins, adding in more emotion to the already heartbreaking "Cheap Thrills."

She never imagined it to sound like this, with her piano and him on the violin, and the rest of the violins, cellos, and basses filling in the gaps between them. With each note she played, she remembered why she went to music school to begin with. Why she loved playing so much. Why she needed it in her life.

❋

"EMMA?" Owen was carrying his case in one hand, the other tucked into the pocket of his peacoat. Practice had ended with a perfect go-through of the first few songs once they were warmed up. It had been, by far, their best rehearsal yet.

"Yes?"

"Listen, I know things are . . . they're, well, bad. I know they're bad. But I just wanted to offer it up. If you wanted to come stay with me instead of at your sister's, I have a guest room and a piano."

"As if that's all a girl could need." She smiled.

"No, I know. It's not home. It's not your home. But the offer still stands. I just . . ." he trailed off, conflict etched into the lines next to his eyes and the way he clenched his jaw. "I lost you for so long. I don't want that to happen again."

"What do you mean?"

He looked back at her, laughing. "You really have to ask, after all this time?"

Emma shook her head. "Owen, really, I—"

"Emma?"

She looked over to see Connor getting out of his car. Swallowing, she turned to face him.

"What are you doing here?"

"I just . . . I had to see you. I had to tell you I'm sorry in person."

She could see Owen backing up out of the corner of her eye. "Connor, I can't do this right now."

"Why not?"

"We're in public."

"I know you asked me to give you space, but I needed to see you. I needed to make sure you were okay."

She could hear the desperation in his voice, the lack of sleep, the too much crying. There were few times she could remember him crying and his voice had been similar: raw, too full, thirsty for something more stable than the experience he was having at that time.

"How could you expect me to just be fine?"

Cars rushed past them, ignorant to the lives that were shattering right on the sidewalk. She needed this to happen on her own terms. It was only yesterday that she sat in Leah's kitchen, unable to tell Molly what she wanted to do.

Him being here was messy, unprecedented. Him being here threw everything off. The desperation in his eyes, the way his voice shook, exploited her own pain. In rejection, she only wanted to feel validation. Connor was the only one who could make her feel that way.

"I didn't do it. I promise. I didn't do whatever she said. I could never do that to you. Please, you have to believe me. You have to believe that you mean too much to me. I could never do that do you."

Emma looked away from him. Cars stopped and they went, controlled by the streetlights. Bass thumped too hard from one car while the gentle crooning of a man's voice left the half-open windows of another. It was a strange clash of music, and of melody.

"I don't know," Emma began, "if I can trust what you say. Rachel said she has proof. Why would she say that if she *didn't* have proof that you two have been sleeping together?"

Connor shrugged. "She's mad. She thought that her and I hanging out meant something more than it actually was. I shouldn't have spent so much time with her. I see that now. She's just trying to break us up. She probably thinks that if we break up her and I have another shot. But Emma, we don't. I promise you that we don't."

She looked back at him, embracing the numbness that passed through her. "Why would she ever think that you were going to break up with me for her?"

"Like I said, I shouldn't have spent so much time with her."

Clenching her teeth together, she pulled her phone out of her pocket. Owen had texted her, asking to let him know how things went. He had been trying to tell her something before Connor interrupted them: another what-if to add to her jar.

"I don't know if I can trust this right now."

"I understand."

"No, I don't think you do."

He stayed silent.

"If I ask for Rachel to send me her proof, will I get anything? Or is she actually making this up?"

She wanted to believe Connor. She wanted to trust that he was good, and kind; that he would never do something so cruel to her. Looking at him now, at the fear that pulled at the corners of his eyes, made her question the lengths he would go to try and make this right —and the lengths Rachel would go to break them up.

"Please, Emma. No. She has nothing."

Her stomach churned with uncertainty. To not trust Connor, to walk away from this, meant walking away from everything she knew. It meant walking away from her home and a life she had grown accustomed to. While it was true that she always thought love was something bigger than comfort, she knew now that this was the way it was supposed to be. If she wanted a home, to be comfortable and secure, Connor could provide that for her.

The feelings of a fresh romance, the swooning and the trying, was long dead for the two of them. This was the way things were now.

"What do you want from me?" Emma asked.

"I just want you to be happy. I want you, obviously." He chuckled nervously. "But I want to make sure you're happy, and that you're okay."

"I just . . . this time away has made me think about what I want."

"Do you not want to marry me anymore?"

"I need music back in my life. I need to put myself first and stop worrying about every one's happiness instead of my own."

She surprised even herself with the answer. The question that he had asked was meant for their relationship and their future. Emma knew now that she could have no future with someone who didn't support her dreams as much as she supported theirs.

"Of course. Anything. But that's not . . ." he shrugged, the question still a sword dangling over their heads.

"I know. I'm still thinking about that. Look, I need to get back to Leah's. We can talk about this another time. I'm not ready."

"So you've been staying at Leah's? Not Owen's?" Connor asked, his smile growing.

"Why would I stay at Owen's?"

Connor looked away from her now. "With how close you guys were in college. I just figured if there was anyone else you'd be with, it would be him."

Emma blushed and she was glad it was dark. If anyone knew her better than Owen, it was still Connor. What he said, though, was something she wasn't even ready to admit to herself, let alone to the man she was supposed to be marrying. Had been planning on marrying.

"No," she said as she grabbed his hand. Fear, of the unknown and of losing everything she did know, surged through her like a tidal wave. It burned her throat and trapped her heart in a vice grip. "I couldn't bear to be with anyone else right now. Not when I still love you."

As she said it, she realized how much she needed him to prove he still wanted her, that he still needed her. The hurt wasn't from the potential of him cheating, but him wanting someone more than he wanted her. Just like needing to prove that she was still a force to be reckoned with on the piano, she needed to prove that she was the better woman. It didn't matter if Rachel was lying or not. So when he leaned in to kiss her, she wrapped her arms around his neck and let him pick her up off the ground. She would let him take her home where they would make love and then fall asleep. She'd trust her gut that this was the right thing to do.

"Can I take you home now?" Connor asked, setting her back down.

"Please."

17

"Are you going to be around tonight?" Connor asked.

Emma looked his reflection in the mirror as she finished touching up her mascara. She shrugged. "It's Tuesday. I was going to see the girls. Amy, Stephanie—you know. I haven't seen them in awhile."

"Oh."

She continued to get ready. Coming back here was stranger than she thought it would be. As much as he swore that nothing happened, that Rachel was making it up, it wasn't the same. Even now as she looked at him she wasn't sure if the remorse she saw on his face was because Rachel had come so far between them, or because Rachel was telling the truth.

"It's only cocktails. I'll maybe be an hour or two."

"Okay. Do you want to hang out later? Watch tv, or something?"

"Sure." Emma shrugged. "Whatever you want to do."

"Or something else. It's up to you."

Emma closed her eyes and took a deep breath in. She didn't want to lose her temper right now, not when he was trying. She'd been back home for almost two weeks and this was the first time, other than going into work, she was spending time away from him.

"Em, what's wrong?" He crossed the distance between them and put a hand on her shoulder. She shrugged it off.

"I just can't pretend like everything's back to normal."

"I know. I'm sorry. I keep telling you that I am. I can't believe—"

"That she'd say that. I know. You've said that."

He frowned. "Then what's wrong?"

"It doesn't feel back to normal, Connor. Do you still talk to her?"

He shrugged. "She doesn't have anyone else."

Emma turned and left the bathroom, her temper rising like an angry sea.

"What?" Connor asked, following her.

She spun around. "After all of this, after me leaving, you still talk to her? Because she doesn't have anyone? Are you serious right now?"

"She doesn't, though. She's has no friends. She doesn't have anyone else to talk to."

"She tried to ruin our relationship."

He sighed. "But she didn't succeed, did she? You're back, and things are fine. Em, what am I supposed to do? Stop talking to her?"

Emma raised her eyebrows. She couldn't believe what she was hearing. On the one hand, she felt sorry for Rachel. Even if her motivates were self-centered, maybe she was just trying to tell the truth. The fact that Rachel had promised picture proof still sat heavy on her heart.

"Show some loyalty."

"I haven't cheated on you."

"That's not what I mean." Emma sighed, shaking her head. "She's just tried to destroy the relationship with the woman you supposedly want to marry—"

"I do want to marry you—"

"And you're still worried about her? And how she's feeling? How about what I'm feeling?"

"What are you feeling?"

"Resentful."

He nodded. "I know. And I don't know what else to—"

"No, you don't know. It's not just about Rachel. It's about everything. I'm there for you for everything, no matter what. I change meetings around, I go to all of your work events—but when's the last time you came to one of my fundraisers? Or even came to the symphony with me?"

He stayed silent, which only made her angrier.

"I'm not okay with anything right now," Emma admitted.

"What do you mean?"

"Us. This. Things need to change. No, I'm not happy about you talking with Rachel, but I'm not going to order you to stop talking to her. I shouldn't . . . it shouldn't . . . " She shook her head. A new flash of pain struck like lightening.

Connor stayed quiet.

"I have to go. I'm late to meet the girls." She wiped stray tears off of her cheeks and double-checked her makeup in the hallway mirror. "We'll talk about this later."

"Emma, wait."

"What?"

He sighed and reached a hand out to her. She looked at him, waiting.

"Please, just . . . don't leave now. Don't leave like this. What . . . what can I do to fix this? What do you need?"

Emma turned away from him and shook her head. His question was bigger than he could possibly know. What she needed was to go back ten years and focus on a future beyond a boyfriend. Sure, her name was on committees and she was thanked in speeches when charities accepted donations, but what she was doing—while it was worthwhile—wasn't enough. She wasn't fulfilled.

That made her more unhappy than whatever was going on with him and Rachel.

"I need . . . something. Something more than fundraising for a symphony I'll never be a part of. Do you know what it's like, being on the outside of something you want so badly? Playing with Owen is just another slap in the face. It's just a reminder of something that I'll never be able to do unless I start playing and composing again. But I'm too busy trying to make sure everybody else is happy."

Her life, as hard as she had worked for it, was never about her or what she wanted. She'd compromised on the apartment and she'd made sure that Connor got the dream job he wanted.

"I thought playing again made you happy. That your job made you happy."

"It does, but it doesn't. I'm playing Owen's music."

"What do you want to do?"

Emma shrugged. "Right now, I need to go meet the girls. But I honestly don't know. I don't. There's not much more I can do."

Maybe she'd outgrown Seattle. Maybe she'd outgrown Connor.

"I want you to be happy, Emma. I want you to have whatever it is that makes you happy."

"I know."

"I thought that all of this was what you wanted."

"No. I've never wanted a life like this."

It was probably the most honest conversation she had with him in their whole relationship.

"I want to write music," she admitted.

"Like, songs for the radio?"

Emma shook her head. "No. Well, maybe. But mostly to play in venues or something. There are some great jazz clubs here."

"Can you do that here, in Seattle?" His eyes lit up.

"I could. But New York might be better."

"You'd want to go back to New York?"

Emma turned away from him. As much as she was hurting with what was going on with him, the thought of going back to New York hurt more. She still shook when planes went overhead, still needed reassurance that the world wouldn't collapse beneath her. But hadn't it already?

"Maybe. I don't know. But really, I need to go."

"Okay. Can we talk about this more when you get home?"

Emma looked back at him. He smiled, sad and hopeful. She nodded. "Sure. I don't know what else I can say right now."

"Maybe while you're gone I can look up some things for you, see if there's any open mic nights, or something?"

"Sure." She didn't want to take the time to explain to him that there was so much more work she needed to do before she could even consider playing in public. He was finally showing an active interest in something that was hers and hers alone.

"I'll see you later?"

"Okay." She kissed him, softly, and pulled away. He pulled her back in for another, pushing her back against the door to the linen closet.

"Save this for later," she said, smiling as she pushed him away. No matter how many times they had slept together since she moved back in, each time felt like she was proving to him that she was enough. She needed him to tell her that he wanted *her*, that he needed *her*. It was no longer about love, but about power.

"If you insist. I love you."

"I love you too."

Pushing her hair behind her ears, she grabbed her clutch off the kitchen table, and walked out into the hallway. She regretted it now, leaving. It wasn't like her to just walk away, especially when Connor was so eager to fix things. She'd stay until things felt resolved, even if nothing ended up being fixed. Now, the second half of a conversation that might not ever happen hung heavy between her and the door. Being the bigger person meant going back in, meant finding out if things could actually be fixed.

"Emma!"

She turned, finding Amy walking towards her. There was no going back into her apartment now.

"Oh, hey. Sorry I'm running a little late tonight. Were you coming to get me?"

"No, no. I just . . . needed to calm down a little before we see the others. Frank's home this weekend."

"You should be with him tonight, then!" She walked down the hall, heels echoing through the carpeted hallway. Amy walked with her, arms linked like high schooler's.

"No, no. It's . . . bad. You can't tell the others."

"I won't, I swear."

"He's . . . oh this is so embarrassing."

"What's wrong?"

"You know how I thought something was wrong?"

"Yeah?"

"He can't . . . he needs to see a doctor. He needs, you know, *pills*."

"Oh. Well, that's normal these days. Even guys who don't need them use them, right? And at least you know it wasn't anything to do with you."

Amy smiled as they entered the elevator. Emma pressed the button for the top floor and took a deep breath. Amy's probably felt trivial in the face of what Emma was going through. But Emma wasn't going to be honest about her situation anytime soon.

"That's true," Amy reasoned. "He's all upset about it though. I mean, I can imagine how he feels. But he's going to the doctor in the morning and everything will be back to normal I'm sure."

"Definitely."

"What about you? How're things with Connor? I've seen him around so much more these days!"

"Oh, they're fine. Things have slowed down with work, so he's actually been home more. It's nice."

"Are you sure?" Amy raised her eyebrows, stopping them before they joined the other girls. "You don't look fine."

"I've just been so busy with rehearsals and with the wedding coming up, everything has just been in up in the air. It'll calm down once the wedding's over."

"When are you going to start planning your wedding?" Amy asked as she led them to join the other girls, who, because of the weather, had elected to sit inside tonight. A light rain tapped on the windows.

"Maybe they don't want to get married," Stephanie suggested. "I mean, they wouldn't be the first couple to just be together and not be married. Even if they are engaged."

"We're thinking spring, but who knows I haven't even started to look at anything," Emma explained. "I've just been trying to find the time."

She couldn't tell them that it was because she wasn't even sure there would be a wedding anymore. Looking down at her left hand, the solitaire diamond sparkled even in the rain. The ring was perfect. She knew that, given an hour on the phone, she could plan the perfect wedding to go with it. It was just the life that would follow the wedding that she was unsure about.

If she didn't trust Connor, there was no point in marrying him.

"That's the same excuse I gave about not wanting to have kids." Stephanie said, raising her eyebrows. "If you don't want to get married, own it. Don't be ashamed."

"No, I do." Emma knew it was what they wanted to hear. "We just have some specifics to figure out."

The girls all smiled, happy, suggesting them open champagne tonight instead to celebrate—something. Emma had stopped paying attention once the conversation shifted to someone else. Looking around at these women, she was happy for them. They knew that being part of this group was where they wanted to be.

But now, more than ever, she wished she was back in Leah's kitchen, drinking a glass of wine and playing with Henry. She wished she was back at Benaroya, rehearsing. Or even at the Conservatory messing around in the recording studio with Molly.

She wanted to be anywhere but here.

What Emma needed to figure out was if she still wanted Connor in the picture, too.

18

"I can't believe we're doing this again," Emma said, looking over at Danielle, who was navigating through terrible evening traffic. She was driving the three of them to yet another bridal shop. They'd gone to three already. Seattle and Bellevue were littered with them. If Emma had to put money on it, she'd wager that there were even more here than there were in New York.

"I know. But we're kind of running out of time. You and Molly aren't exactly jumping at getting it done by yourselves, either."

Emma looked back at Molly, who sat in the back seat, eyes on her cell phone. "You haven't been looking either?"

Molly glanced up and shook her head. "No amount of coffee can adequately prepare me to try and do this again. Can't you just pick something for me to wear? I swear I'll show up in it."

"No," Danielle laughed, "I need to make sure it fits you first. Besides, I think I'm changing the colors."

"Again?" Emma asked.

"You'll understand when you're planning your wedding," Danielle said, throwing a quick glance at her.

"Right."

Emma turned away, trying to focus on the traffic, the buildings as they passed by—anything but the wedding she wasn't sure she'd be planning anymore. Her thumb touched her ring finger. Her ring wasn't there. She must've forgotten to put it on after her shower.

"You guys *are* getting married, right?" Molly asked.

"I . . . of course," Emma answered, still looking out the window. "Of course."

Danielle parked the car and the girls got out, heading into a small boutique. Just like the rest of them, there were faceless mannequins in the front window, modeling the season's latest trends. To the left, bridesmaid's dresses in different colors and styles sat from their hangers, from lightest colors to darkest. To the right, rows of bridal gowns, and mannequins modeling them, waited for them.

A month ago, Emma might've gone to look. Now, she was afraid to. She didn't want to find the perfect dress only to realize later that this wasn't what she wanted.

"Come on, I thought you guys might look good in these ones," Danielle said, leading them towards a display of strapless, floor length gowns. They had a sweetheart neckline and came in pastel colors: yellows, pinks, and purples. Molly picked out a mauve-colored one and held it up to herself.

"Not bad."

Emma touched the fabric, no one color jumping out at her. It wasn't her wedding; she didn't feel like she had a say in what to wear.

"What about the yellow?" Danielle asked, picking the dress off the rack and handing it to Emma.

"Are you ladies doing alright?" A saleswoman, dressed in all black, asked.

"Yes, thank you. Appointment for Hayes?"

The woman nodded, and smiled. "I recognized you. Should I get a fitting room started, then?"

Danielle handed the woman the yellow dress, and took Molly's as well.

"Did you want to keep looking around?" the woman asked.

Danielle shook her head. "I think those are good for now."

Emma looked over at Molly, who shrugged. They followed Danielle into the dressing room, took their dresses, and changed.

As Emma was changing, she took a second to check her phone. She hadn't heard from Connor all evening, which, before, would have been normal. But since she had come back, he'd taken to texting her more often, asking her how things were going when she was out without him.

But so far, she'd heard nothing from him yet.

Emma checked her phone but saw nothing. There was a text from Owen, asking her to call him when she could, which was strange. They never talked on the phone. But she shrugged it off, assuming it had to do with the concert; that he would need her to come to practice more, that he was changing the song list, or something.

"How's it going in there?" Danielle called through the thick curtain.

"Fine. I'll be out in a second," Emma called back. "Are you really sure you want me in yellow?"

"It's not *yellow*-yellow. It's . . . daisy yellow."

"*Yellow Wallpaper*-yellow," Emma said as she changed from her clothes into the dress, thankful for the side zipper. It was made for girls who needed to zip themselves.

Stepping out from her changing room, she was met by multiple reflections of herself on the wall of large mirrors. Molly was already out, hands in the pockets of the dress, eyebrows quirked.

"Damn, Bishop. If you I wasn't madly in love with my girlfriend . . ." she joked.

Emma blushed, and stepped up onto the pedestal, getting a look at herself in the mirror. The dress was flattering, sure, and even the color wasn't bad. The color was more pastel than she thought it originally was, making her skin look more pale and her auburn hair more red than brown.

"Are we done now?" Emma asked, looking at Danielle through the reflection in the mirror.

"Yep. I just needed to see them on you."

"So, this really was pointless? Why'd we have to go to the other stores?" Molly asked.

"We got Emma out of the house."

Emma rolled her eyes as she stepped off the pedestal. "Yeah, yeah. I'm going to go change."

"Sweetie, we've just been worried about you," Danielle said. "Since you went back to him, you've just . . . disappeared."

"Work has just been crazy. And I've been spending more time with Connor."

"Yeah, but how long is that going to last?" Molly asked.

"Everyone goes through phases. Danielle, it's not like things have been peachy with you and Tom," Emma argued.

"I know, but it just seems like . . ." Danielle trailed off. "I just want to make sure this is what you want."

"If this wasn't what I wanted, I wouldn't be with him."

Emma walked back into the dressing room, the weight of what she said sitting heavy on her bare shoulders. She hadn't been completely sure the night she went home with him after rehearsal. Now, weeks later, the only thing she was sure about was that she loved him. She just didn't know if she was still in love with him.

Checking her phone, she saw another text message from Owen, asking her to call him.

Pressing the phone icon on the screen, she balanced the phone between her shoulder and her cheek as she changed out of the dress.

"Emma," he breathed. She could hear him smiling.

"Hey. What's so important?"

He chuckled. "Ah, yeah . . . That. Are you free for dinner? I think we should really talk."

"About what?"

She stopped trying to get dressed now, her stomach dropping. It wasn't until now that she realized how important the concert was to her.

"Nothing . . . bad. Not really. Well, it might be."

"You're stammering. What is it? Am I not playing in the concert anymore?"

"Oh! No. Nothing like that. Nothing like that at all."

"What is it then?" She was getting irritated.

"I really need to talk to you about it in person. Dinner? Drinks?"

"Not tonight. I'm busy."

He paused, and the phone sounded muffled.

"Owen?"

"Sorry. Well, let me know when we're free. We really need to talk."

"Okay. Will do."

Emma hung up, and put the phone back into her bag. His phone call left her unsettled.

"Everything okay?" Danielle called into the dressing room.

"Yeah, I'll be out in a minute."

She re-dressed quickly, and brought the dress out with her. She hated that she still hadn't heard from Connor yet, that Molly and Danielle were waiting for things to fall apart again.

If Emma was being honest with herself, she knew she was waiting for the same thing.

"Ready," she said, coming out of the dressing room.

"Awesome. Let's go. I feel like I'm going to be strangled by tulle," Molly said.

"No, you're afraid you'll want to propose to Laurel," Emma teased.

"Okay. Fine. But come on, weddings are so much fun. It's just a good thing that we're taken, Em, or we'd end up ruining these—"she checked the price tag on the dress—"very expensive dresses."

"It's not like we don't have anyone to sleep with," Emma said.

"But sleeping with someone casually is different. Especially at a wedding. You can't tell me that if Owen had the chance, he wouldn't rip that dress off of you."

"It depends on how drunk he is," Emma said as she handed the woman behind the counter her credit card.

"What?" Molly asked. Danielle just looked at her.

"What? It's true."

"So you did sleep with him. I knew it. I fucking knew it." Molly said, grinning. "Oh come on, now you have to give us details. When was it? Recently? Please tell me you've fucked around behind that jackass' back—"

"Molly, *shut up*." Emma said, her blush deepening.

"Fine, fine. I'll wait until we get in the car. How much do I owe you for the dress?" Molly asked the woman behind the counter, whose lips were pursed.

"With tax, your total is two hundred-twenty-nine dollars."

Molly whistled, and handed over her card. "You're lucky I love you, D."

As they left the shop, Molly shoulder-bumped Emma. "Okay, details."

"What do you want to know?" Emma asked.

"Everything. Anything. Was it good? Was he good?"

Emma shot Danielle a glance as they got into the car. Danielle smiled, looking amused. "Go on and answer the lady."

"It was . . . all right. He was drunk. I don't think you can get a fair assessment of how someone is in bed based on one drunken night."

"When did it happen? Come on, you're killing me!"

"Sophomore year. Right after I met Connor. We were working on our duet."

"So, it was at school? Like, in his dorm room?"

"No. It was in one of the auditoriums." She couldn't meet either of their eyes.

"What else!?" Molly exclaimed.

"On the stage."

"Kinky," Danielle added. "I'm marrying a musician and even I haven't done that."

Emma shook her head. "He got sick after. He was really, really drunk."

"I knew it. I always knew you guys slept together." Molly said, leaning back against the car seat. Emma looked back at her, eyebrows raised. "I'm serious. You guys together . . .you were just always all chemistry."

"Yeah, too bad he doesn't remember."

"Oh, he has to remember."

Emma shrugged. "We've never talked about it."

"But you guys are talking again. You're playing together. It has to come up." Molly said, arms crossed in front of her chest. "I always rooted for you to be together, you know."

"Yeah, yeah."

The fact that her closest friends had wanted her to be with Owen, not Connor, ate away at her. It was fine for her to be angry with him still, but she needed them to reassure her she made the right decision now, and back in college. She needed to know that they had been honest with her whenever she asked their opinion.

"I'm sure you're with who you want to be with," Danielle said.

"I am. Owen and I . . . I don't know. I've had this conversation with Connor a hundred times. But, Owen doesn't get me the way Connor does. He gets the music part of me, but he knows nothing else about me."

"He doesn't need to know that much about you to give you a good time in bed," Molly said.

"I guess."

It was hard to deny the feelings she had for Owen. The more time they spent together, the more they resurfaced. It wasn't just them playing together, but that they were one person when they were on stage. It wasn't a sex thing, but it could be. If Connor didn't want her, then maybe Owen did.

As she looked out the car window, she couldn't help but think that this was how affairs started.

19

Emma put the kettle on, the coffee beans already ground and waiting in her French press. It was a perk that came with working from home, having the luxury to steep her coffee, to push down the wire mesh, and pour out the perfect cup. She wasn't waiting in a crowded line inside a corporate coffee house, or in a car line next to a coffee stand. She could, she supposed, if she felt inclined to send e-mails and make phone calls from the eerily empty Seattle symphony offices but she found more comfort in her own empty apartment.

Sort of.

When Connor had left an hour or two earlier, he'd promised to be home for dinner. He was making an effort at them spending more time together, asking questions about the concert, asking to listen to what she was working on with Molly—but he hadn't brought up the wedding at all. At this point, there would be no time they spent together that didn't have the shadow of Rachel's alleged lies hidden in the corner. She stood next to the ghost of fallen towers, blacking the edges of Emma's nightmares. It was as if the two events were connected; that Rachel had been a plane, and Emma a tower.

She sat down at the kitchen table and opened her laptop. As it shuddered to life, she scrolled through e-mail messages but found nothing of consequence.

The kettle went off and, pulling herself back out of her seat, images of Rachel and New York burned off in the bright morning sunlight that now poured in through the apartment windows. Pulling the kettle off the burner, Emma went through the motions of making her coffee as another e-mail alert went off. Glancing at the clock, she assumed that the e-mail was the latest sale from Kate Spade or Nordstrom. She could set her watch by when those e-mails rolled in.

Yawning, she sat back down with a cup of coffee in hand. Double-clicking on the mail icon, she pulled it up, and was confused by the one unread e-mail.

"Really?"

Rachel's name filled the sender spot, and the subject read: "You deserve the truth."

It sounded like a politician's spam e-mail, them wanting you to sign some new petition about something. But no, this e-mail had a paperclip next to it, an attachment of . . . what?

Emma sat there, staring at the Spam button, wondering if she should just delete the message without even opening it.

If these were the pictures, the proof, it meant that her gut had been right the whole time. That Connor was a liar, a cheater—that he was the plane, and not Rachel.

The more she thought about it, she knew she should've seen this coming. Someone, whether it be Connor or Rachel, would've broken down eventually.

The truth always comes out.

Moving her mouse to the e-mail, she double clicked it.

Heard you were back with him. I just want you to know the truth.
You deserve better than lies.

Emma's hands shook and she shivered in her own sweat. She didn't need to see the pictures. No, this was proof enough. But, in the same way she watched anniversary coverage of 9/11 every year despite being too afraid to go back to New York, she wanted to see the pictures. She needed to have the vision in her mind so that when

Connor came home, she would stay strong. So she'd be able to leave once and for all.

Double-clicking on the file, she watched the download percentage go up and up until it reached 100 percent and the folder opened. Thumbnail-sized evidence of her boyfriend's infidelity filled her the otherwise white screen.

She clicked on a picture and it popped open. It was a picture of Rachel, wearing a button down shirt and a tie Emma knew she had given Connor for Christmas that year and little else. There was a hand, unmistakably Connor's, grabbing Rachel's breast under the shirt. Arrowing over to the next picture, and then the next, and then the next, Emma saw what was really going on when he stayed late at work, when he met Rachel for drinks, when he said he just needed to go clear his head.

Whatever visions of a future that she had with Connor were gone. She thumbed the engagement ring. Why had he even bothered giving it to her in the first place?

How could you marry someone but have no intention of staying faithful to them?

The thought was another strike against her heart as she got out of the chair and crumpled on the floor, arms around her knees. No tears came. As much as she hurt she did not cry. The wind had been taken out of her. As nerves and adrenaline coursed through her, her teeth chattered and her knees quaked. Emma knew what this reaction was, that this was the calm before the storm. Just like when the planes hit the towers, the pain shifted to anger, and it engulfed her.

How dare he.

Her phone went off: a text message from Connor.

Hi babe. Love you. Miss you.

Emma pushed the phone away from her and watched it slide across the wooden floor—a controlled response when all she wanted to do was smash the thing with a hammer. But she wouldn't stop there. She'd kill the laptop, any and all pictures of them, pour red wine over every piece of clothing she bought him, pull the diamonds and pearls off the chains of every piece of jewelry he had ever given her. But no, no—that wasn't the *correct* response.

Taking a deep breath, she smoothed her hair, containing her anger inside of her until it burned in her chest and in her veins.

Seeing his name made things worse. Maybe he did really love her and this thing with Rachel was just something physical. Or he loved them both. Or he was just another cheating, lying boyfriend who couldn't handle his girlfriend being more financially successful than him. Either way, his brand of love wasn't one Emma could stomach anymore. It wasn't just that he had slept with Rachel; it was that he had denied it when she had confronted him about it. It was that he had lied, repeatedly, to her face. This whole life they had built up together wasn't anything more than some fantasy he was trying to live out with her.

She couldn't be apart of it anymore.

Getting off the floor, she walked over and picked up her phone. She would need it, at least for now. Emma was fighting the urge to smash the phone and buy a one-way plane ticket to wherever her parents were now. San Francisco? Santa Fe? She could pack up a few things, drive to the airport, and disappear.

But Danielle's wedding, Owen's concert—she couldn't let them down.

The idea ripped through her in a cascade of different kind of pain.

No. She'd stay. She'd make sure that he knew that she was leaving him. He'd be home in a few hours, which would give her enough time to figure out what she was going to do next. She couldn't stay here, even if he said he'd leave. The comforter in one of those pictures had been theirs.

Hand pressing to the knob of the shower, she turned the hot water up to the point where she almost couldn't stand it. The pictures flashed in her mind on a constant reel, mixing with his promises. That he wasn't lying, that he was faithful, that this was enough for him.

As she got out of the shower, she wrapped the towel around her, and reached for her phone. A missed call from Connor, another text message. Instead, she called Leah.

"You're calling me instead of texting. Is someone dead?"

"Well, it depends on if I decide hiring a hit man is worth it."

There was silence on the other end. Emma rolled her eyes.

"L, I'm kidding. But I need somewhere to stay for awhile. Again. Just until I can find a new apartment."

"Is . . . everything okay?" Leah asked tentatively, testing the water.

Emma looked up at herself in the mirror. She didn't look heart-broken. She didn't look like parts of her were scattered across the kitchen floor. It was the same old Emma looking back at her, calm and poised, ready to take on whatever comes her way.

"No. Turns out I'm an idiot who just believes anything her fiancé tells her. Who believes that her life is actually perfect."

"I can be there in twenty."

"Give me," she pulled the phone away from her ear to check the time, "two hours? I should probably break up with the guy instead of disappearing."

The line was quiet, and then: "Yes, that would be the grown up thing to do."

The sisters laughed and Emma said good-bye, thankful that Leah knew better than to ask questions. Hell, for all Emma knew Leah had known the truth all along and had just been waiting for Emma to come to her senses.

She was leaving him, and leaving here. So much for spending the rest of her life with him. Deep down, she knew this was going to end. She'd known from the moment Rachel tried telling her the truth in that dress shop this was over. But having their relationship end like this, with her being played, with her not even sure what the hell her next move would be, was not how Emma did things. It was supposed to be a cleaner break, something mutual that would've left them friends. Something after the wedding so she could have that one last good memory with him. But that was not how real life worked. She needed to accept the fact that her life was more *Scandal* than *Grey's*

Anatomy. She needed to get this situation handled. There was no McDreamy in this story.

Sliding onto the floor again, she couldn't believe this was happening. This was real, that he was sleeping with Rachel, and that she was leaving him. As much as she wished she could cry, Emma shook instead. She felt cold and sick. If she was going to leave him, she would need to strengthen her resolve. All she wanted right now was for someone, for Connor, to hold her.

He couldn't be the person she turned to anymore.

Glancing at the clock, she saw how little time she had left to get ready. Getting up off of the floor, she walked into the kitchen, her still-wet feet leaving footprints on the wooden floor. Pulling open the door of the refrigerator, she took a half-empty bottle of wine from the shelf, and walked back into the bathroom. Dropping her towel, she pulled the cork out of the top of the bottle of wine, and took a long sip. She needed an outfit—*the* outfit.

"Right," she said out loud, the wine bottle still in her hand. "Clothes."

Back at her closet door, she pulled the plum colored dress off of the hanger. This one was cut just above the knee, had quarter-length sleeves, and dipped low in the front. Connor liked anything that, conservatively, showed off her cleavage. She took another long sip of the wine as she walked back into the bathroom, dress in hand.

"This'll have to do."

So she got ready. She pulled underwear and a bra from the drawer in the bathroom, slipped them on, and then pulled the dress over her head. She garnished her face with war paint: red lipstick that didn't feather and dark liner around her eyes. As she dabbed Chanel behind her ears, she felt the wine settle into her bones. She could do this. She could leave him. She could make him bleed.

Figuratively, of course.

Now ready, she pulled the large suitcase from the top shelf in her closet. One arm-full after another she grabbed piles of clothes and packed them neatly into her bag. Nearly everything, except for her collection of dresses, shoes, and handbags, would be able to come with her. In a separate bag, she put her toiletries, make-up case, perfume, laptop, a few different books of sheet music, and a well-loved copy of "Pride and Prejudice."

Checking her phone, she saw that Connor was due home any minute. He had tried calling her, but didn't leave a voicemail.

Remembering to grab the bottle of wine from the bathroom, which was now empty of all of her things, she poured the rest of the contents into a glass and set it on their kitchen table. As she sat down, she heard the door unlock. Her nerves felt like they were going to explode.

"Hi, babe," Connor called out from the entryway of the apartment.

Emma stayed silent.

"Wow," he said walking into the kitchen. "You look amazing. What's the occasion?"

"Have a seat."

"What's wrong?" he asked, setting down his bag slowly. "I tried getting a hold of you all day. I was worried—"

Emma cut him off. "I got an e-mail from Rachel this morning."

"About?"

The color drained from his face as Emma slid her finger across the screen of her phone. Tapping the e-mail icon, she pulled up Rachel's e-mail, clicked on the attachment, and turned the phone towards him as the pictures loaded.

"This."

"Did you ask her to—?"

"No. But I don't think that's the problem right now."

"Then why did you open the e-mail? Why did you even look at—"

Emma stood up. If anything, this was only making it easier for her to leave. Instead of being apologetic, for giving her any reason to second-guess her decision to leave him, he was blaming her for his inability to stay faithful.

"Well, I'll be sending someone back to get my things."

"What do you mean?" he asked in a quiet voice. She stared at him, at his sad eyes, at how every inch of him looked defeated.

"I mean, I'll be sending someone back for the rest of my things. I no longer live here. I'll sign papers so that you can take over the lease."

"Please," he said, walking around the table towards her. "I know. I know what I did . . . it was fucked up. I don't even know what I was thinking. I just, I felt bad for her, and she . . . I don't know."

Anger, repressed and suppressed, was an earthquake inside of her. She had stayed quiet for too long now. Believing him before was easy, because she didn't want to see the truth. Now, she was forced to face it, to face him for what he was. There was no reason that would ever make her understand what he did. It was a betrayal deeper than him lusting after another woman. This was him lying over and over again. This was him promising that things had been one way and now that she had physical proof, things were another.

It was an unforgivable act.

"You . . . you felt sorry for her, and that's why you slept with her behind my back. Okay."

"Just, please, Emma. I want to marry you. You're the one I want to be with. Let's . . . let's leave for California, or Vegas. We can be married by this time tomorrow. I haven't seen her since that day you came back and told me what she said. I want to be with you, and only you, for the rest of our lives. I was so stupid, Emma. So stupid."

Emma looked at him, and then at the ring on her finger.

"I can't."

Emma took off her engagement ring and set it down on the kitchen table. She grabbed the handle of her suitcase, threw the tote bag over her shoulder, and walked out of the apartment.

20

JULY 2006

In less than a year, Emma would be done with college. For her sister's graduation, their parents took them on an Alaskan cruise. The added benefit was checking out Seattle before the ship left port, since Leah was staying there for graduate school. For Emma's graduation, she decided she wanted a week at Cape Cod. It wasn't big, or fancy, this trip—just a week of relaxing, of not worrying about music, concerts, or boys.

"You know, I'm sorry that we never came here before," Georgina, Emma's mother, said as she pushed too-large sunglasses up over her head. She squinted in the bright sunlight, looking at Emma through one barely open eye.

"I know. But we're here now."

Conversations like this made Emma uncomfortable. Since 9/11, their perspectives shifted around the what-if's: what if her father worked at a different fire house, what if her mother worked in the towers instead of in Midtown, what if, what if, what if. It was a paralyzing anxiety that took over when Emma least expected it. Digging her toes deeper into the warm sand, she looked out on the ocean. She didn't want to think about the what if's. She just wanted to be in the present.

In their tours of the beaches of Cape Cod, Nausset Light Beach was, so far, her favorite. With sand dunes behind her, the only thing in front of her was water and horizon. It terrified her to think about being out there without seeing anything other than water, to think that if she swam out there, she would never be able to reach the bottom.

"Yes we are," her father, Brian, said sleep. He was laying on a separate towel under a large umbrella and sounded half asleep. "This is so much better than the Hampton's."

"It's different," Emma said, leaning back on her towel. "Less familiar faces."

"That's the beauty of it, dear," Georgina said.

Silence passed between them again. It was how these trips went. They would pass small talk back and forth when they felt they hadn't spoken in awhile, and then would fall back into their books or their naps. In the evenings, they would go to dinner—somewhere local, somewhere they could share something that they wouldn't be able to get this good anywhere else—and discuss the books or the dreams they had during their long, lazy afternoons. Thankfully, at least for Emma, the July release of the Harry Potter books meant that they had a built in book to discuss, on top of the other summer reads. Her mother's dog-eared copy of an Elin Hindebrand book lay half-open on her towel, abandoned for the sake of a cat-nap. One of the "Harry Potter" books was next to her dad, but had so far been untouched.

Emma rolled over and picked up her phone. Normally, she wasn't so attached to it on their summer trips. But that was before Connor.

"Texting that boy again?"

Emma looked over at her mom, whose sunglasses were now back in front of her eyes. "Maybe. I don't know."

"Have you heard from him?"

"I have. A little."

"Is he just a friend?"

It was a question that she and Connor left left unanswered before the start of summer break. Connor was a local, so his summers were spent on beaches out on the peninsula, or sailing on Lake Washington. A friend, definitely. But they weren't exclusive. She'd barely seen him since the semester ended

"Or is he more than that? A, oh what did I hear—a 'friend with benefits'?"

Emma laughed, thankful that her father's only response was gentle snoring of a deep sleep. "No. Definitely *without* benefits."

In fact, and Emma would never admit this to her mother, neither of the men in her life—Owen or Connor—were offering her anything in the category of benefit. The junior year concert had been more of a showcase that inflated Owen's already large ego, and Connor was becoming increasingly jealous of how close she was with Owen.

Who decided sex was a benefit when all it did was cause trouble?

Sure, she had slept with Connor, but it had just seemed to complicate things. It solidified that what she had with him was more than the kissing by the waterfront, or in his dorm room, or in his car, but what did it really accomplish for either of them? It wasn't like it was something that could be drawn out, not when there were roommates to consider. It was a means to an end, a rushed display of intimacy. She wondered it would be like when she was a real adult, when she could take things slow, when she didn't have to worry about someone walking in on them. Would it still be just as passionate, just as hushed, like they were sharing the most intimate secret? Or, would the sex fall by the wayside, with late night television or chores taking its place? Maybe then she'd care more about it.

"That's a shame. Take advantage of your youth."

"You're telling me I should be sleeping around?"

"No, not *around*," her mom laughed, "but you're an adult. You haven't had a steady boyfriend since high school. You've got to start thinking about your future."

"A future?"

"House, kids, husband—"

"Mom!"

"What? I'm being practical. My musician daughter, you're going to need to find a support system."

"A benefactor and a husband are two very different things."

"They don't always have to be," she said, sitting up. "I just don't want you to be alone, sweetie. Along and struggling because you have this gift that doesn't necessarily pay well."

It was a familiar conversation, but one that hadn't been touched since Emma decided against going to that conservatory in Boston, or even applying to Julliard. Her parents sat her down, told her that they'd help her pay for college, but she needed to be realistic. Playing the piano wasn't going to pay the bills, or for the student loans. But it was a dream she still pursued, and one she had been encouraged to.

"I know. But it's not like I can just find some rich man to marry."

"Darling, that's what college is for," Georgina teased. While she hadn't met her husband in college, most of her friends did. Emma wasn't sure if she would be falling into the same boat as those women.

"Yeah yeah, a BFA and an MRS in four years."

"You can't say I never taught you anything."

It was Emma's turn to chuckle. She didn't have such a bleak outlook on her possible future. Would it be hard to make a living? Sure. But that didn't mean she wouldn't be able to do it. It wasn't like she had saddled herself with student loans from a college without a reputation, or without connections.

But she couldn't deny that it was still a worry she had. What would happen when she was done with school? Where would she go?

"You mean I can't just move in with you and Dad?" Emma teased.

Georgina sat up and frowned. She must've taken what Emma said seriously. "Sweetie, we don't even know where we're moving yet. Now that your father's retired, we're getting out of New York. We just don't know *where.*"

"You're leaving New York?"

"It's not like you or Leah come and visit us there. It's time for a change of pace. Find somewhere else to call home."

It wasn't until that moment that Emma realized that this feeling, this emptiness that had followed her to Seattle, was that she didn't feel like she had a home. Not since the attacks. Home wasn't somewhere that you felt terrified, where you were constantly looking over your shoulder. Home wasn't a place that you went to sleep at night and crossed your fingers that everything would still be standing when you got up in the morning.

"You guys could move to Seattle, be close to me and Leah."

"So you're going to stay in Seattle after graduation? Do you love the rain that much?"

"It's not that rainy, Mom. It's like New York, but cleaner. There's just a different pace to it, too. Not as fast," Emma said, trying to explain herself. She could pick out the perfect soundtrack to show her mother what Seattle felt like, but words were failing her. "I don't know. I guess I could see myself there, long term. It's so hard to know."

"It'll depend on that boy, I'm sure."

Emma blushed. "What do you mean?"

"Oh, if you and your no-friends with benefits friend, if you two end up having benefits to your relationship. Then, maybe you'll want to stay there"

"I don't know if that's going to turn into anything serious." Her phone vibrated as she said it. Connor.

"See?" Georgina said. "He likes you."

"Maybe it was an end of the year fling."

"Or, maybe he's your future husband."

"Such high hopes on a townie who goes to a state school," Emma countered, knowing how snobbish she sounded. It wasn't like their family had any room to be elitist. They were comfortable, sure, but comfort was relegated to meals and new school clothes when she was a child. She didn't know if her parents struggled to pay bills or went without so she and her sister could have.

"Ah, yes. If you're going to marry rich, you'll need to find someone with a more sensible amount of student debt. Have you tried wandering the halls of Starbucks or Microsoft? There's bound to be a few in there."

"Yeah, probably a few silver fox's. Maybe, I'll find someone old enough that he'll die in a few years, and then we can just live off of my inheritance."

Georgina laughed. "My beautiful daughter, I see no flaws with this plan at all."

"Hey, while we're here, let's just shoot up to Martha's Vineyard. There's bound to be some sensible divorcee's that aren't giving all of their money to their wives in alimony checks."

"Oh, even better."

They both laughed now, loud and long, overwhelmed by the ridiculousness of the conversation. The more Emma thought about it, the more she thought she might be better on her own. If she was going to be chasing auditions or traveling with a touring symphony, it would make sense to remain unattached.

Connor's name lit up the front of her phone again, and she smiled.

"Maybe you do have one of those friends with benefits after all, hm?"

Emma looked over at her mother and shrugged. Maybe she did. Maybe this was just the start of something big for her, and she just didn't want to see it. It scared her to think that she was at the age that she could meet the guy she'd marry.

"Maybe. I mean he is kind of great."

"Do you have fun together?"

Emma nodded. "He takes me on all of these cheesy tourist things. Like, the one day we did this underground tour, and we did the Space Needle. I don't know . . . I just don't think to do those things."

"It's good that he's making you have some fun. You work hard. It's nice to have that balance."

"It . . . it really is."

She never thought of it that way, that he added balance to her life. But the more she let the idea grow, the more it made sense. Her attraction to him was beyond the physical. It was that he helped her come down from the high that came with playing with Owen, that came from staying up for days on end. With him, she could relax.

"Maybe I'll meet him one day." Georgina said, settling back down onto her towel. "I have a feeling that your father and I would like this man."

"I'm just surprised."

"At what?"

"You haven't asked your usual questions. Major, what do his parents do, what does he want to do with his life—you know, that kind of stuff."

"Oh, I'm sure he's a fine pick. You wouldn't still be talking to him if he wasn't."

"What do you mean?"

"Sweetie, I know how you are with guys," Georgina said without looking over at her. "If he didn't have some sort of drive, some sort of focus, you would've cut things off at the end of the semester. No matter how much we joke about it, you do find decent guys. And the ones who aren't don't make it more than a few weeks."

Emma knew it was true. Connor was a business major that already had a fall internship lined up with Microsoft. Any boy she'd been with in the past that started leaning away from college and more towards a summer abroad, or writing the great American novel instead of going to college, she stopped seeing.

"And here I thought I was being discreet about all of that."

"You can't hide things from your mother, darling. Your father," she gestured to the sleeping man, "sure. But not me. You know that."

Emma laughed and lay back down on her towel. The warm summer sun beat down on her. She could feel it in her skin, the way it mixed with the salt water and the sand. This was better than sitting at the piano, or staying up late with Molly. This was better than so many things.

Except kissing Connor.

If she had to be anywhere other than right here, she'd want to be in his car, or in his dorm room bed, kissing him. That was the only thing better than this.

21

The crying started as soon as she got to Leah's.

It was small at first, just silent tears that fell down her face, ruining the makeup that she had put on. But they tears began to build the more she replayed the entire day in her head. The e-mail, him saying those things, him wanting to elope, her leaving—it was all over in a matter of a half hour.

No goodbye's. Nothing.

He had been her home for years and now that was done. Over with.

Burned down.

It had been two hours now. Two hours of sobbing, of quietly crying, of going through whatever reserve stash of tissues Leah kept in the various rooms of her house that Emma found herself in. She moved from living room, to guest bathroom to try and regain her composure, to the kitchen floor, back against the kitchen cabinets like she used to do when she was little.

"Are you . . . are you okay?" Leah asked, coming around the small kitchen island.

"I'll be fine."

"Do you need anything? I'm sure Jacob can go off your ex if you want."

"Wine."

Emma was so thirsty. While she knew she should have water, she preferred the numbness that came at the bottom of a bottle, rather than the clarity of water. She was already going to be emotionally hungover tomorrow, so she figured if she was physically hungover, at least there would be a real excuse for feeling so shitty.

Being the pulled-together big sister that she was, Leah went to the wine fridge, pulled out a bottle, and handed it to Emma.

"I had Jacob run out and grab your favorite bottle."

Emma unscrewed the top of the wine bottle and chugged, not caring if she was practicing proper wine etiquette for once. She wasn't even sure if that kind of thing mattered when you were drinking an $8 bottle of wine, or if it was just the educated snob in her that looked down on this entire scene. She was just glad that her brother-in-law cared more about her sister than Connor had cared about Emma.

"I'm sorry about all of this."

Leah took out a bottle of her own, closed the small refrigerator door, and joined her sister on the kitchen floor. It sent a dust cloud of memories pulsing through Emma. It was how they got through things: through death, through bad breakups, through their lives pulling apart.

"Don't be sorry. I'm just glad you left the bastard. You deserve so much better than . . ." Leah trailed off, shook her head, and took a sip of wine from the bottle she'd pulled out. "Better than Mom."

Emma turned her head. "What?"

"Yeah, Dad cheated on her a ton. You were just too young to remember. I don't think he does anymore. Then again, I'm not there to see it." Leah chuckled. "She loved him, still loves him. For her it's just part of being his wife."

Emma put her head back against the cabinet counter. She'd always idolized what her mother and father had, always wanted the fairy tale they peddled to her as an adult bedtime story. Maybe Emma hadn't been listening right, maybe she'd just ignored the writing between the lines because that's not what she wanted to hear.

"Well, good for mom that she's still with him, I guess."

She wouldn't bring herself to say the words she was feeling. She knew they weren't for her father, but for Connor.

"Please don't take that as me thinking you should stay with Connor. You deserve someone so much better than that."

"Maybe," Emma considered. "But really—I don't even want a relationship right now. I don't. I just want to get my life back. I don't recognize who the hell I am right now. This isn't what I wanted. The life with Connor, yes it was nice and perfect, but Leah . . . none of it was me."

All of a sudden the weight left her chest. None of this was who she really was. Sure, she'd grown since college, but Owen had been right that first night: she wasn't the same Emma. She was a shadow on the window looking into the life she knew she wanted. Leaving Connor wasn't just about leaving the man who hurt her, but about leaving the life she knew she didn't want. She didn't even miss the apartment now that she was safely hidden in Queen Anne. There were no traffic sounds, no sirens wailing, no sound of apartment doors closing down the hall or the sound of someone else using the bathroom through her bathroom wall. This wasn't fake elegance and fake privacy.

What Leah had was a real home: a husband and a kid who loved her unconditionally.

"This is what I want."

"Exhaustion, dirty diapers, and a toddler who'd rather pee on the carpet than in the toilet?" Leah grinned and Emma laughed.

"Maybe one day. But, God, I've been so caught up in wanting to live this life of fifty-dollar bottles of wine, of having the fiancés who worked the good job, of having views of the Sound and having people know who I am. But they don't." Emma took another long sip of wine. "They just know the person that I show them. Even Owen."

"You can't hop right in bed with him, you know."

Emma blushed. "No, I can't just hop into bed with anybody. I've never been able to just, you know, jump from bed to bed. I mean you have some crazy power that I only wish I'd possessed."

"It was fun while it lasted, but I couldn't imagine not having Jacob in my life."

"Oh, I know. I was just always so envious of you. Whenever you'd tell me about your boyfriends, the attention they gave you, the power you had over them . . . " Emma trailed off, wondering if she, too, had had a similar power over Owen and Connor in college.

"It was a power, sure, but I was just like Rachel once. I had an affair with a married man. I remember thinking that maybe he'd leave his wife for me, that I deserved better. But one morning we sat there afterwards and I just knew it. I knew that I'd never be able to be with him. I'd never trust him not to find someone else behind my back."

Taking another drink from the bottle, Emma considered what her sister said. There were family secrets and habits that were getting passed down from one generation of woman to another. It was inescapable. Maybe it wasn't just their family, but their gender. Or the human specifies as a whole. It wasn't just the fact that everyone was programmed to think that being with one person was the end-game, but that you were supposed to find Eternal Happiness with that one person. The second someone got bored with their life, they blamed it on their relationship and went looking elsewhere. It wasn't their job, or anything else in their lives that could possibly be making you feel this way. Wasn't that what everyone always said?

But then, in straight relationships, the woman would get blamed. Emma had to fight not to think that she did something wrong, that she hadn't done enough. There were even people saying that Hillary couldn't be President because she couldn't even keep Bill happy. As if what qualifies a woman to do anything is based on whether or not the man that they're with can stay loyal to them.

"I don't even know if I'm mad at Rachel. It's not her fault that

Connor couldn't turn her down. I mean, yeah, if she knew he was with me when they first started sleeping together then she probably shouldn't have gone after him. Assuming she's the one who did." Emma sighed. "I don't even believe the story Connor told me."

"You're not mad at Rachel at all?"

"A little." Emma shrugged. "But it was Connor who cheated on me. No matter if Rachel pursued Connor, or the other way around, it was Connor's choice to sleep with her. To betray my trust. To break up our relationship."

"That's awfully big of you," Leah said, eyebrows raised.

"Yeah, well, we'll see how I'm feeling tomorrow. I think I just need time to process what even happened today."

"You know you can take all the time you need. Jacob and I, we're more than happy to have you here. And Henry loves whenever you come to visit. He'll really be able to spend time with you now."

Spending time with her nephew was something she had wanted to do—had added to the list of things she knew she need to do. But with Owen, Connor, the fundraisers, the girls in her building, family had fallen by the wayside. Her Conservatory family wasn't even truly family to her, but distant relatives she felt this deep, but stale, connection to. She loved them, but not as much as she loved the people in this house.

"Thanks. I think this is exactly what I need right now. I need to maybe cry myself to sleep, but then just figure out what I'm going to do tomorrow. I have the weekend to pull myself together and get back to work and then, I don't know, maybe—"

"You don't have to figure it all out tonight. Don't. Go take a long shower or a bath, and go to sleep. If you have trouble, there's some NyQuil in the cupboard. But if I know my sister, you'll be asleep in about . . ." Leah picked up the empty bottle that now sat between them. " . . . thirty minutes, give or take time for throwing up."

"God, *Le-ah*. I'm an adult now. I've learned to hold my alcohol."

Leah stood up and offered Emma a hand, her smile sad. "I just wish I could've protected you from all of this."

Emma pulled Leah in for a hug. She knew if her sister had told her that she thought Connor was cheating on her, Emma wouldn't have believed her. She never dreamed that any of this was even possible. But she also knew she didn't know who she would've turned to tonight.

22

—————

The caller ID flashed *Georgina Bishop*. Emma looked at it and waited. Maybe if she moved slow enough the call would go to voicemail. There were too many things Emma didn't have the answers to right now. She wasn't sure if she was ready to face her mother's disappointment just yet.

The phone stopped ringing. Emma closed her eyes and put her head back on her pillow. Well, Leah's guest room pillow. She'd been living with Leah for a few weeks now. Sure, she'd been looking at places but nothing had really caught her eye. Nothing felt like the home. Not the way New York did before the attacks, or the way being with Connor felt. This was Leah's home. These were Leah and Jacob's things. The black and white photos on the wall had been pictures they took on one of their trips out to the peninsula. The bed she was sleeping in was a choice they made together on what belonged in the guest room. But Emma knew her mother, and this phone call would be a "get your life together already" phone call. A, "stop putting so much thought into a temporary residence and just move out of your sister's place already," phone call.

After a few seconds, the phone started to chime again. Emma opened one eye, and then another, before rolling towards the bedside table. Georgina again. Even from halfway across the world, her mother would not be ignored.

"Hi Mom," Emma said after sliding her finger across the front of her new phone and placing it at her ear. She'd thrown her phone off the end of the pier that Ivar's sat on after a week of "I'm sorry" e-mails and text messages from Connor. He hadn't gotten the hint.

"Sweetie, hi, listen, I know that everything is up in the air for you right now but the museum is open and we have to go. We can't avoid it anymore."

It all came out in a rush of one breath. Of all the things that she hadn't wanted to deal with, New York City, and the 9/11 memorial, hadn't even made the list. She didn't think there'd be a need of even including them in the shit-storm that was her personal life. But now Emma didn't have a choice. It went on the list, nestled in the boxes from Connor's.

"I know, I just . . . I can't right now."

"It's the perfect time. Rip off the band-aide. You can't avoid every-thing that hurts you forever."

Avoiding was what she did best. She was avoiding Connor, avoiding Owen, avoiding moving onto a life that didn't involve the man that she'd spent the past decade with.

"Mom, I need to find a place to live, Danielle's wedding is next weekend, and the concert is coming up," Emma sighed into the phone. September had come and gone too quickly, as it did every year since 2001. But going back there and facing everything—it was too much. Her fiancé cheated on her, sure, but she didn't want to go touch the names of the people who died in the attacks. She didn't want to remember going to school and having the skyline forever changed by the end of the day. Dealing with the hurt Connor caused was easier.

"You can't move on until you make peace with your past. How many times have I told you this?"

"I have, I just—"

"You haven't been back there since you left for college."

"Neither have you, Mother."

"I know. But I'm here now and I think we should go together."

Emma sat up. "What do you mean you're here? You're in Seattle? Why didn't you tell me you were coming? Is Dad here too?"

"Your father is upstate on some hunting trip this weekend. And I told Leah, that's all that matters."

She could hear her mother smiling on the other end.

"I just wanted to see my grandson and my daughters. Is that so wrong of me? And besides, maybe you'll have missed me so much you'll want to come back home with me."

"Mom, I don't think I can." Emma sighed. "New York hasn't been my home for awhile."

"Sweetie, it *is* home. You can call Seattle home all you want, but we're from there. Our roots are in New York, no matter how burned beyond recognition they might be."

"I'll think about it, okay?"

"Yes fine. Well, tell you what. Since you're in Leah's guest room, I'm staying in a hotel—"

"Mom, no, you can—"

"No, I'm not having you bouncing around from room to room just because I came to town. I'm staying in a hotel close by. You and I, we'll go looking at apartments. If we find something that you really love, I won't bug you about New York. We'll just get you settled in and get you ready to be back on stage."

"Is this because Leah wants me out?"

Her mother chuckled. "No, not at all. She's pissed that I want to try and get you out of there. She thinks you need more time around family."

As much as Georgiana protested, Emma still felt like she was the dark cloud hovering in the corners of the happy family's home. She felt guilty for so many things, and taking up this room was at the top of her list. Leah had enough to worry about without taking care of her heartbroken and homeless younger sister.

"So when do I get to see you, anyway? Why aren't you at Leah's?"

"I know my daughter well enough to not just show up at her bedroom door. This gives you time to process."

It was Emma's turn to laugh. "Is process your nice way of saying that you know I'm still in bed?"

"Yes. My flight got in just after ten and I came straight to Leah's. I figured letting you sleep in was what you needed. Now go get out of bed. I'll see you soon."

Emma pulled the phone away from her ear and checked the time. Was it really after one already?

"All right. See you soon."

She hung up and laid back down on the bed. Staring at the ceiling, listening to Henry giggle and scream downstairs, she weighed her options. There was more to her mother's advice than just ripping off the band-aide on visiting New York. Georgina probably thought that going back to that Ground Zero would help get Emma to move past her personal one.

Rolling off the bed, Emma moved downstairs and sat at one of the high stools at the kitchen island's edge. Leah was also at the counter, knife in hand, cutting pieces of food into non-choking hazard sizes.

"So, Mom called me."

Leah raised her eyebrows but said nothing.

"She thinks I should go visit New York, and the memorial."

"Yeah, she mentioned that when she was here this morning. I guess she's coming back over in a few hours, closer to when Jacob gets home from work, after Henry's nap. I can't believe she's here!" Leah's voice was high and happy. It took moving mountains, or worlds crumbling, to pull their mother in from whatever grand adventure she was on. "But New York . . . I told her that I just couldn't do it right now. I can't leave Henry here—Jacob's too busy. And, you know, I just can't. I don't want to remember what happened that day. I just want to live in the now. There's just too much destruction going on as is. I'm not ready."

Emma's gaze lingered on the small television on the far counter. It was muted, but the news ticker at the bottom of the screen told of another suicide bombing in a country that America was far removed from.

"Do you think you'll ever be ready?"

Leah put the knife down on the counter. Henry toddled into the kitchen, his small hands latching onto the top of the island.

"Mommy? Lunch time?" Henry asked, letting go of the counter top and moving his closed right hand in front of his mouth, signing the word for "eat."

Smiling, Leah turned to Henry. "Yes, baby. Eat. Lunch time."

Leah picked Henry up and put him in his highchair where his big blue eyes were suddenly entranced with the television. Emma grabbed the remote and turned the television off. She knew that she wouldn't get an answer from Leah. Not a verbal one, anyway. The truth was, Henry was what Leah cared about now. Henry, Jacob, and her life in Seattle. She

"Do you need help?" Emma stood up. "I'm good for more than taking up your guest room."

Leah smiled. "Figure out what you want to do about New York. Don't let Mom pressure you into something you don't want to do. Go back only if you want to. It's not the end of the world if you go, or if you don't." She paused. "And you know you're welcome to stay here as long as you need to. It just all works into my plan to convince you to move out of downtown anyway."

"To where? Bellevue?" Emma grinned and walked over to where Leah was feeding Henry. "I'm not sure if I'm trendy enough for the Bellevue crowd."

"No, not Bellevue. Here. Queen Anne."

It was Emma's turn to raise her eyebrows. Queen Anne was close enough to the city's true limits that commuting wouldn't be difficult, but Emma wasn't sure if she'd fit in with the Queen Anne crowd, either. Sure, she fit the demo: white, upper-middle class. Plus it wasn't as if she couldn't see the view of the city's skyline from her guest room. When she and Leah took Henry to Kerry Park the other day, Emma could even see the building she used to live in, but felt like it was a world away.

"Maybe. I'll think about it."

"It's a great neighborhood. Great schools, shops, not a ton of tourist traffic except for Kerry Park. The commute down the hill can be bad, but since you do most of your work from home, anyway."

"Yeah, yeah." Emma teased back. "I'll expand my search. Right now the only apartments available downtown are studios going for $4000 a month."

"Shades of New York."

"It's best qualities followed us out here, it seems."

Leah started to say something and then stopped. Instead, she handed Henry another piece of edamame.

"I can ask around to see if anyone knows of anything open," Leah said finally. "Just so you have the option. I know Mom's taking you to look at some places, but I just want you to make sure you find something that's for you. Not something that Mom wants you in, or that you have to worry about sharing with someone else. You need space to figure your life out."

"Yeah, I know, I know. I promise I'll find something I actually love. And yeah, can you ask around? That'd be really great."

"You have to promise me something, though."

Emma rolled her eyes, waiting for something ridiculous to come out of her big sister's mouth.

"You have to start coming over here more after you move out. Sunday dinners. Like a real family."

Sunday's had normally been spent cleaning or catching up on e-mails. It'd never occurred to Emma to see if Leah and Jacob were available for dinner. She always just assumed that they were too busy with Henry, and with their own life, and she didn't want to interrupt any of that.

"Just let me know what I can bring. Every Sunday is yours."

23

The way Emma felt about playing the piano was the way some people felt about running. The faster the song, and the more difficult to play, the happier she was. Her fingers needed to be moving faster than she thought possible. The notes needed to blur together in her head. She needed the challenge the way she needed air.

Looking at the sheet music Owen handed her, she laughed.

"You've got to be kidding me."

He shrugged, eyebrows furrowed as he looked at the song title. "What? I thought we'd start off slower today. Every song can't be a sprint. You need to go easy on yourself sometimes."

Emma looked away from him. There was nothing wrong with Chopin's Preludes. *Op. 28 no. 15 in D flat* was a fine song. A beautiful song; it was a gentle rainstorm when all she wanted the violent tornado of Chopin's *Revolutionary*. Her entire life was in a revolutionary war and the only way she was going to win the battle tonight was to stretch her fingers as far as she could, make them fly as fast as she could. Instead of pieces of her body that she controlled, she wanted them to be ten racing horses, moving together and apart from each other, thundering down a track.

"Maybe we can try an 'Etude' instead?"

Putting her fingers to the keys, she didn't wait for his answer. It didn't matter what she played while they waited for the rest of the orchestra to get there.

Fingers pressing down, instead of launching into *Revolutionary*, she appeased him with a song in a major chord. *Etude No. 1 in A-Flat Major* was light, airy, and feminine—exactly the type of song she should be embracing. The song still sounded like rain, like a chance meeting between two would-be lovers hiding under a building's awning. At least, that would happen in a romantic comedy set in New York City. Here, in Seattle, things were different. The rain fell and you kept on moving. You pulled up your hood, walked faster, always had a hair tie handy just in case you got caught in the rain and needed to throw your hair into a bun. You perfected the art of blowdrying your hair, your sweater, or your coat under the hand-dryer in the women's bathroom and you kept on moving.

She finished the song and finally turned back to Owen.

"There. Light, airy, slower. A sunrise salutation. Can we get on with the real songs now?"

The corners of his lips twitched, hinting at a smile he was trying to suppress. "It's not like I asked you to play *Clair de lune*."

"Oh, look. Your orchestra has arrived." She nodded towards the other musicians who had started to fill the empty plastic chairs on the practice stage. "I guess you'll have to torture me with *Suite bergamasque* another time."

"Careful. I just might." He winked and turned to the other musicians, welcoming them by extending his arm. "Thank you, everyone, for being here today. It means a lot to me."

They pulled out their instruments and began to tune; sharp and random violin notes filled the air. Emma took the opportunity to look at the rest of the sheet music that sat on top of the piano. Since their last practice he had gone through and numbered them in the order that they'd be played at the concert. The first song was going to be the waltz Owen wrote for Danielle and Tom's wedding. Sitting back down with the song's pages in hand, she read through the adjustments that had been made to incorporate more than just a lone violin. From just the violin, the song moved into two violins, then the piano, followed by the full orchestra. The last refrain of the song didn't go back to just the lone violin like she expected, but just the piano and violin. They would waltz together until the final notes rang out and they put their fingers down, the last notes lost in the applause.

That's how it would go the night of the concert.

They would play together, writhing in the pain of the notes and memories, and finish to applause.

Emma blushed. Her fantasy with him had nothing to do with physical touch, and everything to do with playing together. Every now and then she caught herself daydreaming about a man who'd write a song about her, for her, and want to play it with her. A man who anticipated the moves she was going to make, what she would want, what she needed him to do.

If only her definition of home, of what she wanted, was so closely tied into music. Maybe then she'd be able to move on from the idea of Owen.

She knew Owen wasn't fantasizing about her, or a woman like her. He'd want the kind of woman who would follow his lead—that was evident in the way he started today's rehearsal off. He'd want the kind of woman who would be able to put her own career on the back burner while she supported his. Emma was his equal. Standing in his shadow was something she'd do for this one concert, only.

Yes, she was here to support him. To play his music, and the songs they wrote together. To support him on his big night.

But wasn't it her big night, too?

It would be her first night playing on a stage that wasn't in rehearsal, or determined her final grade in a class. It would be her big debut into Seattle's music world. She'd no longer be on the outside looking in.

"Em?"

Emma looked up at Owen, blinking.

"You ready? We're going to run through the first few songs tonight."

"Yes. Sorry," she mumbled quickly. "Ready when you are."

❋

"WHEN's the last time you went dancing?"

Rehearsal had ended and the rest of the musicians were filtering out. Emma looked up at him, eyebrows raised. He must've spent enough time with her in college to know her better than this. Yes, sure, she was musically inclined enough to add harmony into a song someone else was playing, but dancing was a different story.

"I've never gone out dancing."

Connor had never wanted to go out dancing with her. He always wanted to stay in and watch something on Netflix. In a recent late-night Facebook stalking session, she'd seen that Rachel put up pictures of her and Connor out at a nightclub, drinking and dancing together. It seemed that he had no problems going out with Rachel. The night she saw the pictures, she threw up. Now, the thought of them out together only fueled a rage that she hadn't figured out how to douse.

"Exactly." He turned away from her and started to walk towards the door.

"Are you high?" she asked.

He turned back towards her, laughing. "No."

"Are you sure? Because you're acting like you're high."

"No, I'm not high. I just think that we both need some fun in our lives. I'm working twenty-four-seven on this concert and you . . ." he trailed off.

"I'm cleaning up the mess that is my life."

"Your life is not a mess, Ms. Bishop." His smile was gentle and warm. "You're just in-between right now. You need friends who can help you have fun."

"You mean like friends with benefits?" Emma quirked an eyebrow, trying to lighten the conversation.

"No, no. Without. Without complications and drama and wedding planning that makes you want to shoot yourself in the foot."

She had to concede to his point. Danielle's wedding was all set to go. Since the breakup, she hadn't had to play maid of honor and go on cake tastings or dress fittings or do anything that remotely involved reminding herself that she'd be going dateless to a wedding. Anything Danielle had needed was handled by jumping on Etsy and pressing "submit order." That she'd been able to do with a bottle of wine next to her, no problem. But as far as having fun? Even Molly was terrible to be around right now. All she'd talked about was how in love with her girlfriend she was and how she was starting to look at rings. Emma was excited for her, but it wasn't something she could emotionally handle at the moment.

"Fine, you win. But am I even dressed to go out dancing?"

Emma looked down at jeans, the coral tank top she'd picked up on sale at Anthropolgie, and the well-loved cardigan she'd had since college. Going out dancing meant she needed a dress that was too short for someone her age; a dress that fit someone who had thinner hips and thighs than she did. Dancing was for girls who went out in groups and were ten years younger than she was, and who looked ten times better than she did right now. There was no way he could take her out looking like this.

"You look fine. It doesn't matter, I promise."

"It probably does. For me, at least. Don't places usually have dress codes?"

He shook his head. "Not where we're going. Come on, we're going to miss it."

"Miss what?"

"You'll see."

She followed him into the hallway, into the elevator, and stayed silent as they made their way to the ground floor. By the time they walked out onto the sidewalk, night had taken over completely. Above them, stars peeked out through the glow of the city lights and thunder rumbled in the distance. As plentiful as rainstorms were, the thunderstorm was rare.

"It sounds like it's about to rain."

"We live in Seattle. It's always about to rain. Come on," he said, extending his hand to her. She took it, and let him lead her down the street. She was surprised when they didn't walk into the parking garage, and when he didn't call for his driver or a cab.

They walked up 2nd Avenue in an excited silence. He was almost vibrating with the amount of energy he had radiating off of him. As they turned onto Pike, she could see the red glow of the Market sign.

"The Market?" Emma asked.

"Just trust me."

The Market wasn't what she expected, especially for dancing. Everything closed down at dusk.

But then she heard it: the violin, the guitar, the voices and the clapping.

More eager now, she followed him down past The Green Tortoise hotel, and onto the cobbled street that ran in front of the Market. The street had been blocked off and a small band played in the center of a quickly growing crowd.

"What is this?"

"Block party . . . sort of. End of tourist season fun."

Emma watched the men play, their feet stomping against the ground, as people around them clapped along.

"So this is what you do when you're not at rehearsal or composing?" Emma asked, turning to Owen. "You come down among the peasants and play commoner?"

He laughed. "You make me sound so elitist. I like to do this. Look around you. Everyone is letting themselves enjoy the moment instead of worrying too much about what other people are thinking. Concerts can be the same way, but things like this . . . I don't know. They're just different."

As he started clapping along with the rest of the group, Emma could feel the distance between herself and the moment. How she wasn't ready to let go of everything just yet. She could be here, enjoying this with him, but there was still too much she was thinking about. Would Connor have taken her something like this if she'd asked? Looking around, she thought she saw him in the crowd. But when she blinked, the face changed, and it wasn't Connor at all. Just another man. A stranger.

"Come on," Owen said, taking her hand. Thinking that they were going somewhere else, she let him lead her, until he twirled her around.

"What are you doing?" Emma asked, eyebrows raised. She didn't dance, especially somewhere so public. "No, I can't—"

"You can. Just close your eyes."

She narrowed her eyes at him and shook her head.

"Come on. Just close your eyes."

Feeling ridiculous, she finally closed her eyes. As she did, the music seemed to get louder. She could pick out the side conversations, the laughter, and the sound of feet hitting pavement. When Owen took her other hand, she opened her eyes to find him smiling, and moving. Dancing. So she moved with him, mirroring him, twisting when he wanted it, coming close when his hands asked it.

For a long time, they didn't say anything. Thunder continued to rumble, slowly closing in on them, but the trio played on, and she kept dancing with him. It was the way he smiled while he danced that kept her moving with him. If she had seen him like this before, it wasn't without some sort of alcoholic aid.

As a streak of lightning cracked across the sky, the band began to wrap up, thanking everyone for coming out.

"How was that?" Owen asked, a bit out of breath.

Emma laughed. "It was fine."

"Just fine?"

"No," Emma shook her head, her smile big, "it was fun. This was fun."

"Come back to my place with me. There's something I want to show you."

She told herself that it was just another song that he'd want her to play. Just something benign, something platonic that had nothing to do with kissing or taking off their clothes, or making up for the last time they had slept together. It would be about the concert—his concert—and what she could do to support him on his big night.

"Okay."

They started to head in the direction of his loft as the crowd dispersed. It was strange heading this way and knowing she wasn't going back to Connor's. Her being okay with the fact that things were over with Connor came in spurts, like the lighting that snaked across the sky. She was fine with it, until the pressure changed and a memory struck her like a lightning bolt.

Rain started, sporadic and gentle, as they rounded the corner onto 2nd. His building was still a few blocks down, but even with the chill in the air, Emma didn't mind this. They walked fast, smiling, near giggling as the clouds finally dumped on them. Now racing, they sprinted into the lobby of the building, and to the elevators.

"Maybe check the weather next time?" Emma asked through her laughter as she tried to ring out her hair.

"You can't tell me that wasn't fun."

"No, it was."

"Okay then."

She looked up at him and time stood still. Maybe it was the magic of the night, of the dancing and the rain, that had her feeling this way. Everything disappeared. She didn't care that she had to go look at apartments tomorrow, that Connor was still e-mailing her even though he was going out with Rachel. Emma knew what she wanted, and what she wanted was to kiss Owen.

And the elevator door opened to his floor. Emma could feel her heart beating in her throat.

"After you," he said, his hand on the elevator to hold the door open.

Emma walked past him, her body still on fire. He opened his apartment door and let her into the dark space. The only light came from the city lights outside the big windows.

"Come on," he said, leading her into the dark. "You won't bump into anything, I promise."

"So you keep your apartment cleaner than your dorm room?" Emma half-whispered.

"I just have the money to hire a cleaning lady."

Owen turned on a small lamp that illuminated the glossy black of a piano's body. Disappointment sunk into her stomach: this *was* just about his concert.

"Sit, please."

"I . . ." Emma started, looking between him and the piano.

"I wanted a chance to practice with you. The song we wrote . . .it's difficult to play in front of everybody else."

"What do you mean? You played it with me the first time I came to rehearsal."

He took a few steps closer to her, his body all shadow despite the reading lamp. She could smell the rain and the sea on him still.

"Emma, that song. It's . . ." he trailed off, his hand reaching out to hers. "We created something together. Something beautiful and perfect."

"It wasn't me, it was you."

"No, Em. Don't you remember? I was drunk and you took the lead. You wrote this song—I just put the finishing touches on it. This whole thing is for you. It's yours. It's about how much you've influenced me. How blind I was all of those years. I had you, you were right in front of me and I . . ."

"What?" Emma asked, her heart pounding.

"Emma, you're so . . . Infuriating. Headstrong. Compulsive. And despite my better judgment, despite everything, I haven't been able to let you go. I love you, Emma. I always have."

"You . . . barely know me." Emma swallowed, her body burning in a new kind of pain. He gave her every reason why he shouldn't be with her, instead of the reason's why. It wasn't about who she was, but who she wasn't that made him want her. "You said just said that you find me infuriating."

"Yes, but—"

"No. Owen, you can't just come out and say something like this after everything. We're too different. I'd make you miserable. I don't want to sit on the sidelines while you go after your dreams. I've done enough of that and I can't let myself be swallowed in your shadow."

He dropped Emma's hand. "If that's the way you truly feel, then I'll leave it alone. We'll do the wedding and the concert together, and I won't bother you again. Is that what you want?"

"Yes."

"You're sure?"

"I am."

Emma turned and walked back out his apartment door, back out into the rain, into the cold, into a post-Owen future that she wasn't sure she even wanted.

24

Emma stood outside of the townhouse, arms crossed, hating that she took a half-day off of work to do this. She wasn't in the city like she wanted to be. She wasn't still in bed with Owen after he told her that he loved her. She hadn't even made it to his bed. She bolted, running as fast as she could in the opposite direction of something that she had thought she wanted, but didn't?

It was complicated.

"I know, sweetie," Georgina began, "it's not the city. It's not the hustle and bustle of rush hour traffic and homeless people in your doorway. But it's quiet, and it's safe."

Queen Anne was the last place Emma wanted to look for a place. It was a neighborhood for the families who could afford not to move further out into the hilly suburbs, but didn't make enough money to own horse property. It was bright, sunny, and above everything. Looking down on the city was far more appealing from the penthouse loft of some overpriced apartment building than a place with green grass and a deadbolt instead of a doorman.

"We have a lot of natural sunlight that comes in through the windows and a great patio in the backyard that's perfect to sit out on during a rainy day," the realtor explained.

The traditional New Yorker, Georgina wouldn't look at a place anywhere she went without having the buffer of a realtor with her.

"Great," Emma said. "So, can we go in?"

Looking at the house from the outside, Emma had all but written it off. It was yellow with sage green on the outside, with monstrous plants lining the walkway up to the house. It looked charming, sure, but it wasn't something Emma was ready to hand over her checkbook for. She had modern, clean, and upscale just a few weeks ago. Now, she was being taken to places that still cost as much as modern, but would need twice as much to make look modern.

There were two kinds of people in Seattle: The modern, tech-company loving, yuppies or there were the earth-worshipping, vegan-food-eating hipsters that were too cool, or too rich, to settle in Portland. This house looked like it had granola hidden away in every nook and cranny. A New Yorker would not be living here.

Walking up the front steps, hand on the white railing, she saw the long porch, the small rocking chair and plant set out adjacent to the front door. It felt like a home; a place that someone had loved living in. It was still full of life, full of potential to make a family happy. Already Emma knew it was the wrong place for her. This home—this front porch—deserved a family who would love their muddy boots lined up against the wall, a family who would spend time decorating the porch with Christmas decorations, or who would put a window box out and grow their own herbs. It wasn't meant for someone who was single, who had no kids or aspirations of having them any time soon. They weren't for someone who hopped from one trendy drink spot to a country club for a luncheon, to Bellevue Square. The house embodied "down to earth," which Emma was most definitely not.

"Through the front door we have the main living space with tons of natural light, like I said, and original hardwood floors that have been restored," the realtor began. Her heels were a loud click against the reflective surface. Light poured in through the windows whose blinds had been raised all the way, pouring over the white walls and warm honey color of the oak floors.

"This is nice," Georgina commented. "A lot of potential."

"Oh definitely. You're welcome to paint the rooms whatever color you want, the property owner doesn't mind," the realtor added.

"Great." It was all Emma could say.

They moved from room to room and Emma couldn't shake the feeling of being home. It weighed down her already heavy heart and built up a lump in her throat. This wasn't like their apartment back in New York, or her apartment with Connor. It wasn't like Leah's house or the first apartment she had when Emma came out to Seattle for school. It was different. Warm. Inviting. It was a heavy, heated throw blanket you wrapped yourself in on cold, rainy days when you struggled to get out of bed. She didn't deserve a place like this.

"And this is the dining room," the realtor waved a hand towards the empty space right outside the kitchen. It, too, had oversized windows that the daylight poured through. It had something more, though. Suddenly, Emma knew what this house reminded her of: her first piano teacher. The woman was older, graying on the top and sides of her hair that was always down, curled against her shoulders. There was no *Beethoven's 9th* or *Fur Elise* played in that woman's sunroom. No, her upright piano only played songs that challenged her students. She was the gasoline that had been thrown onto Emma's already burning desire to make music.

"I'll take it."

Emma wasn't a New Yorker anymore. Every excuse that she had about this place was because she thought she didn't deserve it. Someone else, someone with a different life, would breathe life into this empty house. But this house was already breathing life into her. Standing in the center of the would-be eating space, Emma knew what needed to go there. Emma knew she'd spend many dinners sitting on a piano bench writing songs of her own.

"That's great! Your application was already approved so—"

"When can I move in?" Emma asked, pulling her checkbook out of her handbag. "I'm prepared to give you first, last's and the security deposit right now."

"Oh, wow! Great. Let me call the owner real quick."

As the realtor walked back into the front room, Emma avoided her mother's gaze. Maybe it was impulsive. Maybe Emma really just didn't want to look anymore and saying yes to a house was easier than cramming her life back into a small apartment. She could get a dog, even though the yard was the size of a postage stamp. A small dog, but a dog that still commanded respect. A dog that wouldn't make her feel like she was living in an empty house full of the ghosts of someone else's past.

"That was easy," Georgina said finally. "I guess I won't make you come back to the city with me after all."

Emma sighed. "Mom, I didn't pick this place just so I didn't have to go to New York with you. It just . . . standing here, it feels like a real home. Or a place that could be a real home for me. No sirens, no listening to my neighbors through my bathroom wall. It's a great space and I can easily fit a piano here."

Georgina smiled, "I'm glad, sweetie."

"Can I think about New York, though? Maybe I can fly out after the wedding. Maybe for Christmas."

"Whatever you're comfortable with. You can't rush this. I just want to make sure that you're happy and healed." Georgina crossed the space between them and put her hands on her daughter's shoulders. "This, today, is the first step towards being happy. To do something I was never able to do."

"What's that?"

"I will never be able to be like you. I'd never be able to go out and live on my own. My whole life is your father. I see that in Leah, too. But you've been able to forge this path for yourself and you don't let anyone get in the way. You're stronger than me and Leah."

Emma turned away and stepped toward the new windows she'd be looking out of if and when she got a piano to put in the empty room. Strength wasn't something she thought she had. It was the opposite: she felt weak and naive. She had believed Connor's lies and went on supporting him and staying with him. She let herself get so swept up with Owen in undergrad that she never bothered to make a name for herself. Emma even gave up on trying to find a grad school program because she didn't want to move away from Connor. Connor and Owen were the suns of her universe and she moved in a close orbit around them, waiting to be sucked in by their gravitational pull.

"No, I'm just better at hiding it."

Even now, she was thinking about going to New York, not with her mother, but with someone else. With Owen. It wasn't that she didn't want to go with her mom, it was just that she couldn't be weak in front of her. She wanted her mom to know that she was alright, that going back to New York was exactly the thing she needed to heal. The reality was that, yes, maybe she'd go to New York, but she didn't think she'd be able to go to the memorial.

Memorial. Like thousands of bodies didn't die on that ground.

"Are you okay?" her mother asked.

Emma turned back around. "I'm fine."

Thankfully, the relator came back into the room. "I'm so sorry, it turns out that the owners accepted the application of someone else just as we got here. I can find more places like this for you to look at, however. If you're looking to stay in Queen Anne, you have so many wonderful choices . . ."

Emma tuned the relator out. Looking around the house, she sighed. "That's fine, we'll keep looking. Do you have any more to show us today?"

"Of course!" the realtor said and led them out of the house.

Leaving the house with the promise of being able to look at another place only a few minutes away, Emma took one more glance at the cottage.

"It reminded me of the house we rented at the Cape," Emma said finally.

"You're right." Georgina smiled. "It doesn't remind you of the New York apartment, though?"

Emma shook her head as she opened her car door. "Maybe in color scheme, but it was definitely more Cape Cod."

They were silent as they drove to the next place, a townhouse with views of Lake Union. It was a place Emma had already written off as being a poor version (in view, not price tag) of her apartment with Connor. Nothing could really compare to the view of the Puget

Sound, to the convenience of living in the city, of the short walk to the Market or the office. What benefit would this place offer to her?

"I think we're here," Georgina said finally, turning down the jazz music that had been playing to fill the empty space the lack of conversation had left. "That's lovely, by the way. What we were listening to."

"Oh. Well, it was me."

"You didn't tell me you have a recording!"

Emma looked ahead and unbuckled her seat belt. "I know. It's nothing, really. Molly and I were visiting Conservatory to give a talk about what to do after college and we were able to use their recording studio a few times. I've just been so focused on Owen's concert that I needed a break from it all."

"Hm." Was all Georgina said before exiting the car.

"Hm?"

"It's just an interesting revelation to hear from you, dear. I'm glad you're playing new things. You sound beautiful."

"Thank you," Emma said a the realtor approached.

"Now I know you said you were interested more in townhouses than houses because of the price and this one I have a really good feeling about," the realtor explained as they walked up to the front door of the townhouse. "I've worked with this property management company for a long time and they're really great about everything. And I already check to make sure it was okay to put a piano in here and they were more than fine with it."

Emma nodded. It hadn't occurred to her that having a piano in her living space wouldn't be an option.

"You have your own garage under here," the woman said, gesturing to stairs. "And up there you'll see how much natural light you'll have in your townhouse."

Looking up at the white building, she did see what the realtor was talking about. There were big picture windows that faced out to the Lake. It didn't stop Emma from wondering if "natural light" was a buzzword that every realtor was using these days, as if not every house that they'd show their clients would have windows.

"Great. Can we go look inside?"

She felt bad, but Emma was getting impatient. It didn't matter to her how the outside looked, but how the inside felt.

Walking inside, she tried not to judge the plain, too-white kitchen and the odd lofted bedroom. It was modern, there was no denying that. The boots of her heels were a soft click against the spotless hardwood floors as she walked around.

"This is a newly renovated space, so you'd be the first to live in it."

"Really?"

The realtor nodded and smiled. "Oh yes. And if you're flexible with your move-in date, we can even have it painted for you in colors you'd like. The lease agreement would give you the specifics—no dark colors, nothing that would be difficult to take off or paint over. But you'd be more than welcome to make this place your own."

Emma nodded as she tried to picture herself here. Colors on the wall, a piano, her things—did this place feel like home, the way the last place did?

"Would you like to see upstairs?"

They went through the motions of seeing the rest of the house: the walk in master closet, the master bathroom with the large tub and oversized standup shower. The double sink stung, reminding her of her apartment with Connor but pushed past that. One day someone would share that other sink, or they wouldn't. Being alone was something Emma knew she needed to get used to. Being alone was something that she needed, period.

"This is all really great. Would you be able to double-check on the availability?"

It wasn't the heart-bursting love she had felt for the first place, but something that felt more comfortable. It was easy being in this space, a space that no one's ghost would haunt. It would be all hers to decide what to do with. To fill with her own memories, instead of trying to find comfort in someone else's.

"Are you sure, sweetie? You felt so sure about the last place." Georgina said.

"I know. It just sounds like the best I'm going to get for the price I can afford. I really don't want to keep looking," Emma admitted.

"Plus, the open floor plan is perfect for me. There's so much I can do with this space, I could—"

"Record your own music right from your living room. I have an oriental in storage that would fit right here," her mother said, her arms gesturing to the space in front of the fireplace. "And, you won't need a formal table if you just put bar stools against the kitchen counter and a guest bed in the other room for when your parents want to come visit you."

"Are you sure you're on board with this?" Emma asked. "I thought you wanted me to come to New York?"

"I think you should go back to New York at some point, sweetheart. But I can see that this is where you need to be. You're not going to be able to find a space like this in New York, sure, but it's more than that. You'll come back to New York when you're ready."

25

MAY 2007

"I can't believe it's today!" Molly said, throwing the door to their dorm room open with a loud bang. "And I'm making mimosas."

"How nice for you," Emma said, rolling back over. It was too early. She was too hungover to be dealing with this. Her head pounded in the afterglow of another night fighting with Connor. He didn't want to believe that the relationship was over just because school was done. Sure, she was sticking around Seattle—but only long enough to figure out what her next plan was, her next step into adulthood. She couldn't live with Leah and her fiancé forever.

"Oh, come on hun. Chin up. Or drink until you're happy."

"I feel like shit."

"Break ups do that. How'd it go with lover boy?"

Emma turned back towards Molly and sat up as she wiped the sleep out of her eyes. "Oh, as expected. A lot of crying, a lot of yelling. Connor asking if I was dumping him for Owen."

"What part of, 'I'm breaking up with you,' did he not understand?"

"Probably the, 'I don't want to be in a relationship,' part."

Molly handed Emma a plastic cup. "Here, you need this."

"Plastic cups? Fancy."

"Snob. It's all I have. And what did he think, that you were just going to stay here—"

"—With no job, no way to repay my student loans—"

"And just be with him forever? I mean, he's like your first real boyfriend. You need to branch out. And it's not like you were going to move in with him and his roommates."

Emma's stomach churned. Whether it was from the hangover, or the new addition of booze, she couldn't be sure. It hadn't been her first real relationship, just the first one where she had seen potential of a future. But he was staying here; he would never move away from Seattle. He had his new job at Microsoft that Leah's fiancé helped him get, pre-breakup. He had his family, his whole life, here. No, not a life.

Roots.

He had roots here.

It wasn't something she could fault him for having, either. It was something she envied. She just didn't know what that was like, and she wasn't ready to find out. Living with her sister was just something temporary until she figured it all out. She'd work somewhere part-time, at least, to get money put away until she figured out her next move.

"Branch out. Yeah. How about I get through graduation first, and then we'll see what happens."

"Where are you off to tomorrow?"

Emma shrugged. "Mom and Dad actually want to do a road trip. We're going to go down the coast, and then over. Try and hit up some national parks."

"That's so awesome. I wish I could do stuff like that with my parents."

"Yeah, it's cool. It just kind of sucks that after that, there's no plan, other than coming back here and living with Leah while I figure everything out."

"Just go with the flow, or whatever the kids these days do."

Emma rolled her eyes and threw a pillow at Molly. Molly ducked and stuck her tongue out. "Come on, you need to start getting ready. We've got to line up in an hour and a half."

"Shit, really?"

"Yeah. You slept all morning."

That's what happens when you break up with a guy you might actually love, Emma thought as she gathered her stuff and went to shower. It wasn't even like she wanted to break up with him; she just knew she had to. There was no future when she had no idea where she'd end up. The thought of staying with someone who was so driven, while she was so lost, bothered her. She couldn't just follow him around like a puppy. She needed to forge her own path.

At least that's what she was telling herself as she cried through her shower.

"Oh, sweetie," Molly said as Emma walked back into their room. "Come on, let's get your face together. At least graduation's outside. You can wear sunglasses. And if anyone asks why you're crying, it's just cause you're going to miss me so much."

"Obviously. Why else would I be crying?"

She let Molly touch up her face with gels and creams she vowed to learn how to use one day. When it was time to go, she put on her cap and her gown, and walked arm in arm with Molly.

❀

IT WAS FINALLY OVER. College. School.

No more classes, no more papers or tests, or having to get up early just to have class cancelled. But it also meant no more staying up until four in the morning with Owen because he wanted her help writing a new song. It meant no more getting silly with Molly on Thursday nights watching *Grey's Anatomy* and picking out what Seattle things they got wrong.

This was the third picture she was standing next to Molly and

Danielle in, the fifth time her mom had to step away to touch up her running makeup, and the second time Emma had seen Owen.

As much as breaking up with Connor hurt, she didn't want to think about what it would be like to leave everyone, especially Owen, behind. She hadn't seen him much after their final concert. The final concert that she thought that they'd be playing the duet they wrote together, but couldn't. It just wasn't right for the concert, Owen had said, and he composed something else for them to play together. A different duet, but one lacking the intimacy and emotion of their original one. In Emma's opinion, and their professor's, it had been subpar from what they had been working on all year. But still passable. Still well done. Still worthy of a good grade.

"Hey, I'll be right back," Emma said to Molly and went off to chase after Owen.

"Owen!" she called. He turned around and smiled at her.

"Emma. Hi."

"I just wanted . . . I hadn't seen you all day, and . . ." Words were failing her. The weight of the moment was crushing her.

"I know. When do you leave?"

"Tomorrow morning."

"Where to?"

"Portland. We're just going to take the summer and see . . . everything."

His smile grew wider. "I'm jealous."

Emma rolled her eyes. "I know about the audition, Owen. I helped you apply, remember?"

They'd spent almost as much time on their final showcase as they had searching the internet for positions that they could apply for. Real ones, real symphony spots. At least, Emma told him she was researching for a piano spot in a symphony. They were few and far between; it'd be easier for her try and get some notoriety playing a dead white man's songs in different college campus performing arts centers. She was good, but wasn't destined to be one of the greats. That part of her life had been sealed when she gave up her space in the Boston conservatory.

"I was . . . I didn't want to make. . . " he sighed. "It's going to be weird, not having you there, playing with me. You always anticipate what I'm going to do. You've spoiled me."

Maybe she'd spoiled him, but he'd ruined her. The past four years hadn't been about making the grades, but about winning his praise, about making sure he had every opportunity to go off and do something better than—well, whatever Emma ended up doing. She worked so hard to make sure that he was happy, to see if she could get him to see her as anything other than his backup singer, so-to-speak.

"It's true. But you'll survive," she said, laughing.

"What will you do after your road trip?"

"I'm not sure. Start looking for somewhere to work, I guess. Not that many auditions come up for piano, but I was thinking maybe check out some of the smaller cities, even their theaters."

"Interesting." He paused. "Have you considered staying in Seattle?"

"I haven't ruled it out, no. "

"Maybe you should. You know, Emma, I've been really fighting with myself not to say this, and I just—"

"Emma!"

Emma turned as Connor ran up to them, red faced and winded.

"I thought . . . I can't . . ." he tried, but he was pulling in deep, big breaths in between his words.

"What?" She asked, turning away from Owen. "Connor, I can't do this again. I told you we're—"

"No. Move in with me. I got a place in Belleview, and I can afford it. You can figure out—"

"Connor, that's... No." She doubted it as she said it. It felt like too much now, since she had nothing. "I've got plans, the road trip."

"No, I know. I mean after. After your road trip, you can come back here. We can figure it all out. But, god Emma, this can't be the end of us. I love you. There's no reason we can't do this."

She turned to look at Owen, who only shrugged. As much as she wanted him to finish what he had started to say, Connor's offer had been the first relief from the pain she had been feeling all month. If she did this, if she moved in with him, she didn't have to give it all up: Seattle, Connor, Owen.

"Owen, I'll say good bye before I leave, okay?" Emma turned back towards Owen, who only offered a small smile in return.

"Sure. I'll see you."

When he walked away, she knew then that she wouldn't. She couldn't.

"So what do you say?" Connor asked.

"Connor, I don't know. It's a lot to think about. I already figured out where I'm living, but I need to figure out what I'm doing with my life. I can't . . . "

"Don't decide anything. Just promise me . . . promise me that you'll just give me a chance when you get back from your trip.

"I will." The lie slipped out as her parents came up to her. "This is Georgina, by the way. My Mom."

"Nice to meet you, Mr. and Mrs. Bishop," Connor said.

"Oh, god. No. No no no. Georgina is fine." She smiled wide as she shook Connor's hand.

"So you're the guy who's been keeping my Emma happy," her father said, shaking Connor's hand.

Connor smiled but it never reached his eyes. "I've been trying to, anyway. But I should really get back to my parents. They're waiting in the car for me. It was nice meeting you . . . Em, I'll talk to you when you get back from your trip?"

Emma nodded. He came over, kissed her cheek, and walked off into the crowd.

When he walked away, Georgina raised her eyebrows. "So that's Connor. Who was the other guy?"

"Owen."

"Uh huh. And you're with Connor . . . "

Emma shook her head. "We break up last night."

Georgina pursed her lips. "I'm not surprised, with the way you'd been talking at the Cape. But just make sure you're thinking things through, sweetie. Don't feel pressured to come back here for him, or feel pressured to end things because you're not sure about your future. You could have a future; here, with him. Or you can have a future with someone else in a million different cities."

"Can we get out of here now?" Emma asked.

"You didn't get to say goodbye to Owen," her father reminded her. Georgina shook her head.

"She'd go say good bye to him if she really wanted to."

Georgina wrapped her arm through Emma's, and they walked back towards the car. "You've got so much ahead of you, sweetie. So much that you don't even know yet. In ten years from now you won't even remember this day. You'll be settled into some new life, with a man and a family. You'll have a life that's so much bigger than what you've put into your boxes from your dorm room."

Leaning into her mother, Emma so badly wanted to believe her. That she'd have something bigger and better than three boxes of papers and pictures, of clothes that she'd been wearing for the past four years.

She didn't want the past four years, and the thousands of dollars in student loans, to have all been for nothing.

26

The blue light of the laptop threw harsh shadows over the otherwise serene guest room. Pieces of Emma's life were starting to fall into place. She had a place, for starters. The busy season—the Pops concerts, the holiday music shows—was starting soon and it meant a big opportunity to get donors for the symphony, and for the hall itself. In just the few days since she'd signed her lease and picked out colors for accent walls, Emma had everything at Leah's nearly re-packed and leads on decent looking furniture, even if it was from Craigslist. Georgina had left, but promised to ship some things as soon as she made it back to New York.

The problem was every piece of furniture she owned was at Connor's still. Maybe she should've been more aggressive and taken it with her but, if she was being honest, she didn't want anything from the life that they had shared together. It was tainted now. She didn't want any part of the life that they had shared together.

Scrolling through Overstock, Emma tried to get excited about all of this. It was a new start, a new life, a new chapter--or whatever clichéd expression she was supposed to be embracing. The truth was that she was single at thirty, in a job that she was good at but that her heart wasn't it. A family was not on her horizon. Maybe internet dating was. Or hitting up casual drinking holes in search of a connection she knew she'd never find.

"Em?" Leah's voice filtered through the door.

"Yeah?"

Emma glanced at the clock. Eight-thirty. Had she been up here all evening?

"You have a visitor."

"I . . . what?"

"Tall, dark, handsome?" Leah whispered as she came into the bedroom and turned on the light. Emma recoiled from the brightness. "He said that he just needed a few minutes of your time. He seems upset."

Sighing, Emma got out of bed and walked in front of the floor length mirror set up in the corner of the bedroom. If Owen had showed up here, it would've been for a good reason. The last time she had seen him, she'd left things very clear: she couldn't return the love he thought he felt for her. At least not right now.

"You look fine. Go put the man out of his misery, I've got to get Henry into the bath."

"Jacob's not doing it?"

The normal routine was Jacob did bath and bedtime, but the past few nights Emma noticed Leah doing them all on her own.

"No, he's stuck at work still. But these things happen. It's not a big deal."

Emma nodded but felt the familiar twist of pain and anger in her gut. She'd believed Connor when he said he was working late, and ignored it when they became two ships who passed angrily in the night.

"Are you sure?"

"Oh, it's really fine. He gets caught up in a project and can't take himself away. Relationships are about sacrifice and compromise, Ems. It's not all fun family nights and sex. I've had to learn to live with disappointment sometimes, but Jake always makes up for it when he gets the free time."

"But isn't that settling?"

Leah shook her head. "No, not when Jake makes me feel as happy and loved as he does. Someone will be worth it. Maybe it wasn't Connor, and maybe it's not the guy we've kept waiting downstairs. But someone's going to make all the disappointments seem worth it."

Pulling her hair back in a quick, but messy, braid that fell over her shoulder, Emma resigned herself to going downstairs. "Thanks. I'll make sure this is quick."

"Oh, don't worry about us," Leah said, squeezing Emma's shoulder. "Worry about you for a little while, hm?"

❊

WALKING downstairs felt like an awkward prom reveal.

Owen waited there at the bottom, his back to the stairs, arms clasped behind his back as he looked at the picture of a very young Emma and Leah that hung in the photo collage that Leah had artfully hung on one of the walls in the living room.

"You're here."

Owen turned and smiled. "I am."

Emma waited for him to continue. Her heart beat heavy in her throat. She'd been ready to face him in rehearsal, at the wedding, at the concert. Seeing him here, with Henry's toys scattered and his giggles descending down the stairs, was like seeing him in a different life. This is probably the kind of life he would've had if he hadn't been a brilliant musician, or if he let someone into that cold and empty loft of his.

Oh right. He had tried to have Emma be that girl, but she'd turned him down.

"I wanted to check on you, to make sure that you're okay."

"I am. Why wouldn't I be?"

He took a few steps closer to her. "I sprung a big thing on you the other night. It wasn't . . . It was wrong of me to do that. You've barely been broken up with Connor, and we have so much coming up. It was very wrong of me to put my own feelings on you too."

"Sometimes I'm not sure if you're a real person."

Owen chuckled. "What do you mean?"

"You just decided to stop by my sister's house to apologize for telling me how you feel because you recognize that it was too much for me to handle right now."

"Yes?"

"Unreal." Emma rolled her eyes and shook her head.

"Is something wrong?"

It was Emma's turn to laugh. "No, it's just that not too long ago, I would've dreamed of you telling me that you loved me. I would've given anything for you to notice me like that. But right now, I'm just not ready to let myself love. I'm not . . ." she paused, looking away from him, trying to figure out what to say next. "Owen, I don't want you to be the rebound guy. It would've been so easy for me to stay with you the other night and just let myself get wrapped up in you and your life. But I can't."

Pain blossomed in a new part of her heart. She wanted him to take her somewhere, to make her forget about what happened with Connor, to make her feel wanted and loved. But she knew she hadn't even begun to heal.

"I understand. I can't promise that I'll wait around for you—"

"I didn't ask you to. I didn't ask you to come here, I'm not asking you to do anything," Emma shot back in a hoarse whisper. He wanted so much, too much, from her. In college he had wanted her ability to play piano, her ability to mix modern pieces with classical. Now, he wanted her to play a song she'd never wanted to play in public. He wanted her to play a full concert. He wanted her to be ready to love him now that he was ready to love her.

"Maybe that's the problem," Owen said.

"What is?"

"What do you want from me, Emma? What can I do with you, or for you? I know you need your space right now. I know we have the concert coming up, and the wedding. But I'm always asking you to do things for me. Tell me, please. What can I do for you?"

"Come to New York with me."

The phrase fell out of her mouth before she could stop it. Before she even knew that was what she wanted. Not to go to New York with someone who knew the city intimately, who had ghosts and memories of their own. But a stranger she could guide around, someone who knew what happened on 9/11 but didn't live through it in the way she had.

"Are you sure?"

Emma nodded slowly. "Yes. I think. I'll cover the hotel, the airfare—"

"It's okay, Emma, I can cover my own. When do you want to go?"

Part of her wanted to drive to SeaTac right now but she knew she couldn't. It was the week of the wedding and she'd need to spend as much time with Danielle this week as possible.

"After the wedding? I'll look at flights."

Owen nodded. "So, we're good."

"Good . . . friends?" Emma asked. She knew it wasn't what he was getting at. They'd never just been good friends. They'd always been partners in one way or another. She'd always been pining after him, thinking he never wanted her for anything more than her mind.

"On good enough terms that you'll let me dance with you at the reception?"

Emma grinned. "I think I'll be comfortable with that."

"One more thing before I go . . . I know you're staying here, with your sister. But I know there are a few openings in my building—"

"Thank you for checking, really. But I've already found a place. I move in the first." It was still the beginning of October, but already November was coming too fast.

"Well that's really great."

"With enough room for a piano," she added. It felt important to say.

"Good. I am happy for you, you know. My ego is bruised, I'll admit."

Emma shrugged. From upstairs, she could hear the bath water turn off and the soft murmurs of Leah getting Henry ready for bed. The house was otherwise quiet, just like the neighborhood. It was quiet enough that she could almost hear leaves blowing down the street, skittering across dimpled pavement. There was no sound of bus breaks bouncing between tall buildings, or people yelling at each other down the street. Here, looking down on the city, everything was calm. Peaceful. Safe.

"It's probably good for you, you know. Getting knocked down a peg or two every once in awhile."

"I'd give away my best violin to be knocked down a peg or two every day by you."

She blushed now, not totally believing his words, but she understood the weight of what he was saying. It was all too perfect—too much like she'd always dreamed it would be.

"You should go now."

He nodded. "I know. But if you need something, anything at all, just call me."

"Thank you."

"And I'll send you my schedule. I'm honored that you asked me to go to New York with you."

Emma smiled as she ushered him to the front door. "I'm glad you've agreed to go with me, as my friend. No expectations."

"That's all we'll be, unless you'd like it to be otherwise."

Closing the door behind Owen, she sighed. He was saying everything that she wanted to hear—everything she'd wanted Connor to say when they'd been together. Owen was even going to come with her to New York, something that Connor never offered to do with her. Maybe when they'd first gotten together, if Emma had been brave enough to go back, Connor would have gone with her. But that was how relationships always were in the beginning: full of hope and false promises, fantasies about a future that would never happen.

27

Standing at the bar, Emma was on her second Cosmo of the night. She was avoiding Owen, especially after having to rehearse walking down the aisle with him. The winery's label was one of her favorites, but tonight was a not a night for grapes, but for hard liquor. Liquor that would help her feel stronger than she knew she was right now.

"My son talks a lot about you," a woman said as she came up next to Emma. She was older, but had aged in a way that would have been labeled "gracefully." Her long hair was pulled back in a gray bun and she had small diamond stud earrings sparkled in the dim light. She wore a black turtleneck and khaki pants, with a silk scarf wrapped around her neck.

"I'm sorry?" Emma asked.

"Owen. He talks so much about you. He always has. It's nice to see that you're spending so much time together."

"All nice things I hope."

She nodded. "Of course. He's quite . . . taken with you. I've never seen him act this way. Usually, and I do love Owen as equally as I love Thomas, but Owen is more selfish. He isn't that way with you."

Emma blushed, looking across the room at Owen. "I hadn't noticed."

"Of course not, dear. But that's fine. You only seem him how you want to see him, or how he lets you see him. And vice versa. I mean, to him you're this inspiring thing, this talented and ambitious woman who is a force of nature."

It was so strange for her to be hearing this from Owen's mother when she didn't even think these things about herself. A force of nature? Surely not quiet and timid Emma Bishop. "You must have me confused with someone else, ma'am."

"Oh no. You're Emma Bishop, aren't you?"

"I am."

"Then I'm talking about you, my dear. Just be careful with him. You know, he's waited for you for quite a long time. I told him he should move on, and there were a few girls here and there—nothing serious, obviously—but he would always feel incomplete with them in his life. He was much better off without them. Much better with you."

"Thank you, ma'am."

"Oh no. Call me Betty, sweetie."

"I'm so sorry I haven't been as in touch with you about the wedding as I should've been. I—"

"Oh, stop. You have had a lot going on these past few months."

Emma hadn't been aware of how close Owen was to his mother. He was always so quiet, so quick to take personal calls out of earshot. Perhaps it was because she, Emma, was the topic of their conversations.

"Well, thank you. Again." Emma picked her glass, which had been refilled, up off of the bar. "And it was really nice meeting you, finally. I should go find Danielle and make sure everything is set for tomorrow."

"Ah yes. Of course, dear. We'll catch up tomorrow."

"Of course."

Emma found Danielle, Molly, and Laurel at a table in the corner.

"Emma-bear. There you are!" Molly said, wrapping her arms around her.

"Sorry, I got caught up talking with Owen and Tom's mother."

"Oh, isn't she just perfect?" Danielle asked. "She's been so helpful with everything. I didn't think that this would all come together the way it did, but between her and my mother, and you guys . . . It's just going to be perfect."

"Of course it will be! Is there anything else you need done for tomorrow?"

Danielle shook her head. "No, everything we need to get ready is already here. Hair and makeup are coming at eleven, photographer's coming then, too. All the favors are here, and will be put out tomorrow—I think we can relax now, Em."

"Actually," Owen said as he approached the table. "Do you mind if I steal your maid of honor for a bit? There are still some things to discuss."

"Em, you have a key card, right? We're heading upstairs."

Emma nodded. "I'll see you guys up there."

"It won't be long," Owen reassured them before leading Emma away from the table. It was quiet in the room; Emma hadn't noticed how it had emptied while she was talking to his mother. Only a few people, some groomsmen and some, what she assumed to be, relatives that were still chatting with Owen's parents remained.

He stopped them in front of the windows, where the, outside, the vineyard stretched out before them into the seemingly never-ending darkness.

"I saw you talking to my mother."

"I was. She's nice. Very . . . open."

He smiled, looking away from her, his gaze focusing on the Sound. "Yeah, I hadn't . . . I didn't think . . ."

"What, Owen?"

"I have a feeling I knew what she said to you, and I didn't want things to be different or difficult between us."

"I don't know what you mean."

He shrugged. "I just, I didn't know how to tell you."

"Tell me what?"

Instantly her heart started to race, a blush rushing across her skin. She hung on his answer, not realizing how much she wanted to hear him say this, if it was what she thought he was going to say, until now.

"That I knew."

"Wait, knew what?"

"That Connor was cheating on you."

"I . . . You, what?" Emma asked in a whisper. Her hands shook and she felt like she was going to throw her very expensive wine up, all over his shoes.

"That day that I called, that you were out with the girls looking at bridesmaid dresses. He called me, asking me for help. He wanted to know how to stop. How he could be a better man for you, and... There's no excuse. He told me what had been going on, and I didn't tell you. I thought that's what my mother was talking to you about."

Emma shook her head slowly. "No, she was saying how good I was for you. How un-selfish and un-self centered you are with me. Why didn't you tell me? Why didn't you tell me before I got—"

"Would you have believed me? Without Rachel's e-mail?"

"Did you tell her to e-mail me?"

"No! No. I didn't. I wanted to talk to you in person about the whole situation. I didn't think it was fair to you to just tell you over the phone, or in an e-mail. I didn't want you to think I had other motives."

"You could've told me this any time you'd seen me over the past few weeks. When you came to my . . . Leah's house. When you brought me back to your apartment."

"I know, I know. I didn't want to ruin your happiness."

"What part of my life do you think I'm happy with right now? This is as low as things are going to get for me. Any of the times you've seen me would've been the perfect time to tell me. Before I got Rachel's e-mail would've been the perfect time to tell me. When I went back to him!"

"It wasn't my place to tell you. It was Connor's."

"If Danielle, or Molly . . . if they'd known, they would've told me."

Emma crossed her arms in front of her, the vodka from her Cosmos selling into her knees, her elbows, into the part of her mind that could even consider Owen's point of view. No, she'd seen *The Wedding Date*. She'd watched too many romantic comedies to know that that letting him just get away with this wasn't going to be how this worked.

"You're right." Owen sighed and looked away. "I should have told you. I wanted to protect you."

"I don't need protecting. I need a man in my life to tell me the truth."

"I'm sorry. I don't—"

"No. You don't. I have to go. I need to think."

Emma turned away from him and walked through the party, out into the rustic lodge-looking lobby and to the elevators. For the next twenty-four hours this was her home. She'd get no distance to process what Owen told her, not when she'd have to be walking down the aisle with him tomorrow.

The elevator door opened on her floor and she walked down to the room she'd be sharing with Danielle and Molly for the night. The door beeped after she inserted the key card, and she pushed it open. Danielle and Molly were sitting on one of the beds, glasses of champagne in hand. Emma heard the door close behind her and immediately started crying.

"Emma!" Molly shot up off the bed. "What's wrong!?"

"Owen. He knew. He knew Connor was cheating on me."

"What!?" Molly yelled. "You have got to be kidding me."

Emma shook her head and headed for the open bottle of wine. "Yeah, he knew after we ran into Rachel while he were dress shopping. Apparently, and get this, Connor *called* him to ask him what to do. That he couldn't stop sleeping with Rachel."

"Fuck him," Danielle said quietly. "Fuck them both. Owen's just as bad as Connor. It's all a big betrayal. You should be pissed. Do you want me to switch the order around so you don't have to walk down the aisle with him?"

Emma stopped pouring the glass of wine.

Wasn't that what sparked this whole thing? She had thought about it so much that initial night, and so many times afterwards, that she'd be walking down an aisle with someone who couldn't even bring himself to propose to her yet. Part of her hoped that by walking down the aisle with Owen, but looking into the crowd at Connor, she'd be able to finally end her infatuation with Owen. She'd know once and for all that it was Connor she wanted to be standing in front of their friends and family with, not Owen.

"No, I still want to."

"Sweetie, don't hurt yourself if you don't have to."

"No, I need to figure this out. I need to know how I feel about him and if I can't stomach him tomorrow, then I'll know."

Molly sat back down on the bed next to Danielle. "And then what? Everything just goes back to normal and you'll . . . what?"

Emma shrugged. "I'll finally be able to move on from this weird triangle I've put myself in. I can finally move on from this stupid crush."

28

As she walked into the ballroom, arm linked with Owen's, she was stunned by the beauty. The day before, the room had been simple and empty. Today, candles flickered on tables while floor-to-ceiling windows provided a view of the mountains at sunset. The Cascadian range was a silhouette against a golden sky and soon the stars would be out. It was a perfect fall day.

The ceremony had been short and painless. Even the pictures that followed were simple. They had gone up to Discovery Park, where the colors on the trees had begun to change over, and where evergreens mixed with Oak trees that began to boast deep reds, oranges, and golds. When it got too cold, they all went back into the limo, and headed back to the winery.

"Would you like a drink?" Owen asked as he shrugged off his jacket, leaving it on the back of his chair. He was seated next to her at the bridal party table. Danielle and Tom sat alone.

"Sure. Vodka Sprite, with a lemon?"

"No problem."

Emma pulled her phone out of the wristlet that matched her bridesmaid's dress. Three texts from Connor, two missed calls, one voice mail. She cleared the screen. It had been a month since she had left him, and up until now they had maintained radio silence. She wasn't going to ruin her night by breaking that now.

"So, you and Owen?" Sarah asked. She was a friend, or acquaintance, really, from college who had driven up from Portland for the wedding.

"I'm not sure what you're implying," Emma countered. "Owen is just a friend."

"Right. He's pretty attentive for just a friend. I can't believe you guys are still trying to pass this off as nothing."

"What do you mean?" Emma asked.

"You know, like in college. When you'd be all, 'Oh no, he's just a friend and there's nothing going on' when there is so something going on."

Emma looked over at the bar as Owen was walking back with their drinks. He smiled as their eyes locked. What he said to her the night before was stuck on permanent repeat. The fact that she didn't say anything back, that she turned and walked away, only made this conversation even more unbearable.

"See?" Jen, another old college friend, grinned. "The way he looks at you, the way you look at him—there just has to be something."

Emma blushed. This conversation wasn't something she'd have with girls she hadn't talked to since her last day of undergraduate classes. She needed Molly, who was preoccupied with Laurel, or even Danielle. But you couldn't pull a bride away on her wedding day to talk through a personal emotional crisis—especially when you'd already talked it to death the night before.

"Here," Owen said as he sat the glass in front of her. "Did you ladies want anything?"

Amber shook her head. "No, I'll go grab something in a minute. They should be starting dinner soon, right?"

"Hopefully. I'm ready to dance," Owen said.

"You're always ready to dance, but usually only for street musicians. Is this a new found love, or one that is alcohol induced?" Emma asked.

"I'm sliding gracefully away from being sober, Emma dear. But yes, I do dance other places than in the middle of the street. Sometimes even in my underwear.

Emma rolled her eyes. "Well, I'm sure all of Belltown gets a nice show when you do."

"The very best."

"What are you guys talking about?" Molly asked, hands on her hips. Emma hadn't noticed that she came over to the table.

"Oh, just the time he dragged me after rehearsal one night to go out dancing, and we ended up listening to this band playing outside of Pike's Place. And he made me dance."

"Wait, you guys are together?" Sarah asked.

"No, no. I'm single."

"Weren't you with that Connor guy, or whatever?" Jen asked.

"I was. We broke up."

"Oh! Okay. I thought I saw something on Facebook, and then I saw that you were doing some concert, or something. You need to be more clear with your updates." Sarah said, taking her phone out of her bag.

"Yeah, hun. We can't properly stalk you." Molly added with a wink.

"I'll try and get better at it. Should I be posting minute by minute updates?"

"Oh yes. We need to know what you're eating, thinking—pictures help, too. Especially of cats." Molly teased.

"I guess I should get one. Isn't that what single spinsters are supposed to do? Adopt a cat?"

"I think spinster is a bit . . . outdated." Owen commented. "A cat would be nice. Dogs are work."

"But Emma with a Golden Retriever, walking around the city center? She'd be a postcard!" Sarah exclaimed.

"Or get a cat," Jen suggested. "You could be Seattle's Holly Golightly."

"I'm pretty sure my new place doesn't allow big dogs like that. I was thinking about getting a small one though. Or a cat."

"Oh, you'd be perfect. And Mr. Owen here is a very good fit for your Paul Varjack." Sarah said, pointing at Owen, who said nothing.

"I think they're going to cut the cake," Emma said, hoping for some sort of out of this conversation. She was thankful no one else seemed to near getting married. If she never had to sit through a conversation like this one again, it would be too soon.

Dinner, cake, and the first dance all passed without disruption. Emma delivered her speech, with the added help of a second drink, without blushing or crying. Owen's speech had been funny, yet touching, with anecdotes about when Danielle and Tom had first gotten together and how he hoped that he, too, would find someone to love the way Tom had found Danielle.

"Care to dance?" Owen asked as the dance floor opened up to everybody. It was a slower song; old, something that she couldn't place.

"Sure," Emma answered as she took his hand. It was the first time she remembered touching him. As she laced her fingers through his, her pulse beat faster. A blush spread across her face.

"You okay?" he asked as he pulled her closer. The scent of his cologne was soft, but comforting. She wasn't sure she had ever smelled it on him before. "Are we okay?"

"We are."

"Just making sure."

He turned them in a slow circle, rocking back and forth, mimicking the other couples. She liked dancing with him, the way she anticipated where he would move and when. It was like when they played together, but almost better somehow. There was nothing riding on this, sure, and it wasn't like they could be out of tune when someone else was playing the music. It was just easy, simple--the way all things with Owen had a tendency to be.

The night continued on with ease. Emma drank more than she had in a long time, but she was also having the most fun she had probably ever had. There was nothing to care about here. She had no boyfriend running off to be with his ex. She had no expectations of the way the night was going to go. Dancing, drinking—these were the only two things that mattered tonight.

"Another dance?" Owen came up behind her as the songs slowed down finally. Danielle winked at her from across the small dance floor.

"If you insist." Emma smiled. Flirting felt good.

They turned in their small circle again. Her arms wrapped around his neck as he pulled her closer. She could feel the heat from his body, smell the alcohol on his breath. It was the closest she had been to someone, physically, in months.

"Emma?"

"Hm?" She looked up at Owen who was staring down at her intensely.

"I really want to kiss you right now."

"Oh?"

"I've been wanting to, for a very long time. But you haven't seemed ready."

"I'm ready now."

As the distance began to close between their mouths, Emma could feel her heart beating in her throat. When they finally touched, she felt like her body caught fire. Mostly-sober, very adult Owen kissed better than twenty-one-year-old Owen.

"Emma?"

She froze, eyes flying open. Turning around, Connor stood behind her, wearing a suit.

"You weren't answering any of my calls or my e-mails. I had to come see you."

Owen stepped next to Emma. She waited for him to touch her hand, to fight this battle, but he stayed quiet. This was hers to handle.

"Connor, please leave. This isn't the time or the place."

Too many questions, too many vodka-bathed thoughts were filling her head. It wasn't fair, that he was here now, that he was ruining this for her.

"Can just come with me for a minute? Just talk to me. The way things ended . . ." he trailed off, his voice catching. She felt bad for him, but only for a moment. What he had done was unforgivable. "You just have no idea how much you mean to me."

"Come on," she said, walking away from the dance floor. She wouldn't let him cause a scene. Not here. "Owen, I'll be right back."

"Oh, you're with him now?" Connor asked, anger riding on the edge of his voice.

"I'm with no one. But we were in the middle of a conversation."

"Well, sorry I interrupted," he snapped.

"You have no reason to be angry at me. We broke up because you were still sleeping with your ex-girlfriend. How I spend my time repairing myself, and who I date after, is none of your concern."

They had walked into the lobby. Emma was doing her best to keep her voice down, but was failing. The only other time she had been this angry, this embarrassed, was when Rachel had told her the truth about what happened.

"I didn't realize that when you weren't taking my phone calls it was because you found someone else. Or, were you with him before we broke up?"

"What the hell are you talking about? Are you forgetting that you are the one who cheated on me, repeatedly, with your ex-girlfriend?"

"And I apologized for that. But I'm not going to sit here feeling bad if you were with him."

Emma took a deep breath.

"I was not with Owen before we broke up. Nor am I with him now. We were just dancing and talking. Not that it's any of your goddamn business anymore. So, if you would, please leave. I am done with this."

"He kissed you! I saw it!"

"Good bye, Connor."

"Wait! Stop. I'm sorry. I fucked up, I just . . . I saw you two, and I thought . . . I didn't mean any of that. I just wanted to come here and apologize. I miss you Emma. So god damn much."

"But that doesn't change anything."

"Just please give me another chance."

Emma shook her head as she crossed her arms in front of her

chest. For a moment, she wavered. He looked on the verge of tears, which made her heart ache. She had put so much time and effort into their relationship, thinking it was one thing when it had ended up being something else entirely. He had bought the ring for her, had planned on marrying her—despite the fact that he couldn't seem to get over Rachel. But the ring meant something. The ring was something he never wanted to give Rachel.

"You had enough chances to stop sleeping with her. To put me first. And you didn't. Every time she asked, you went to her. No matter how many times you probably told her that it was the last time, you still went back to her. You got me a ring. Great. You love me. But you love *her* more. I refuse to be someone's back up. The person someone comes home to after they've been out with someone else. I'm supposed to overlook you sleeping with someone else because we live together? Because, eventually, you come home to me?" Emma shook her head. "No. I deserve more than that. Way more than that. And if you can't see that, then you're not the man I thought you were. And you definitely don't deserve me."

By now, guests from the wedding were wandering out. Looking at the large grandfather clock, Emma saw that she missed it: her chance with Owen, the rest of the wedding. On a night that was supposed to be anything but about Connor, he had stayed at the center of it. All focus would have to be on him.

"I'm leaving now."

"Wait, Em—" he grabbed her arm, but she backed away from him. She could see Owen on the far side of the lobby, watching them for a minute, before he left without saying a word.

"Goodbye, Connor."

She walked away from him for the last time.

Her heart beat in her throat and her ears as she moved through the hotel, finding the elevators, and taking it to Owen's floor. The way the night ended was, by no means, how she wanted it to go. She had so many things she wanted to say to Owen, so many things that hadn't been talked about last night--and then Connor showed up. She needed to clear things up.

She needed to finish what had already been started.

"This is a surprise." Owen said. He was still in his tuxedo, though the shirt was untucked and he had taken off his shoes. The bowtie was sitting on the table behind him, the jacket still in view. He still looked good.

"Yeah, well," Emma faltered. The liquid courage she had gained at the wedding was fading. Connor showing up had been something she hadn't thought would happen, but she should have known better: she knew him, she knew what he thought would make things better and still she had felt blindsided by his presence. But nothing had changed for her. She didn't love him anymore.

"I just ..."

"Came to get this?" He offered her the wristlet she had forgotten about completely as she dragged Connor out of the wedding.

"No." She sighed. "Just that ... I don't know."

He nodded.

"I love you."

She reached out, grabbed his shirt, and pulled him towards her. Standing on her toes, she kissed him and he kissed her back.

Wrapping his arms around her, he picked her up, carrying her into his hotel room, continuing to kiss her even as he closed the door behind them. It wasn't what she had planned on saying to him, but it got her point across.

Afterwards, as they lay tangled up in the clean, white sheets of his bed Emma wasn't sure she had ever felt so relaxed, so happy, or so loved ever before.

"What're you thinking about?" he asked, playing with her hair as she rested on his chest.

"I could get used to this."

He laughed, the sound reverberating through his chest. "Yeah, me too."

29

OCTOBER 2005

"Emma Bishop, as I live and breathe," Owen said, leaning against the door frame of Emma's door, red cup in his hand. It was part custom, but mostly habit, to keep the door propped open while she was getting work done. Unlike freshman year, when she'd feared the strangers who would linger in her doorway, she knew everyone now. Their presence, for the most part, was welcome.

"Well, you did stumble down to my door."

He looked up, and around, and then took another long sip from his cup. She only had a desk light on, and it cast long shadows across his face. "I did. But it was for an important reason."

"And what reason is that?"

Emma turned away from the piles of sheet music she had been looking over. With finals approaching, and with that a showcase concert, she hope to have felt more prepared than she actually did. Owen being here, standing in her doorway, only made things worse.

"I want you to duet with me."

Emma raised her eyebrows. It had been mentioned before, years ago: during their first class they took together. They had played a duet together then, sure, but composing something together was a much bigger commitment than she was looking to make. The thought of it made her blush; spending hours with him, close, making music--it would do nothing, if not make the crush she had on him worse.

"You've said that before."

"I know, but seriously, if you don't play with me I'm going to fail." He crossed into the room and sat down on her bed. She could smell whatever cheap alcohol he had gotten access to from where she sat. If anything, it helped her keep a level head about this: that he was here, that they were alone.

"You're not going to fail. You're the best musician in our year."

"No, I'm the best composer. There's a difference. No one else interprets my stuff the way you do. You get me, Em."

Her phone vibrated, alerting her to a text message.

"Who's that?" he asked.

"No one important."

It was actually a guy from her piano lab who wanted her to help him with a project. With it being as late as it was right now, she doubted he wanted actual help with a project. Only Owen was crazy enough to want to work this late, and this drunk.

"So, I have your undivided attention because I really ... you need to come with me. You need to listen to what I wrote for us."

Emma glanced at the clock on her desk. "Owen, it's almost midnight. Molly'll be back soon. I should really get to sleep."

"It's mid-term time of term. Live a little."

"I really can't."

He stood up and held out his empty hand, the other still holding the red cup. "Come on," he begged. "Come with me."

"Where?"

"You'll see."

Emma looked at the clock again, and then back up at Owen. He looked glazed over. Whatever he'd been drinking had reached his eyes. Going with him didn't feel right, but she stood up anyway. In all of her years in college, she hadn't strayed or gone after the experiences she assumed she was supposed to be having. She didn't fuck around with guys, and she never skipped class. If she followed him now, it would be the most daring thing she had done since she left New York City.

"Fine. But you only have me for an hour."

He smiled. "Deal."

She grabbed her phone and keys, and tucked them into her back pockets, before following him out into the brightly lit hallway. They walked without speaking, cutting through the maze of hallways and out into the cold spring night. Goose bumps flashed across her skin as sea air brushed against her cheeks, but she didn't complain.

"Don't tell," Owen said finally as he pulled a set of keys out of the pocket of his jeans.

Emma tilted her head to the side, brow furrowed. He shook his head and opened the door to the music building.

The hallways were dark, lit only by the red glow of the emergency exit signs. She followed him, silent still, until they came to the auditorium doors.

"Still coming?" he asked in a whisper.

Emma nodded.

They walked along the carpeted aisle, and as they approached the stage, Emma could see the violin case resting against the piano bench.

"You planned this."

"Maybe."

Instead of taking the stairs, he set his cup on the edge of the stage and pushed himself up. Turning towards her, he offered his hands to help but she declined. Instead, Emma took the stairs. There were many things on private bucket list, things that she would never share with anyone, and playing like this—in an empty, dark auditorium, haunting the building, was at the top.

"I'll show you what I've been working on and you can fall in, okay?" he asked, appearing more sober now that he got his violin out of his case.

"Do you have sheet music for me?"

He shook his head. "It's still being worked on."

Sitting on the bench, Emma placed her hands on the cold keys, and waited. He pulled a long, low note out, and then another. The melody felt sad, longing even, as if the song was about someone he wanted, but couldn't have. She closed her eyes and let him play on, noting to herself the moments where piano might work, where he needed something to harmonize with him. Where he needed support.

As he began the song again, Emma opened her eyes and began to play. Slowly at first, waiting for his approval of what she thought might sound right. He wasn't the best at composing and she tried to fill in the spots he missed, the parts of the puzzle that he couldn't see.

Suddenly she noticed that the violin had stopped, even though she'd kept playing on. Pulling her fingers from the keys, she looked around for him and found that he had disappeared. Getting up, she tried to use her phone for a flashlight.

"Owen?"

"In here," he called from the side of the stage. Walking towards the sound, she entered one of the aisles between the different layers of curtains.

"I don't think we're supposed to be back here."

For her, it was a space reserved for the juniors and seniors that had been invited there. She had played a few times on this stage, sure, but she had never entered from the wings.

"Too late for that, come on, you need to watch this."

She took his outstretched hand and followed him to a drafty corner of the backstage where television screen glowed in front of him.

"Look," he said, pressing a button as the screen changed to when they had started playing. At first it was clumsy, but after a minute they had synchronized. She watched herself, listened to the way she played, listened to how they played together.

"Emma, this is . . . you are . . . "

She could still smell the alcohol on his breath. And, as he leaned in to kiss her, she could taste it, too.

"Owen," she pulled away from him, but her body felt like it was on fire.

"Em, I've wanted you for so long. But if you don't want to, that's okay. It's okay."

"Here?" She looked around. He took her hand again, his palm damp with sweat, and led her to the space between the curtains. Shrugging off his jacket, he dropped it on the floor, and reached back her again. His hands wrapped around each side of her cheeks and he bent to kiss her with her fire this time, more desire.

As she let herself lay down with him, and felt the weight of him on top of her, she got lost in what was going on. Just like when they were playing together, she moved with him, anticipated the harmony, and drowned in the moment.

Afterwards, as her bare skin touched the cold wood of the stage, she looked over at him. He was looking up at the ceiling, his hands moving as if playing an imaginary violin. Suddenly, he stopped, got up, and stumbled towards the nearest garbage can.

"Owen?" Emma called out, quickly dressing.

"I don't feel well," he said, getting down on his hands and knees, and throwing up again.

"Here, your clothes, and, um, I'll go get you some paper towels or something?"

In all honesty she didn't know what to do: run back to her dorm, or try and help him, or cry.

This was a night she had been dreaming about since she had met him. Now, the memory was tainted with the smell of vomit and cheap vodka—a memory that, at this point, she wasn't sure if he would share with her in the morning. Whenever Molly had come back to the room and got sick from drinking, she'd never remember what happened the night before.

"No, it's okay. Just go," Owen said, wiping his mouth. He pulled his boxers on, and then his jeans. Even in the glow of the emergency exit sign, she could see traces of vomit in his long, dark curls.

"I can't just leave you like this," Emma argued.

"No, please. This is embarrassing. I'll be fine."

Backing away from him, she turned and walked quickly off stage and out of the auditorium. She felt guilty for leaving, but the embarrassment over what happened, both for her, and for him, was what pushed her back to her dorm room.

"You were out late," Molly said as Emma walked into the room.

"Yeah, I was out with Owen."

"Oh?" Molly said, eyebrows high, too excited for three in the morning.

"Yeah, but I really need to crash. I'll tell you about it in the morning."

Emma changed quickly into pajamas, throwing the clothes that smelled like his cologne into her hamper, and got into bed.

She rolled away from Molly and, as she fell asleep, she didn't know what she was hoping for more: that he would remember what happened, or that he wouldn't.

30

Being back on the subway was like playing the piano again. Emma stood, gloved-hand on the metal pole, anticipating when the train would stop and go, her legs apart just so to balance her weight. When Owen had suggested getting a car to take them to their hotel, Emma laughed. No, she had said, if she was going to go back home this was the way it needed to be.

Had it been her senior year of high school again, she would've been standing there with headphones on, listening to classical pieces over and over again. Now, she wanted to take in the soundtrack of the city. Besides, it was getting close to rush hour; musicians were bound to be hopping in and out of cars, hoping to catch a quick buck off an in-awe tourist.

As the train pulled into the 42nd Street station, she went to move forward, but then remembered Owen. In the past when she traveled, it had only been with her mother, and they always anticipated when the other one was going to move. Owen was a stranger to this city. He had no idea.

"Come on," Emma said as the doors opened, her hand reaching out to him. He grabbed it, and they exited the too-full car like salmon trying to move upstream. "This way."

They moved down a long hallway that was full of people and noise. Everyone was focused: they had a train to catch, or they needed to get out of the underground.

"Why didn't we come up at Grand Central?" Owen asked as they began to climb the large staircase up to street level.

"You'll see. Everyone needs to experience this once. And I really do mean *once*."

As they came up on the street, Emma was overwhelmed by the city: horns and sirens bounced on the wall of buildings that lined the street. Times Square grew up around them, too full of people. Tourists, cameras in hand, mixed with the people who sold bike tours, who sold demo tapes (no, not sold—asked for donations), who sold their souls to pay the bills by wearing animal costumes. If it wasn't the people shouting around her that made her feel overwhelmed, it was the advertisements that smiled down on them from every surface. Broadway shows, television shows, and even clothing companies had bought up every inch of free space, just to try and get the attention of those thousands of people who came through the square every day.

"Wow."

Emma looked up at Owen. Like a child too caught up with what was on television, his eyes, open wide, reflected the blue glow of the screens around them. It helped soften the blow of the smell of urine, of the feeling of being overcrowded, and all the other reasons why she hated Times Square.

"Everyone needs to experience it once," Emma repeated. "The next time you come back here, you'll be avoiding Times Square like the rest of us."

"I can see why. Have you ever done New Year's Eve here?"

It was one of the first personal questions she could ever remember him asking. What her favorite composers were, sure, but this was outside of their musical world.

"No. It's a bit much. Just being in the city is hectic enough. Some people are really dedicated to doing New Years here, though . . ."

"Dedicated?"

"Diaper dedicated. If you try and make it out to use the bathroom, you lose your spot."

He whistled. "Isn't our hotel near here?"

Emma nodded, and pointed in the direction of American Eagle Outfitters. "It's just off that street. Next to the Church of Scientology."

"Interesting. What if you spent New Year's Eve there, instead of out here."

"That would be more fun, I think. If you have windows on the right side of the hotel, I'm sure you can even see some of what's going on."

Emma didn't want to admit that, if she was spending New Year's Eve in a hotel room with Owen, watching the ball drop would not be high on her priority list. She and Connor had always gone out, always been social and networking for the holiday. She couldn't remember ever spending the night with just one person, in something so intimate. The idea appealed to her.

"Maybe we could do that this year."

Emma raised her eyebrows.

"If this trip goes well, I mean. And you want to come back. "

"Let's . . . go get checked in. January is still a few months away."

Heading in the direction of the hotel, Emma avoided eye and hand contact with him. His suggestion surprised her. Sure, she was staying with him for this trip, and they had only reserved one room for the nights they would be here, but it wasn't as if she was sleeping in his bed back in Seattle. She hadn't spent the night with him since the wedding.

"Ma'am," the doorman said as they walked into the sleek, dark entryway of the Paramount Hotel.

"Thank you."

On the second floor of the main lobby, a DJ stood at a table, generating the perfect soundtrack to the evening. A couple sat with their laptops on a leather couch, sipping wine, while woman in a suit stood at the main counter, checking in.

Emma and Owen walked up to the counter after the other woman finished.

"Checking in. Last name is Bishop."

Emma handed over her credit card and driver's license. Owen went to hand the woman his as well, but Emma swatted him away.

"Thank you Ms. Bishop. Here you go, your room number is 9016. You can take the elevators there, to the left, and the lounge is open for dinner."

"Thank you," she said, taking the room keys from the woman, and turning back towards Owen. "Ready?"

Owen nodded and followed her to the elevators.

They went to their floor in silence. As the elevator doors slid open, slow and methodical, they were greeted with the local time and weather on the black wall.

"Which way—?" Owen began to ask.

"Over here." Emma said, leading them to the right and down the hall of identical dark doors.

Sliding the key card in the door, it clicked and beeped, granting them access to the suite.

"You didn't have to get something like this," Owen said, walked into the living room. Unlike the hallway and lobby, everything in here was bright. Large windows looked out over rooftops, the St. James Place Theater sign glowing red against the indigo sky. Emma remembered now, as she looked out on the city, that it never got truly dark here.

"You don't like it?" Emma asked as she set her bag down on the coffee table.

"It's just too much. You have to let me help you pay for the room."

"It's how I like to travel. This has nothing to do with you."

Owen shook his head. "I have no doubt that you have expensive tastes, but—"

"I would've gotten this room whether you were with me or not. Stop fretting," Emma teased.

"I'm not fretting."

He walked over to her and placed his hands on either side of her face. She stopped breathing, waiting for him to kiss her. She didn't realize until now how badly she wanted him to kiss her.

"See? Now you're fretting."

He pulled away, moving towards the bedroom, and flicked on the light switch. Emma stayed where she was, taking the moment to collect herself. She felt like she was in college again, that they were back on that stage. The lines between then and now were too blurred. At least if history was repeating itself, she thought, it came with hotel rooms instead of dorm rooms.

"So, what do you want to do for dinner? Go out? Room service?" he called from the other room.

"I don't know. We could try the hotel restaurant," Emma called back. She assumed that the couch doubled as a sleeper. Moving the coffee table, she pulled the cushions off the top, and pulled the bed out.

"What're you doing?" Owen asked, peeking his head out of the door that divided the living room from the bedroom.

"Making up the bed. What does it look like I'm doing?"

"No. Stop. You're not sleeping out here."

Emma looked up at him and blushed. "I didn't want to assume anything. I wasn't sure . . ."

"Come on," he said, holding up his key card. "Dinner first, and then we'll worry about this situation."

"You're just trying to get my drunk so you can take advantage of me," Emma teased.

"If I remember right," he began as he opened the hotel room door, "it was you who took advantage of a drunk me. Both times. Come on."

"I didn't . . . you remember that? The first time?" she asked as they stepped into the elevator.

"Of course I do."

"Oh."

Emma blushed. The elevator doors opened and they walked out, heading across the lobby and through the open doors of the hotel's small restaurant.

It was dark, just like the rest of the hotel, with gold and metallic accents. Small windows were set far back, looking out on what the nightlife of Midtown Manhattan had to offer. While there were high, leather backed stools at the gray, steel-looking bar, there were leather booths tucked on the sides and in the back of the small wine bar. The whole experience looked to be intimate, with small tables and comfortable chairs and tea lights in the center of the tables.

"Would you like a table, or are you sitting at the bar?" the hostess asked.

"Emma?" Owen asked.

"A table would be fine."

"Of course. Sit anywhere you'd like."

Emma walked to the long, gray couch and sat behind one of the small tables, leaving Owen to sit either next to her, or in one of the deep arm chairs, upholstered in a white and gray chevron fabric. When he sat in the chair, she felt disappointed.

"Do you know what you'd like, or do you need a moment? We do have a small menu," the hostess said, handing it to them, "and we do have a full service bar."

"I'll take a cosmo," Emma said as she looked over the menu.

"And for you, sir?"

"I'll . . . have a Smoky Scotsman, please," Owen said, ordering one of their signature cocktails.

"Perfect. I'll get those right away."

"So," Owen said as he turned towards her. "I'm a little out of my element here. Does anything look good on there?"

"A few things. I'd hope they would be up to your standards, though. I know you're used to getting spoiled by Michael."

"He's a great waiter. Don't tease."

"I'm not. I'm just not sure you know how to order in any other restaurant anymore," Emma teased, handing over the menu to him.

"Do you know what you're getting?" he asked?

"I do."

"Well, come on. Give me some guidance."

Emma shook her head, relieved that she saw their hostess coming back with their drinks. "You're on your own."

"So cruel." Owen said, smiling as he shook his head.

"I know." Emma teased back.

"Are we all set?" the hostess asked.

"Just an order of French fries for me, please."

She needed her favorite comfort food now more than ever.

"Same." Owen said, handing the menu back.

"I'll put this in right away."

"Well," Owen began as the hostess left, "I don't think she looked very pleased."

"She doesn't know who she's serving tonight, that's all."

"You mean, people who are going to spend more money on alcohol than on food?"

Emma rolled her eyes, but still smiled. "No. She doesn't know that being a picky eater is your thing."

"My *thing*?" He repeated as he lifted up his glass. "I didn't realize I had a thing."

"Owen, you definitely have a thing."

He laughed before taking a long sip of his drink. Emma did the same, enjoying the way the vodka settled in her fingers and elbows immediately.

"This is surreal, you know," he began, "us being here, together. I never thought in a million years."

"And I never thought I'd be coming back here, least of all with you," she said. "But my whole life is kind of surreal right now."

"You thought you'd be coming back here with Connor?"

Emma flinched. "No. I didn't think I'd be coming back here at all."

She cursed her mother for bringing it up at all. Everything was fine before the phone call. She was wallowing in the hurt that was left in the wake of leaving Connor. It wasn't like she needed even more emotional trauma at the time. And yet, here she was.

Because facing what happened on September 11th was easier than facing Connor.

No. That was a lie. That wasn't even close to the truth. But the vodka was setting in and her thoughts were melting together.

"And why not?"

"It hurts too much, Owen. Being here physically hurts." She took another drink, almost emptying her glass. She would need a refill soon.

"I didn't realize—"

"No," Emma shook her head, "I didn't mean that at you, just in . . . in general. I don't know. It's just a lot of pain all at once."

She had never spoken so candidly with him before. It was weird.

"But, it's going to be okay—or whatever I'm supposed to say here."

Emma laughed. That was the Owen she knew.

The hostess dropped off their fries and they asked for refills on their drinks. Emma could feel the drink in her legs and her toes, the way she didn't move stiffly but in a smooth, fluid motion. She liked this feeling. Warm, Molly called it. She was feeling warm.

"So you remember?" she asked before biting into a fry.

"Remember? Oh! Yes. You didn't think I did?" Owen asked.

"No. We never talked about it so—"

The hostess brought over their drinks and took the empty glasses away.

"—I thought you didn't remember. You were pretty drunk."

"No I wasn't."

"Owen, you puked afterwards."

"Well, when you put it that way," he joked. "But no, Emma. Of course I remembered. It was a great night. We finished the duet that night."

"We finished the duet, and then we never played it for anyone. You just made it different for your concert."

"We should play it for someone."

Emma shook her head, laughing. "You don't even want to play it the way we wrote it."

"No, I do. I just . . ." he trailed off.

"What?"

"I couldn't play it while you were still with Connor. It felt . . . wrong. Like we were lying to him, or like you were cheating on him."

She took another drink and digested his words. It was, the more she thought about it, like she was cheating on Connor when she played that song. The way it was conceived, the way it was celebrated

—the whole point of that song, she now realized, was that night. The night they broke into the auditorium and had sex on the stage. And wrote that song.

"I concede to your point."

"You see what I mean, then."

"Yes. Quite so."

Owen drank fast now, the liquid in his glass disappearing faster than Emma could drink her cosmo. Pushing away his now empty glass, he looked up at the hostess, who was sitting on her phone.

"Another drink, or?" he asked Emma.

"Sorry about that, is there anything else I can get you?" the hostess interrupted.

"No, I think we're all set," Emma said, looking to Owen for confirmation. She could keep drinking, but she didn't want to feel terrible tomorrow. Well, more terrible than she already knew she was going to feel.

"All right, here you go," the woman said, handing over the check. Owen took it and signed it quickly, scribbling a tip down, and handed it back to her.

"Here you go," Owen said, standing up. "Have a great night."

"You too."

Emma followed Owen out of the restaurant and up to the elevators, giggling as they walked.

"Are you giggling?"

"No. You're giggling."

"You're drunk," he countered.

"Hardly. I'm just . . . warm. That's all. Emma Bishop does *not* get drunk. She just gets warm."

"Ah, yes. How could I forget?"

He pressed the number for their floor and she waited as the elevator went up slowly to their floor. It felt like forever, being in here with him, waiting to get back to their hotel room. Maybe this was the way it would've been if Connor hadn't showed up that night. Or maybe she would've never had the courage to go to Owen's room. Not that it mattered now. It happened. And now she was about to spend the next two nights in a hotel room with him. The thought sobered her a little.

The elevator doors opened and she walked out, Owen following her. He let them into the room, and she walked to the bed, and threw herself on it, bouncing a little as she landed.

"I've never seen you like this before. Other than the night of the wedding."

"Like what?"

"Uninhibited."

"It happens. Usually at the bottom of a bottle. But, it happens."

"Maybe you're going to be the one who throws up tonight," Owen chuckled.

"Maybe. Probably not. We have a big day tomorrow."

"Oh?"

"We're going to the Memorial."

That thought was sobering enough for her.

"Ah, yes. Are you sure you want to go still?"

"I need to go, Owen. It has to happen so I can go back to Seattle and just . . . I can move on. And make roots. Or something."

"Or something."

"You're teasing me."

"Only a little."

Emma rolled her eyes. "Fine. Tease me. So be it."

"There's something I never thought I'd hear you say."

Taking one of the pillows, she threw it in his direction. He dodged it, picked it up, and tossed it back to her.

"I don't remember you being this much fun in college," Emma commented.

"I don't remember you being this much fun, either. Can I sit down without you hitting me with a pillow?"

"I suppose." She scooted over, pulling the bottom of her dress down as she sat on her knees. "Was I really not much fun in college?"

"You were fun enough. A little quiet. A little caught up with your work."

"You're one to talk."

"I don't know what you're talking about," he said, glancing sideways at her. "I was always the fun time guy."

"No. You were always the, let's practice until three in the morning to get this piece right, guy."

"And the show up at your dorm room drunk with an idea for a new piece, guy."

"Well, yes. That, too."

Emma laid back on the bed. She could hear sirens and horns even through the thick windows. They hadn't even bothered to close the curtains. She could see the bluish glow of Times Square thrown down the street, bouncing off of the brick and glass of the buildings. Sleep was coming for her. She could feel it settle into her limbs and on her eyelids, luring her away from the moment. She knew she should get ready for bed: wash her face, change, and make up the sofa bed. But she didn't move, not even when Owen laid down next to her.

They stayed there in silence, in the darkness, listening to the city.

31

Emma was surprised that she could walk down the street to the 42nd Street station, hop on the blue line, and still take it all the way to the World Trade Center. It wasn't just the initial shock of forcing herself to do this thing that terrified her. Sure, that was a big part of it. Her hands shook, sweaty against the cool metal of the pole she held onto as she stood in the subway car. Every part of her body screamed at her, demanding that she run the opposite direction, away from danger—away from the memory of debris and ash falling like snow.

The other shock was that nothing had changed, really. There was no added security, no scar left on the wrist of her city. Even in the aftermath of Hurricane Sandy, she had assumed that things would just be different. You couldn't drive through Times Square anymore, but other than that, things were the same.

It still only took twelve minutes to get the World Trade Center station. The closer they got to their destination, the emptier their car became, but the more full it felt. As physical bodies left, ghosts replaced them. As they pulled into the station, Emma got chills. The white letters of the station sign were too bold against the black background and, as they stepped out onto the platform, the station was too empty.

She didn't want to be underground anymore. It felt too much like a tomb.

Steering them in the direction of the exit, she raced up the stairs, and out onto Church Street. The sun was bright for mid-October. Emma pushed the sunglasses that had been on top of her head back down onto her nose.

"You sure you want to do this?" Owen asked again. It was the fourth time he'd asked so far.

"Yeah. We've made it this far."

She led them up Church Street, walking past the Federal Building, and into the shadow of the new World Trade Center building. She had seen in the background of their travels yesterday, but hadn't acknowledged it. Now she had to. It was next to her, complete, no longer just an idea.

1776 feet. Taller than the towers had been.

1776. Suck on that, terrorists.

She kept walking.

Crossing Liberty, she turned up the street, bracing herself. She was thankful that Owen stopped asking questions, that he let her lead them on this, and that he was here at all.

"Tribute Center?" he asked, motioning towards people lined up outside of glass doors. Putting a hand over her eyes to shield the sun, she looked up at the sign. She hadn't heard about it, just the Memorial and the museum.

"Maybe after."

"Okay."

Holding her breath, she walked through the group of people lined up outside, waiting for their guided tour by someone who had experienced 9/11—someone who'd been here, who had lost a loved one, who had been just late enough to work that day to miss everything.

She walked fast past the 10/10 fire house, her resolve beginning to crumble. This was too much: too much sadness, fear, and hatred all in one day.

As if sensing this, Owen took her hand and squeezed it.

"There's the entrance," Owen said, giving her hand another squeeze.

"I know. I just wanted to see this first. My dad told me about it."

She walked up to the bronze memorial and she felt almost better seeing the flags, stuffed animals, and candles still set up against the wall. She wanted to touch it, to feel the faces and the hands and the names of the first responders who had died that day. She wanted to touch the smoking towers, and the pieces that had already started to crumble. It was beautiful and horrifying. It was almost worse than being in the memorial itself.

"Okay, let's go."

Emma walked up to the corner, Owen still holding her hand, and crossed the street in the direction of the memorial entrance. It was now or never. She could do this now, reclaim her city, or get back on a plane tomorrow and hide in Seattle forever. But maybe New York wasn't her city anymore. Maybe it was just the place she lived once, loved once, that would always be in her heart but would never again be her home. Just like Connor.

Once they got together, he was the one who talked her through her panic attacks. They spent every anniversary of the attacks together, with her watching the footage from *The Today Show* from that morning. He made sure that she ate, that she was woken up from nightmares, that she made it through the anniversary each year. But they had never talked about visiting the memorial. Not even once.

Handing the woman their tickets, they went through the process of entering the memorial; the long gates, the metal detectors, the other added security features that almost had her longing for the security checkpoint at the airport. At least that was less extensive.

But then it was time.

At first, when they entered the memorial, it looked like another park had cropped up in the middle of downtown. A park of mirrors, surrounded by mirrors.

"You can do this," Owen whispered.

She kept moving.

Through trees, along the concrete path, she walked past laughing kids, and past strangers smiling and taking pictures. Her anger flared, but she kept moving. She didn't stop until she reached the North Pool. She didn't expect it to be this beautiful. Maybe it was just the weather, or the kids laughing, but now that she was here, the pain that had been radiating through her body since she turned onto Liberty Street had subsided—at least for the moment.

Taking a few steps forward, she touched the smooth surface of the pool's edge, her fingers tracing the outline of a stranger's name. A stranger that she would feel forever connected to. That they would all feel connected to.

Hearing the sound of a plane made her look up and a shiver worked its way through her. It reflected in the surface of the new World Trade Center, and kept going. Like it was supposed to be there.

"Strange," Owen commented, stepping closer to her.

Emma shrugged. "Our plane took us pretty close on the way here."

"True."

"It doesn't mean I like it," she added.

"I didn't think you did."

She moved down one side of the pool, careful to look at each name. To pay her respects. Yellow roses stuck out from some of the names and she wished she knew the meaning. She hadn't researched much before the trip. If she had, she would've over-thought the whole thing and cancelled. It was better that she lept into this blindly.

"I . . ." Emma started, then stopped. She felt anxious now, her hands shaking, her knees quivering as she stood at the corner of the North Pool. "I think I've had enough."

"Okay."

He didn't question it, but instead led her to the exit, where she had the option of going into the gift shop, or going out on the street. She picked the street.

"How're you doing?" he asked, standing in front of her, hands on her shoulders.

"I think I want to go back uptown."

"Where to?"

"Central Park."

The ghosts would understand, wouldn't they? She had made it here, had gone in, had seen their names. But there was only so much of it she could take. Being here reminded her of why she'd left New York in the first place. She needed to get back to the places that she loved.

"Okay. How do we get there? I can pull it up on my app . . ." Owen started, but Emma shook her head.

"We can just go back the way we came and get off at the Natural History Museum."

"Like, the museum in that movie?"

Emma stopped and looked at him. "'Like that museum in the movie'? Who are you. What have you done with sophisticated, very adult Owen?"

He smiled. "I have many secrets."

"And your secrets are that you watch kids movies, alone, in your big empty loft after dinner alone?" She stopped walking. "Sorry, that came out . . . mean."

"It did. But it's true. I love those movies."

"You're ridiculous."

"Yeah, but you're not shaking anymore."

She couldn't argue with that.

❀

THE RIDE WAS SHORT, which she was grateful for, and as they entered the Park, she could feel herself relax. It was more beautiful to her than even the view from Owen's loft: trees beginning to change over, leaves sprinkling the cement paths, flowers still in bloom.

"I can see why you like it here," Owen commented as they began to walk through Shakespeare Garden.

"It's better in the summer. It's humid, very humid, but the flowers are all blooming. These ones, these are all flowers mentioned in Shakespeare plays."

"It's fitting for you."

"What do you mean?"

"Just that you'd like it in here. You're a little like Ophelia, aren't you?"

"Does that make you Hamlet?"

He laughed. "No. I haven't been visited by the ghost of my dead father recently. And I don't think my mother is having an affair with my uncle. So, I think we're safe."

"But your father isn't dead. And your mother isn't crazy."

"No," he chucked, "as you can attest to."

"I like her."

"She likes you. You might even be invited to a holiday dinner or two."

Emma looked up at him as they walked. It wasn't just that his mother liked her, it was that he wanted her around longer than just this weekend, and was thinking beyond the end of this month. She wasn't sure if she was ready yet.

"It's only October. I've got time to figure holidays out. I need to figure everything else out, first."

"Actually, Thanksgiving is a month away. But you're right. You need to figure out the small things first. Like a job," he stated.

"I have a job."

"Not a job that makes you happy. I've watched you, Emma. You're good at what you do, but you don't love it. You don't love it the way you love playing the piano, or the way I love you."

They rounded the Loeb Boathouse, and kept walking past a photo shoot. What were normalities here were quickly becoming normalities in Seattle. Despite all of the strangeness, Emma could a part of herself growing back that she thought was long gone. She could feel herself allowing his words to sink in and they didn't scare her. The memorial, the deaths, the planes, the unmarked graves where people laughed and played—they were things that scared her. She didn't want to forget the past, to forget all of the pain and heartache. But she also wanted something more, something bigger than she had with Connor. Something bigger than she even felt for the piano.

"I love you too."

Owen stopped walking and took Emma's hands in his. "I wanted you to know that I have no expectations from you. You're healing, and we're figuring this out. I just want you to know that you're loved. That someone cares about you."

"I appreciate that."

He squeezed her hand and they kept walking, fingers laced together. This was their first time exchanging the phrase other than after Danielle and Tom's wedding. She needed something without expectation right now. It wasn't that she didn't want to be with Owen —she wanted to be with him now more than ever. It was getting over the fear that he'd hurt her, that he'd betray her the way Connor had. That now that they'd slept together, he'd lose his allure and she'd start looking for someone new.

"The New York Phil, they're holding auditions. Next month."

"For piano?"

"Yes. Perhaps you'd like to make a name for yourself in your own orchestra."

She let the idea roll over her as they left the park and walked back to the hotel. It wasn't a dream she thought she'd be able to pursue anymore. Like so many other things, it had been lost with age or she had talked herself out of wanting it. Her focus shifted to Connor, to a life around him. Now, she was just lost.

"It's something to consider. I'm just not sure that I'm ready to come back here. Besides, I just signed a lease."

He grinned, his smile bright in the late afternoon sun, as they meandered back through Times Square. "You did. So, now what do we do?"

"Now, as in five minutes from now, or now, ambiguous future now?"

Owen tilted his head back and forth, comically weighing the options. "Five minutes."

"We're getting pizza."

"From where? The Scientology church?"

Emma laughed and stopped in front of the small pizzeria that deserved the term "hole in the wall." It was a common sign of a good pizza place.

"No. Here."

Owen crinkled his nose in disgust.

"Such a snob. No, we can take it back up to the room."

"I'm no such thing."

Emma ordered the pizza, two slices of cheese, and leaned against the counter as they waited for the slices to be heated up.

"You are. But it's not unwarranted. It's even charming sometimes."

He chuckled. "Only sometimes?"

"Yes. Only sometimes. Like when we go to Purple Cafe, and Michael is there. Or when you're trying to pick what music to listen to, you're a bit of a diva. But, otherwise, you're okay."

She took the pizza boxes and walked back out onto the street, Owen following.

"I'm not that much of a diva, am I?"

"You like your loft at exactly sixty-eight degrees, your wine fridge organized by place of origin, and your shampoo is more expensive than mine."

"Okay, okay. You got me there. But I'm not the one who refuses to do something perfectly acceptable as means of income."

"Teaching?"

"Yes, teaching. You'd be great at it."

"It's just not something I ever envisioned for myself."

"Look around, love. None of this is what you imagined for yourself."

As the elevator doors closed on them, there was a sinking feeling settling in her stomach. He was right; none of this was what she thought she wanted for herself. But she was writing and playing music again. That was something. Something that she'd share with him when the time was right. For once, she had something that was all hers and she wanted to keep it that way. Just for a little while.

"I think I have something else going for me, but I'll keep it mind," Emma conceded as they walked back into the hotel room. House-keeping had been there: the bed was made, and there was a bottle of champagne in a bucket of ice sitting on the coffee table. "Did you do that?"

He picked the bottle up from the bucket and examined the label. "No, I would never buy this—" He paused. "Ah, I see it now. The snobbery."

Emma laughed, sitting cross-legged on the couch, pizza boxes still in her hand.

Owen picked up an envelope next to the bucket and opened it. "The card is a thank you for visiting and the bottle is complimentary."

"Whatever, come on, open it. We have twelve hours left in New York City. I plan on enjoying it."

32

——————

Moving into her new townhouse was easier than she thought it would be.

Just a few days after she got back from New York, the property manager called to let her know that everything was ready for her. Then a few days later, movers picked up pieces of furniture and a few boxes that she'd been storing in Leah's basement, and took them to the townhouse. Her townhouse.

The new mattress she bought to put on the bed frame she'd made, with Jake's help, was upstairs in the master bedroom. A couch and a few bar stools were in the main room. Boxes of clothes and shoes were already unpacked in her closet.

"You really don't have much," Leah commented, scanning the labels of boxes that were spread out in the open area of the living room.

"I know, but that's okay. I'll build as I go."

"What about cooking supplies? Dishes? You can't live on take-out forever."

"I'll just come eat at your house every day." Emma grinned. "But seriously, Mom's sending me some stuff she's had put away for me I guess. It'll be here tomorrow or the next day. She e-mailed me the tracking info."

"It's still missing something," a deep voice said. Emma turned around in time to see Owen come in through the doorway. She'd told him to stop by to see the place and that she, Leah, Molly, and Danielle would be in and out all day.

"Yeah, a decent wine selection," came Molly's voice from upstairs. "But lucky for you fools, I found the box with the booze."

"Oh no," Leah teased. She found your secret stash."

"You have a few really good bottles of champagne! Em, can I open one?"

"Good god, no. Those need to be chilled!" Emma called back. "I've got some in the fridge you're welcome to open though."

"Allow me," Owen said, walking across the entryway and into the kitchen. "Do you have glasses yet?"

"There are plastic cups in the cupboard above the fridge. I'm lucky I have a set of sheets and towels right now, so judge me for plastic cups."

Owen chuckled. "I wasn't planning on it."

Emma turned away from him, feeling the blush she'd felt so many times in New York return to her cheeks. She hadn't told anyone, not even Leah, about the night she'd spent with him—any of them. Now that he was in her space she felt too aware of him, too giddy with anticipation, too wrapped up in what could be and what might be.

"Where do you want it?" a winded man shouted from the open doorway.

"I thought that they already dropped off everything?" Leah asked.

"Oh, oh!" Molly shouted again from upstairs and came thundering down. "I know what this is."

"In front of that window," Owen said, pointing.

Emma looked at the mover, and then back at Owen. "What is it?"

Owen ignored the question and pulled the bottle of champagne out of the fridge. Only it wasn't champagne it was—

"Prosecco? Did you not think moving into a new house was cause for celebration?"

"Not a big enough celebration."

"Your expectation of what is a celebration must be very high," he said.

Emma rolled her eyes towards Leah, who grinned.

"You can blame our mother for that. Prosecco for every day, for pre-dinner bubbles, but champagne is for the best occasions. For weddings, funerals, engagements, and the announcements of babies."

"Hm. What about piano's?"

Emma shrugged. "I suppose that would be an acceptable reason, but I don't have a piano or champagne, so we'll have to test that theory out at another time."

"Or not."

Just as he said it, moving men carried a large, covered object into the room. The shape was unmistakable but Emma couldn't believe it. She talked herself down from paying to have movers haul one of the free upright pianos that were always advertised for free on Craiglist. None of them had stuck out to her, had called her name. Finding the perfect piano was like finding the perfect home, the perfect mate—she'd know it when she'd know it.

Worried now, she moved closer to the thing, the movers were situating it, flipping it carefully down. No, it wasn't an upright like she thought. Finally, they peeled away the protective blankets and layers to reveal the black baby grand piano underneath. Its body reflected the gray light pouring in through the large windows and the soft brown of the floor. Hypnotized, Emma stepped closer to it, ran her fingers over the soft keys, over the lid.

"This . . . is mine?"

Owen had come around from inside the kitchen and stepped closer to her now.

"Emma, this is yours. And this," he took her hand and put it on his heart, "is yours. The only difference is that you've had my heart for much longer than I've had this piano waiting for you."

Emma's stomach dropped. "What is this?"

"It's my promise to you, Emma, that one day I will ask you to marry me. It'll involve a ring and a thousand rose petals. But today, I'm giving you something you deserve more than a ring. I'm giving you what you've always wanted but have been too shy to do for yourself. This piano is for you, but is also a symbol of my love for you. Of how much your happiness means to me."

"Oh, Owen." Emma struggled to stay tear-free. To stay calm and clear headed. "This is . . . it's too much."

"No, you deserve so much more than this. But this is a start. A start for us, if you'll say yes."

"Say yes?"

Emma looked around now. Leah was in tears and Molly was filming. She had to remind herself that this wasn't a marriage proposal. This was something else, a proposal of a different kind.

"Be with me, officially. Let me love you the best way I know how. Let me share my world with you and be part of yours."

Sighing, Emma closed the gap between them and kissed him. "Yes."

ABOUT THE AUTHOR

Hailing from Buffalo, NY, Nicole is a freelance editor and writer with bylines at Femsplain, Hello Giggles, Brit & Co, and more. She has her BA in English and Creative Writing from Southern New Hampshire University and is pursuing her MFA in Writing through Savannah College of Art and Design.

When she's not writing, reading, or improving her craft she's traveling around the country or spending time with her two large dogs, three needy cats, and one supportive husband. Nicole is a self-proclaimed coffee snob and has a soft spot for a good craft beer.

For more information:
www.nicoleatone.com
nicole@nicoleatone.com

ACKNOWLEDGMENTS

I am grateful for all who made the existence of this book possible. Among them:

Erin Niumata, Marissa Fuller, Kisa Whipkey, Tehlor Kinney, and Whitney Davis, whose combined editorial guidance gave me the push I needed to make this novel ready for the world.

Ashley Ruggirello, for the 1st edition's beautiful cover and interior design.

My amazing group of writer and blogger friends, whose outpouring of support has made working on this project worth it.

My large, family, whose unwavering support gave me the confidence to follow my dreams and guidance when I stray off the path. Especially my brothers, whose Hoover's fries helped me write this book. And my mom, who introduced me to the Cape Cod.

And my husband. Thank you for the morning Starbucks deliveries, indulging in my bad editing eating habits, and for supporting me.

I wouldn't have been able to do this without you. Any of you.

.

www.ingramcontent.com/pod-product-compliance
Lightning Source LLC
Chambersburg PA
CBHW051425170626
46809CB00006B/2331